Beautifully Boundless

Book Three in The War at Waversea Series

Maddison Cole

Love is deaf. You can't just tell someone you love them, you have to show it.

Disclaimer

Please note some content in this fictional novel has been exaggerated for the purposes of your enjoyment, such as the available technologies and studies for chochlear implants. I have been inspired by the ladies who gave up their time to be interviewed by me as part of my research. You are all incredibly baddass and I hope I've done you proud.

Contents

Antonio

Six years ago...

I peer around the dumpster, my heart thumping at a million beats a minute. I shouldn't be here, but I haven't got a choice. The guy who introduced himself as Clayton met me a few streets away, as scheduled. We're both initiating for the GDK gang tonight and then our fates will be sealed. I reckon our paths will cross often, being the newbies and he seems like a decent guy, but honestly I'm just glad to not be doing this alone.

The metal door across the alley keeps drawing my eye, my leg shaking nervously. Graffiti covered brick walls close us in on all sides except the entrance we walked through, the same one allowing the multiple sirens racing past to fill the tight space with their flashing lights. I heard talks of the gang hitting various spots tonight, mostly to keep the police busy and give themselves a better chance at cashing in on a bigger haul.

I know my motivations are the same as everyone else, but it still makes me sick the guy who's built this jewelers from nothing is about to lose his entire livelihood while he sleeps. But I also see the image of my cousin in my mind's eye and know I can't back out.

He's a scrappy boy, a few years younger than me, with gingerish blond hair turning redder with every passing day. We were both so young when he came to live with us after his parents died in a fire, not having any other family left. If I mess this up, we'll both pay the price and the Cornstone's will be on their way to extinction.

"Where are they?" Clayton asks again, and once more, I don't *have an answer for him. I sigh, leaning against the dumpster until two shadows step into the alleyway to join us. Khan leads the way, dressed all in black with a balaclava covering his face. The tell-tale scar is just visible on the edges of the eye holes, the one that fuels many rumors of machetes and even an axe. The man trailing behind is Vince, dressed the same and looking bored as if this is another standard Saturday night for him.*

"Take these," Khan hands us each a semi-automatic hand-gun. "Shoot anyone who gets in your way. You don't have long, so no messing about. Grab the jewels and meet us back here." Without waiting for a response, the thug kneels to pick the lock and holds the door open for us. The minute my foot steps over the threshold, I'm a criminal, but I can't back out.

Dekken doesn't know it, but the GDK have had their eyes on him for a while now. He likes to act tough, being white in is this neighborhood is a tough ride so he puts on a gangster-wannabe front. One the GDK have noticed and want to exploit, figuring he will fly under the radar in places they would look suspicious. But I can't let that happen. So here I am, taking his place and keeping him safe. He's such a smart kid and out of the two of us, he's going places. This is in-evitable for me anyway, so it might as well mean something.

Pushing the gun into my pocket, I stride inside ahead of Clay-ton. The building is silent, my ragged breathing filling the space as I navigate the hallways I studied on the blueprints. The vault is fairly standard, requiring the code I was given from an assistant who is taking a cut of our takings. I punch it in, twisting the handle which resembles a steering wheel and pull the door open. And that's when I see it.

Just inside the entrance is a red button, no doubt linked to the alarm system Vince should have disabled in advance. I try to ig-nore it, looking around the floor to ceiling drawers spanned across each wall with the jewels hidden inside, but my gaze is drawn back. I'm not a saint, but stealing a man's only income seems immoral, even to seventeen-year-old me. It's hard enough to build anything on these cut-throat streets, especially when you open a jewelers with the knowledge everyone is going to go after you. Maybe it's not too late to find a way for us all to come out of this unscathed.

Clayton hovers behind me, seeming like he's going to turn and run but that'll fuck this up for everyone. Shoving him in ahead of me, I shout an order with more conviction than I feel. "Don't just stand there, empty them out!" He moves suddenly, diving from one drawer to the next and filling the duffle bag he brought as I copy on the other side with less haste. Looking over my shoulder to see him fully invested in looting the place, I edge back towards the entrance.

It's clear to me now, even if we both walked out of this alive tonight, our future is written in stone. At some point, this life will swallow us whole and deliver us to hell before we even had a chance, and there's no way to stop it. With Clayton caught in the act, he might do a little time for his first offense, but the jeweler will keep his business and I'll skate by my initiation. If anything, it buys us all some more time to find a way out.

I picture my cousin, his brown eyes staring at me with admiration, the way he rambles on with the word vomit he can't control. I can pack his shit by sunrise and have him far away from here. We can start again, even if it's on the streets, and work our way up. He needs me to save him from this life, and that's the only thought I have when I smash my fist into the red button and run away.

Harper

Rhys once asked me what my biggest fear was, and I didn't have an answer for him. Now I do. It's not my lack of senses as I sit in the deathly silence and pitch black, or the unknowing of where I am or who took me. It's the thought of being alone. The notion I've been awakened from the delusion of not needing anyone, only to have my heart torn to shreds by my own doing.

All I can see in my mind are their eyes, pleading with me to make an impossible choice where I would lose either way. But I still don't regret my decision. I can't lie to myself any more than I could lie to them. From Clay's strong, protective arms to Rhys' cocky smile which infects my own every single time. My heart wants what it wants, and it seems she's a greedy bitch. A bitter smile pulls at my lips, despite the emptiness in my chest. For one moment, I'd felt adored and cherished, and that's more than others get in a whole lifetime.

I'm not sure how long I've been laying here, but the throbbing in my neck has finally eased. My head is cushioned by a pillow, a spongy mattress beneath my sweats as I huddle on my side. Using my hands, I've explored every inch of the room which doesn't seem to have a door. Wood panels line the walls and floor, the rough grooves giving me multiple splinters and broken nails as I tried to pry my way out.

I'd found out the hard way the ceiling slopes so I can't stand upright unless in the center and there's no furniture. Only this bed and a bucket in the opposite corner I will not be using.

I'd rather die from kidney implosion and let whoever brought me here try to clean my defecated waste from the mattress. Not the poetic way I thought I'd go out, but I'm pretty pleased with my stubbornness in desperate times.

I wish I could remember anything beyond leaving Rhys' house but it all becomes foggy after that. Maybe because my heart is clinging to the last words he said to me, begging me to show him how to love. Whether through denial or stupidity, the idiot should have been able to see what love is, since the truth of the emotion was shining in my eyes for them both to see. I bore my heart out, only to be rejected by one and caged by the other.

Feeling restless, I sit upright and swing my legs over the metallic bed frame. I could shout for attention but what's the point when I can't hear any response I might be graced with? With there being no windows, it would have been a curtsey to leave a lamp or something. What if there's spiders surrounding me, or rats in the walls? I draw my knees up on instinct, pointlessly looking around. It's no use, I'm completely isolated until I'm visited by my captor. *If* I'm visited.

I don't like to think anyone would deserve this fate, but I can't for the life of me understand why I've been granted it. I'm a loner, sure, and talking to me before my morning coffee is a no-no, but I've never done anything to warrant being locked away in the dark. Especially if my abductor knows I'm deaf, removing another one of my senses is plain cruel. I could be in a wooden crate surrounded by people for all I know, or in a shipping container headed for Madagascar. No, that's ridiculous, too many movies Harper.

I wonder what the guys are up to right now, or if they know I'm missing. The trickle of a memory filters into my mind of changing into my sweats by the trunk of my car and hugging Addy goodbye. That's right, I was heading back to Aunt Marg's to home-school my way through my degree since staying was no longer an option. Not when my heart would break every time

I saw Clay and the misery my selfishness has caused. Emotions tumble through me, from elation they won't be worrying to sheer dread no one is looking for me. No savior coming to my rescue this time.

Rolling my shoulders, I step into the middle of my wooden cage and reach upwards. Doubling over, I touch my toes to stretch my hamstrings. I'm not a physical person but even I can tell my joints are tight and limbs are heavy. Who knew all it took was no other option to tune into my body's needs and start stretching. Maybe I should drop down into some burpees and by the time I'm finally visited, I could knock my captor on his or her ass. It's a pretty fantasy but I know I'd either die of muscle shock or piss myself by the time I've done two, probably both.

By the time I'm limbered up, impressing myself with the length of my lunge, some of the tension has drained from my body. I'm Harper fucking Addams, I've looked death in the face and said, "Not today, thanks." I'm a deaf girl who attends a mainstream college, well attended. I've managed to draw a guilt-ridden jock out of his shell whilst simultaneously wrapping the college bully around my little finger. Not to mention various attacks, public sex tape and a fire. I can handle a little kidnapping, no sweat.

I bounce on the balls of my feet with my fists before me, punching the air as confidence flares to live in my chest. I don't need saving, I'll save my damn self.

"Pssssst." The noise echoes inside my skull, causing me to shriek and fall to my ass. My funny bone smashes onto the wood floor, and it's anything but funny. Groaning through clenched teeth, I cradle my arm against me whilst words flare to life in my head. "Oh shoot, I'm sorry. I didn't mean to startle you but I didn't want to barge in which would startle you more so I...-"

"Kenneth?!" I shriek, not knowing how close or far away he is. I look around in the dark uselessly, a shudder rolling over my spine. Is he here to save me, or is he trapped too? Flashes of his red curls burst to life before me, visions of his oversized tux jacket and the creepy-ass keychain he gave me. We hugged and a sharp sting dug into my neck before it all went black. Kenneth? My mind starts reeling as I pull off one sneaker and jump back to my feet, brandishing it as a weapon.

"Look, this isn't what you think it is. I have coffee and donuts. I'm going to come in and we can just talk, okay?" I murmur my agreement, eyeing the space around me for a glimpse of light opening in the walls. A second later, a hand lands on my shoulder and I scream so loud, I hear myself in my own head. A pale blue light flashes in front of my face, one I'd know anywhere. My microphone clip.

"How did you-" I step back, the back of my knees hitting the bed and I flop onto it. Kenneth switches on his phone's flashlight, blinding me in the process like a vampire rising from a century-long coma. I'm pretty sure I hissed and everything. Moving away, Kenneth slowly sits on the floor and places his phone light up, illuminating the space. Like I'd already discovered, wooden slopes meet to form a pointed arch like that of an attic and there's no door visible.

"Where did you come from?" Kenneth doesn't respond, for once, the shadows on his face catching between his furrowed brows. Sliding a travel mug and paper bag towards me, I slump onto the floor but keep my distance. "How do you know I won't throw that coffee in your face?"

"It's iced," he replies hollowly. Damn it. Reaching out, I grab the offerings and return to my spot with my back pushed against the bed frame. He looks different, and in more ways than just physical. His hair is slicked back and he's missing his glasses, but his posture is too straight and the deep breaths causing his firm chest to push against a white tee are worlds away from the quivering, chatty boy I knew.

"I didn't want it to go like this," he murmurs into the microphone clip flashing against his collarbone. My hand hovers over the bag, wondering if I should trust eating food he's presented me with, but if Kenneth really wants to drug me again, I'm sure he would find a way. Pulling the first iced bun out, I scoff it in four large bites. Picking out a second, I lift my eyes to stare into his.

"What did you drug me with Kenneth, and how long was I out for?" He doesn't move or answer, just watches me until I begin to squirm. For someone who never shuts up, his newly found silence is more unnerving than if he were rambling on about voodoo and human sacrifices. To fill the awkwardness in the air, I focus on polishing off the rest of the donuts and downing the coffee which spreads a chill in its wake. I huddle my hoodie closer to my body, digging for the resolve I conjured before he appeared.

This is Kenneth, geeky Kenneth who is prone to crying and flinches at his own shadow. I'm not scared, just unsettled so I push my nerves down and sit straighter to mirror him. He's also changed into a hoodie and dark trousers, maybe jeans, and sneakers with a glow in the dark tick printed across the side. An upgrade from the tatty tennis shoes he usually wears.

"Kenneth, we're friends, right?" After a beat, he looks away from my stare and nods slightly. I smile, assured the boy I knew is still in there, which means I can work my way around him. "Clearly, there's been some kind of mistake, or whatever it is we can talk about it."

"You've never wanted to listen to me talk before. Everything you want to now know, I've told you multiple times before but you turned your receivers off." This time it's me who looks away when his eyes swing back to mine accusingly. Damn, he's right.

"I can only apologize for getting so wrapped up in my own thoughts, I couldn't handle yours as well. But I'm all ears now, as long as you leave the mic on, that is." I smirk in a half-assed attempt to joke with him, my kidnapper. Pushing myself up onto the mattress, I cross my legs and pat the space beside me. I could be inviting a maniac serial killer to share a bed with me for all I know, but my instincts tell me Kenneth won't harm me. All he's ever wanted is a friend. Or I'm about to find out the hard way how very wrong I am.

Rhys

"Stop that," Clayton nudges my foot with his to halt the insistent shaking. Slouching back in the armchair in the lieutenant's office, I raise my leg and dump it across Clayton's lap, shaking it ten times faster. Grunting, he shoves me off and stands to pace. "I'm nervous too, you know."

"I'm not nervous," I reply, turning to watch him. "I'm irritated as fuck. We should be out there looking, not stuck in here waiting. How can it take so long to catch some carrot-topped dweeb who will spill his guts to every gas attendant or motel manager he meets?"

"Clearly we didn't know him as well as we thought." Clayton scrubs a hand over his face, his black eyes sunken and the creases in his forehead becoming a permanent fixture. I scoff, moving to stand in front of him.

"Not we, you. I've known about his fetish for gutting defenseless animals since day one. He's on his last warning with Dean Lawrence for letting himself into the labs at night and killing the test rats." We share a look of dread but I push it aside, refusing to even acknowledge the thought of him hurting my girl. He's dead either way, but if there's a hair out of place on Harper's head, he'll suffer unimaginable pain before I give him the peace of death. Which is why I need to get out of here and find him first.

With such a depressing workspace, it's no wonder the lieutenant isn't in any rush to return to us. The walls are an off-yellow from age, heavy wooden frames showing medals and certificates in every empty space. Pride of place above the cushy chair is a large photo of the balding man meeting the president, not a moment I'd be particularly proud of but each to their own. Other than the three chairs and central desk, there's only a pine bookcase with a locked cabinet at the bottom – yes, I checked.

Still in my slacks from last night, I pull at the itchy neckline of the t-shirt I was presented with to replace my torn shirt. Apparently, a lot of the traffic coming through the cells here are barely dressed prostitutes or druggies swap the clothing off their backs for another fix, so the station keeps stocked on men's one-size-fits-all t-shirts. The alternative being everyone gawking at my tattoos and the trail of blood from the self-supplied gashes lining my chest, I put on the damn shirt. The polyester scratches my supple skin, tenderised by a lifetime of expensive fabrics.

"Oh for fuck's sake, here." Noticing my itching for the millionth time, Clayton yanks his shirt over his head and offers it to me. I copy his action, swapping t-shirts like best butties and finding myself more comfortable but smelling like him. I don't know what's worse. I stroll around the room, ignoring Clayton's protests as I drop into the lieutenant's chair. It's much plusher than the one I've been waiting in for hours whilst being totally ignored by the officers rushing past the glass window. Black leather and reclines far enough to hang on the precipice of comfortable and threatening to collapse, which I test multiple times, pushing it back just that little bit further until I'm sure I'm a goner.

"I can't take this anymore. I'm leaving." Clayton strides for the door and I sit forward to link my fingers on the wooden desk before me.

"And where are you going to go? If these fuckers manage to pull a lead out of their ass, we need to be ready. Not separated across the state."

"Why would I work with you? You're a mess." I nod in

agreement, pulling the t-shirt away from the gouges on my chest which are starting to seep again. I should probably get those looked at, after we have Harper back.

"I know you hate being around me, and I don't really give a shit. But," I interject as he reaches for the handle once more. "There's only one way I'm still functioning right now, and it's through believing I can still fix this. Harper wants both of us, but I can't take her rejection again if I turn up to save her alone. I seriously...can't handle that again." I huff out a breath, my shoulders sagging at the thought of her tear-filled eyes. How she pulled out of my grasp and nothing I said or did could convince her to stay.

"Tell me the truth. Do you love her?" Clayton sits in the opposite seat, his black eyes boring into mine. His chest is heaving, misery etched into every crevice in his fatigued face. He looks like a man broken, and it's only my years of concealing my pain keeping me from appearing exactly the same. He may have been the one to walk out on her, on us, but the weight of emotion he bears for our girl is evident for all to see.

"As much as you do," I nod. Something shifts in his gaze, a hint of surprise tugging at his eyebrows. Whether from my confession or the truth of his own, I'm not sure. One thing is for sure, we won't find her or win her back separately. So we're doing this. "Okay, let's be logical. Tell me what you know of Kenneth, lay it all out and we can unravel this shit heap."

A brief moment passes where neither of us move until Clayton resigns with a sigh. He scoots the chair closer to the desk, pushing the notepad and pen in front of him over to me. Even though we've already given our statements and are waiting for the others to finish theirs, Clayton relays every scrap of information he can remember whilst I make notes. Alongside a list of what was found in the wardrobe, I write down all the times one of us was targeted. The hacking, the blackmail, the sex-tape, the fire.

"So, this Antonio could be the young boy from the

photos you found. Do you think the other one was Kenneth?"

"I don't know, maybe. I didn't look long enough and now the police have everything. You know, when I found my locker and Jeremy's jacket with murderer written on it, I thought it was referring to my brother. But if Kenneth thinks I'm responsible for Antonio's death, his attacks would make a lot more sense."

"And his motive is a lot more dangerous. This isn't some jealous backlash or a creep's weird game. It can't be a coincidence you are sharing his dorm, given his apparent hacking skills." I tap the pen against my lips in thought, trying my hardest to not let the worry show through. There's no point both of us being a mess, I'm just surprised I'm the one who's managing to keep a level head so far.

By the time I've finished translating Clayton's brainstorm onto paper, my patience has well and truly waned. Scrubbing a hand through my hair, I push to my feet and throw the pen down. Folding the paper, I shove it into my pocket and lean against the window. It's been a rough twenty-four hours, the sun having set on a whole day of her missing, not only in reality but missing from my soul. I've done everything I can to distract myself and cooperate, the way she would have forced me to. But it's like missing a limb, forgetting an integral part of you isn't there until you go to use it and remember all over again, it's gone.

My heart pounding against the wall of my chest mocks me, since I vowed to give it to her. Every thump resounding in my chest is a thump she should be feeling, with her hand or head resting on me, I don't care. But I need her back, and I'll move heaven and fucking earth to make sure that happens. So, in the grand scheme of things, being amenable with Clayton isn't a harsh compromise, and I fucking hate myself for not seeing that sooner. She was never going to choose, I should have foreseen it and stopped backing her into that corner until she broke. But that's me all over, I break everyone around me so I don't have to.

"Hey, look. Something's going on." Clayton's voice pulls

me back to the here and now, so I force a long exhale out and turn to face him. Beyond the glass window separating us from the main department, uniformed officers are crowding around a white board. Harper's college ID photo sits top and central with webs of marker tying her to drabs of useless information. As the crowd shifts, we see a detective pinning up two new images with a relived smirk on her face.

Both are hazy, but the orange of Clayton's scrap-worthy truck would be recognizable through smeared binoculars. The first shows the front view, a shadowed figure sitting behind the wheel with his seemingly asleep passenger strapped in beside him. Her body is slouched against the window, only the belt keeping her upright as a mass of hair covers her face. The second image shows the rear of the truck traveling on the freeway, a sign for the I-80 East overhead.

"He took your truck?" I grit out, my eyes glued on the slumped figure as my blood begins to boil. It's not that I wasn't raging before, but having actual evidence the slimy fucker took her has my anger bursting through the self-erected damn that was keeping my shit at bay.

"Fuck, the keys were in my room. I didn't even think to check when I found out she was missing. But at least there's one positive, I know where's he's heading. That's the freeway to Detroit, he must be going back to where Antonio lived."

"That's a whole day's drive, he might just be arriving. I can have my private jet here within the hour. If they stopped off along the way, we might be able to beat him to it." Clayton and I share a wicked grin before realizing we agreed on something and twist to look anywhere else. I yank out my phone, shooting a quick call to our family-owned charter company to find out the jet is still nearby.

I shudder at the thought of my father lurking around after the shitshow that was supposed to be my birthday party, probably keeping tabs on the investigation from his office at Waversea. We can't have anything ruining his precious college's reputation now, can we? Nudging Clayton, I jerk my chin towards the door for us to leave when it suddenly opens, the lieutenant stepping through.

"Sorry to keep you waiting, gentlemen." The man is a few inches shorter than us both, the shiny patch on top of his head catching the light. A thick mustache stretches across his upper lip and the strain of his shirt shows how he prefers to spend his decent salary. At the Cheesecake Factory. Rounding the office, he drops into his leather chair heavily and gestures for us to take a seat. "I have a few more questions for you if you don't mind.

"Actually, we're fucked and have stayed far longer than necessary. If your questions are urgent, you have our cell numbers. Otherwise, we're done here." I stride out of the office without waiting for a reply, sensing Clayton on my heels. Multiple eyebrows raise as we stride through the center of the desks, my eyes not wavering from the hazy image until we've passed it. Hold on Babygirl, I'm coming for you.

Harper

"Hang on, I want to make sure I understand. Antonio's initiation to the GDK gang was on the same night as Clay's, and it all went to shit. But Ken - sorry, Dekken," wow, that's going to take some getting used to, "Clay was just a boy himself. He lost his brother that night too."

"I went to every court hearing and listened to Clayton's confession myself. He tripped the alarm, he took too long to leave the building and the police were about to turn up, so the thugs had to drop the 'dead weight'. It's his fault my cousin is dead." Another tear leaks from his eye, my heart breaking for all the boys affected by this terrible night. But I can't help the protectiveness I feel towards Clay. I know how much he's beaten himself up about this, raked with guilt a lesser man wouldn't survive.

"He was just a dumb kid Dekken, you all were," I whisper, careful not to agitate him whilst in this vulnerable, yet unpredictable state.

"Ask me how long after Antonio's death it was until my uncle committed suicide," he challenges me with a direct stare. When I don't ask, he answers for me anyway. "Two weeks. I was an orphan and they were the only family I had left. You have no idea what it's like being thrown into care in the slums as a thirteen-year-old. It was hell, Harper. I was beaten daily by the boys in the group home." Dekken's eyes close briefly as he expels a shaky breath.

I know I should be scared, finding out the guy I believed I knew is completely different. He has a different name, a hidden and tragic past, a pain I know all too well. So despite myself and the fact he is my kidnapper, I push onto my knees and lean into his shoulder. After a tense moment, his arms circle me and Dekken pulls me into his side, his face finding my neck as he cries.

Tears pool in my collarbone beneath the hoodie, my own joining as I succumb to the loss we've both had to endure. There's no competition of larger or lesser pain, no comparison of stories. Just the agonising emptiness coiling around us until it's hard to draw breath. I know the strength of this emotion, and the need to blame someone.

If the drunk who crashed into my parent's car all those years ago had survived, I can't say I'd have done any different. Whether through luck or misfortune, the man I could have sought revenge on met his quick end already, and I wasn't forced to lose myself along the way. Which Dekken clearly has and I can't say I blame him.

"For what it's worth," his muffled voice sounds against the microphone long after his tears have dried. "I am sorry. I wanted to hurt him, and you were an easy way to do that." I nod in understanding, not knowing what's going to happen from here.

"Please don't leave me in the dark again. It's horrible missing two of my senses, I can't even talk to myself for company." Stealing himself, Dekken leans back and moves to stand. His phone still lays on the floor across the room, the flashlight illuminating us amongst the shadows. I stand with him, refusing to be intimidated.

"Harper," he breathes, hanging his head slightly. I've had plenty of opportunities to overpower him and lunge for his phone, but I'd rather not handle this the hard way. When the one who kidnapped me appears so defeated, it's hard to remember who the victim is here. I grab for his hand, pleading him with my eyes. Indecision mars his features, his hand pulling out of my grip. "I can't. Everything was all my doing until…the recording, but I'm not the one calling the shots anymore."

My brow furrows at this, my hands grabbing for him as he retrieves his phone and turns off the light. I stagger forward in the dark, my outstretched arms meeting the air. I spin, hunting for the blue flashing of my microphone clip which has vanished as quickly as my captor has.

"Dekken. Dekken! Please don't leave me here, I hate being…" *Alone.* I finish the sentence in my mind, hating to show weakness. For a moment, whilst consoling Dekken, I'd forgotten I'm not the one in control here. That we weren't just friends having a heart to heart, huddled on the bed like we used to in his dorm. He'd been there for me when my heart was breaking for Clay, the one reassuring constant I could lean against. All the while he'd been hurting so much more.

"If you're still in here, I want you to know I'm so sorry for your loss, and I understand your pain. I'm not fighting and I'm not running. You were there for me once when I needed a friend, and I'm here now. Let me out so I can help you. It doesn't have to be this way." I trail off, giving up hope he's still close enough to hear me.

Stepping on something, I drop to my knees and find the paper bag I left beside the bed. Damn, I wish I'd saved some of the donuts for later, who knows how long it'll be until I'm next visited. A shudder rolls through my spine as I realize I can't see or hear Dekken coming, meaning he could be jerking over me sleeping for all I know. *Ew, no. Hopefully he's not that…deranged.*

I also suddenly regret downing the coffee, the need to relieve myself building in my bladder. The pressure increases as I stand to pace, which soon turns from a slight hop to a full-on wee dance. Adding to my reservations from earlier, I'm now acutely aware someone could be lingering in the room or burst in unannounced any second. No, I stand by my stubbornness, I will take the kidney infection over being caught squatting over a metal tin.

A groan passes my lips, the ache growing in my lower body until it's all I can focus on. I try to sing a little song and sit on the bed, but it only makes it worse. My mind fills with the sounds of gushing rivers and thundering waterfalls, accompanied with the images to match. My resolve dwindles, the urge to alleviate this ache too much to bear. *Fuck, I'm gonna have to use the bucket.*

I wake with a dull headache, a constant throb of boredom which isn't helped by the light bleeding through my eyelids. I throw my hands over my face with a groan, shifting onto my side. Wait...light? I bolt upright on the mattress, ignoring the stab behind my right eye. On the other side of the room, I find what appears to be a bedside lamp, except the bulb is bordering fluorescent. I follow the cable to where it disappears into a square floor hatch, of bloody course. I'm clearly in an attic so why wouldn't it have the classic trap door?

There's a small crate containing a travel mug and a box of donuts, but that's not what has me moving from the safety of the bed. A stack of books taller than the lamp beckons me closer, the multiple worlds within their pages waiting to whisk me away from here. I skid to my knees in the sweatpants I'm thankful once again I changed into. *Fuck playing prisoner in an evening dress.*

I'm still not feeling the hopeless dread my predicament would usually bring, probably because my kidnapper isn't the big, bad psycho I was expecting. Insane, most likely, but not beyond overpowering if I am forced to take that route. For now, I'd like to believe I still have a chance to talk him down.

Darting back across the room, I hoist the mattress from the bed frame and chuck it to the floor. With my arms filled with the pillow and duvet, I shove it along with my foot until I've created a cushioned nest in the sloped corner. Pulling the crate towards me, I sigh to find the coffee in the thermal travel mug still hot. A fantasy novel meets my hand first, a donut second and I'm sold. Always one to make a good thing out of a bad situation, I figure a little reading retreat isn't the worst fate in the world. But then I remember my guys.

Are they worrying about me? Do they even know I'm missing? Maybe this will give Clay the opportunity to get over me while I find a way out of here. And Rhys...well, I just hope he isn't hurting too much, and he isn't projecting the pain I saw in his eyes onto anyone, most of all himself. Where Clay would mope, it's hard to know which way Rhys' mind would go. Would he turn in on himself and hide away like before or fuck me out of his system with a cocky screw-the-world smirk on his face? I frown at the thought, jealously coursing through my veins so I flick open the book and try to lose myself in an alternative universe.

Except it doesn't work. Not when the wolf pack running through these pages have a dominating, muscled savior and tattooed alphahole who are constantly bumping chests. Fuck my life. I lean back on a huff, placing the book down gently as I don't have the heart to throw it. Clearly some overbearing power is steering my mind back to the boys I yearn for, the ones I walked away from.

Closing my eyes, I allow the feelings I've been pushing away to surface, but I was unprepared for the freight train of emotion that barrels into me. I'm consumed, drowning in a sea of guilt and misery I shouldn't have unleashed. Tears sting my eyes, the moment I broke their hearts staring back at me in my mind. Even after I've talked or fought my way out of here, I'm returning to Aunt Marg's spare room with her cats as my main source of company. I know I need to keep moving forward and push myself to finish my degree, but I'm stuck wondering what the point is.

"Hey," a soft voice sounds in my head. I smile despite myself, happy for the distraction. "Can I come in?"

"Um, yeah sure." I call out, probably louder than necessary. I watch the hatch door open, bringing a stream of light with it before Dekken's head pops in and looks for me. I remain where I am, watching his eyes brighten as he spots me and the smile he can't hold back. It's stupid and weird, and I know I shouldn't be comfortable being held against my will. But that's when it hits me. Maybe it started out that way, but I'm not here against my will anymore, I'm hiding. Hiding from the world, the pain I've caused, my own feelings.

"So this," Dekken gestures around the attic before leaning forward on his forearms, "wasn't planned. And I don't want to keep you up here, but I can't let you go either. The doors are locked, the windows are bolted and shatterproof. But I'd like you to join me, if you want to?" There's vulnerability in the way he ducks his head, a complete role reversal happening before my eyes. I nod, crawling towards the hatch while forcing away the 'Beauty and The Beast' alarm bells blaring to life in my head.

But I hold onto the control Dekken has given me, whether he's realized it or not. Besides, Stockholm syndrome can take a backseat since I'm happy to have access to a real toilet. Maybe a shower and, oh god yes, all the coffee.

Clayton

Stepping out of the jet's open door and pausing at the top of the metal steps, I stretch my neck side to side and inhale deeply.

"Smells like home," I breathe, sensing a shadow moving in behind me.

"Smells like pollution, if you ask me." Rhys nudges his way around me and jogs down the stairs. Standing off to one side, a man waits for us in a suit, despite it being the middle of the night. Beyond the hangar doors, clouds cover the blackened sky, blocking out any light the moon and stars may have provided.

I follow the pair, circling the stationary jet for my eyes to fall upon our rented ride. A black Ford Raptor winks back at me, boasting over thirty-inch, all terrain tires and a slick paint job. Over the windscreen sits a row of fog lights above a cab big enough for five and an open back. Rhys strolls to the rear, popping open the tailgate and reaching for the two duffle bags waiting there.

"When you said hire car, I expected something a little more discreet," I grumble as Rhys throws a bag into my gut. Catching it easily, I find a range of men's clothing and toiletries inside since we didn't stop back at the dorms to grab any supplies for the trip. Seems like he's thought of everything. I raise my eyebrow, watching the cruel smile lift the corners of his mouth as he pats the back space.

"Kenneth's got a truck, we've got a truck. I'm not taking

any chances if he tries to make a run for it and besides, there's plenty of room back here for a dead body." I stare after Rhys as he returns to the man holding out the keys, not entirely sure if he's joking or being serious. Rounding the passenger side, I hop inside and throw the bag into the backseat. Fuck, this is seriously a nice ride. The leather seats are wide enough to fit me comfortably, red trim around the edges and headset. Rhys settles in beside me, still smiling but there's no humor to it.

We've barely acknowledged each other since leaving the police station, only speaking if absolutely necessary. He had his eyes closed and headphones in for the entire three-hour plane ride, but the continuous shaking of his foot told me he wasn't asleep. Even though the jet was more spacious than my childhood home, there wasn't enough room for me to pace so I'd settled for chewing my nails. I'm on the verge of an emotional wreck, whereas Rhys is rigidly straight-backed and stone-faced. Scarily so.

Hooking his phone onto the dashboard holder, I see the address he acquired from a poor private investigator he woke and barked down the phone at for Kenneth's records to be sent over ASAP. Turns out his real name is in fact Dekken, Antonio was his cousin and there's a string of group-homes linked to his name. But his uncle's old place is our main interest, which is where we'll start. I recognize the street name but can't say I've ever been over to that side of town, preferring to keep to the hood I knew when younger.

Peeling out of the hangar, Rhys takes a moment to enjoy the sheer size of the metal monster beneath us. Skidding around the tarmac a few times before exiting onto the main road, he makes short work of the remaining distance between us and my hometown. Dodging between the lanes of the highway, he sniggers when I not-so-subtly click my seatbelt into place.

"Since we've got some time where you can't pretend to be asleep, maybe we should...talk," I try weakly. A raised eyebrow is the only response I receive. Each light passing overhead illuminates the dark ink on his arms, the demons and angels watching me carefully as his hands grip the wheel. The tension he excludes is stifling, but Harper managed to see past all that to what's underneath. Which I now realize, I have no idea who that is.

It's easier to pass a person off as evil or plain dark, without taking the time to understand why. He isn't just spoilt, he's damaged. But why? Harper knew the answer and it tied her to him irrevocably. She couldn't choose between us, yet I couldn't accept her proposal. If anyone is to blame for her missing, other than 'Dekken', it's me. The three of us could have spent the evening at the party, sharing dances and stolen kisses, if my ego would have allowed it. But mostly, whether by me or Rhys, Harper would have been safe.

Instead, we hadn't slept in over two days and are across the country hunting for her. Our tie, our purpose, our girl. Once I get her back, I need to fix what I broke and accept Rhys will be in my life for the foreseeable future.

"I mean," I clear my throat. "Maybe we should take advantage of this time to work out...whatever."

"There's nothing to work out on my end. Rescuing Harper is the only thing that matters right now. But don't be fooled, I'm seething inside. I'm not into dudes, and if I were you'd be my last choice. But when you rejected her, you rejected both of us." I turn to look out the window, the weight behind his words settling on me. I knew he would be pissed at me as usual, but his openness took me by surprise. "I was ready to throw everything at making it work, and your reservations ruined it."

"I didn't realize you felt so passionately about...us." The word sounds foreign on my tongue, a shudder rolling through me as I even consider stepping into this uncharted territory.

"Feeling anything is still quite new to me, and it's easier for me to hold onto the rage. But once we get her back, I can't let her go again. I don't have the words nor do I understand my own reasoning, but I have to fix this. Which starts with apologising to you, I guess." My head whips around, certain I misheard him. His face is shrouded by shadows and I'm unable to decipher. So long passes, I think it's all I'm going to get until he eventually continues.

"I was caught up in hurting my dad, and after years of hearing how much he loves his college and the fucking praised scholarship program, I targeted you. I didn't even know you, I just needed you and the rest of them gone to hurt the man who hurt me." My eyes drop to the barely visible raised bump on his neck which I've seen Harper absentmindedly stroke when she thinks no one is watching. It's not hard to imagine exactly how Rhys' father hurt it, and it's in more than the emotional sense. Damn.

No more words are said as we take the exit and edge closer to the flag on the map, not I don't have anything left to say. Has his apology resolved all of our conflicts? No, but it is more than I ever believed I would get. It's a testament to how much he cares for Harper and how far he will go to prove it.

Turning onto Hamilton Avenue, it becomes distinctly clear we are in the right place. Each run-down building is a replica of the last, crumbling brick and boarded up windows displayed across each shop front. Roofs slope and tents occupy every spare gap on the sidewalk amongst the scantily clad women on street corners. They eye us with dollar signs in their eyes as Rhys slows to a casual pace, many chasing the Ford and shouting promises of a good time. We roll by the community high school Antonio must have attended, the wall either side of the locked gates covered in graffiti tags.

The residential part of town isn't any better, and I thought I had a rough upbringing. This place makes my street look like Sunset Boulevard, the stench of deprivation strong even to me. I close my window, sliding further into my seat as if the poverty can reach out its claws and drag me back in.

Rhys comes to a swift stop, hopping out the cab and leaving the engine running. I look beyond him to see what has his shoulders bunched. The orange glow of the streetlamp shines upon an old-style mailbox on a bent metal pipe, '139 Bakersview' printed across the side. Behind is merely the foundations of what used to be Kenneth/Dekken's uncle's house. All that remains is a heap of splintered wood, which I can tell is charred black from here.

I remain seated, watching Rhys stomp over to the mailbox and smash his fist into the side. It flies from the pipe, falling on the grass where I imagine two young boys used to play. Seemingly unsatisfied, Rhys stalks forward to crush the offensive yellow box beneath his sneaker until it's as pitifully destroyed as the house it belongs to.

I take back what I previously thought. I'm not the one on the verge of an emotional breakdown here, he is. Flopping back on the head rest, I blow out my share of frustration. I'd been silently confident with Rhys' resources, we'd be able to cut Dekken off before he managed to get Harper into a place she couldn't escape from. But now what?

My road trip companion jumps back into the driver's seat, slamming his door shut and gripping onto the wheel. His chest is heaving and I notice droplets of blood seeping through the t-shirt I gave him, unfortunately my best one which I'll now have to incinerate. Grabbing his phone from the dash, I see him scan through the email from the PI for the list of group home addresses.

"Rhys, it's stupid o'clock in the morning. Even if anyone there knows where he might be, they are less likely to talk if we wake them up."

"I'll make them talk!" He smacks the wheel, gritting his teeth loudly enough to make me cringe. Of all the people I had to be stuck with, why'd it have to be a ticking time bomb? My instincts scream at me to get out of the vehicle and leave him behind, but instead my hand tentatively reaches out and settles on his shoulder. His violent flinch tells me all I need to know about how many people have consoled him before, the grand total being one with emerald eyes and a heart large enough for them both.

"We're no good to her like this." Rhys closes his eyes, visibly reining himself back in with a series of deep breaths. Apparently my choice of words were fitting since he drives out the other side of town and a couple miles along the freeway, not speaking a word until we pull into a hotel car park. With our bags in hand, I follow him into the hotel lobby and watch curiously as he throws a wink to the bellhop who holds the door open for us. All the tension has left his posture, the cocky shit I'm familiar with returning as if he's practiced this version of himself a million times over.

"Welcome to Hotel Indigo," a cheery blonde smiles from behind the desk. Dulled floral wallpaper fills the space behind her, the peeling corners a running theme through the rest of the décor. The gold-painted vases are chipped, their artificial bursts of green leaves drooping with age. "How long will you be staying with us and how many rooms would you be needing?" Rhys' instant answer has my jaw dropping, and I don't pick it up until he's paid and I've stalked him into the elevator.

"Why the fuck are we sharing a room? Rhys? Rhys! You told the woman we're on our honeymoon!" My voice trails down the hallway as he keeps his back to me, not giving a fuck who I'm waking up. He continues to ignore me, twisting a key in the lock and pushing his way into *our* room. I scoff at the double bed, remaining in the doorway. I'll sleep in the hallway if that's my only other option, but he can get fucked if he thinks one apology means we're suddenly rubbing butts in a grimy hotel room.

"Shut the damn door already," he stalks into the bathroom with his duffle bag slung over his shoulder. I see the grouchy bastard is back in full force and wonder if this is another character he plays or the real him. Grimacing, I step inside and close the door. Hearing the shower switch on, I seize the chance to change into a clean set of clothes and spray myself before he returns in a pair of black boxers. Scrubbing his wet hair with a matching hand towel to the one I spotted in my bag, Rhys switches on the boxy TV and slips into bed.

"Yeah, no. I'm not doing this, give me the keys to the truck. I'll sleep in the backseat." He doesn't make a move to do as I've asked, leaning his head back and closing his eyes. "You're not even watching this!" I moan like a little bitch, reaching for the remote on the mattress but he beats me too it. Reclining with his arms crossed and a glare directed at me, Rhys reminds me of the big bad wolf after he's eaten the grandma, waiting for his real prey.

"I'm a complicated man, but this is quite simple. I can't stand silence. Back on campus, I left my doors open to any shit-face who wanted to hang out there, often throwing parties I didn't even attend just for the noise. Maybe also for the pretense of not being utterly alone in this fucked up world that's never wanted me." Rhys sighs deeply, returning to face forward although his voice continues to carry. "My demons find me when it's too quiet, and right now, thanks to our connection with Harper, you're the closest thing I've got to a friend. So ...get in the damn bed, leave the TV on and don't. Fucking. Touch. Me."

Harper

"You're not half as angry as I'd expected," Dekken speaks carefully. My microphone clip is sitting between the buttons of his flannel shirt, paired with casual jeans on the bottom, designer if I'm not mistaken. His clothes are already worlds away from the shy, geeky boy I knew, but his reclined position and widely spread legs in the armchair are straight up weird.

"I think I'm still processing." I mumble from my side of the living room. The house is old, the garish carpets and wallpaper transporting us back in time a few decades. I haven't noticed any evidence of technology or modern appliances. A low coffee table divides the room, the repetitive tick of a grandfather clock by the staircase floating to the mic.

The longer the silences rings out, the more I feel the need to fill it. "Well, this is awkward." *Oh yeah bravo, that's so much better than the silence.* Dekken blows out a breathy laugh, shifting forward to lean on his thighs. A hint of muscle pushes against the material of his shirt, piquing my curiosity of how much I actually know of the man before me. For the hundredth time in the five minutes I've been down here, he pulls his phone out from beneath his thigh to check the screen. I can see from here, there's no new notifications so he slides it away once more.

"We could...play Scrabble?" Dekken asks shyly, ducking his head. The corner of my mouth lifts in a half smile, assuming there's not much else to do until I figure out what's going on here.

"Sure, why not?" My eyes track the phone gripped in his hand as he disappears up the stairs. His breath fanning across the mic reaches me even at this distance, as does the rummaging of boxes containing counters and multiple pieces.

Quickly darting across the room, I peek through the closed blinds to see a dirt track stretching into the distance and no sign of another building or life anywhere. Clay's truck is sitting by the front porch, the sun gleaming off the orange hood. I try the window, finding it expectedly locked before easing the blind back into place, unaware of how much noise I'm making. I hear a door close and freeze, until the sound of Dekken peeing filters into my head. Gross.

Edging the room, I note the front door is locked from the inside with a padlock hooked onto the chain. A little excessive, but if I had been as erratic as expected, it would be logical – for an insane kidnapping psycho. Looking around an open archway, I find a kitchen and backdoor, blinds blocking out the light on every pane of glass. Hearing the flush and splash of tap water, I dive back onto the aged sofa and act casual. I hope.

Dekken appears in my view, an easy smile playing on his lips. Setting out the Scrabble board, he crosses his legs on the rug and I slide down to mimic him across the table. He offers me the bag of tiles to pick first and we fall into a relaxed game as if we're old friends waiting out a power cut. Using the back of an old envelope, Dekken keeps score while I thrash him time and time again.

"Another one to you," he smirks, resetting the board. Even without the non-stop babbling, I can see the gangly college kid I'd befriended shining through. His flame-red hair is tamed and pushed back, revealing a strong jaw line I hadn't noticed before. But it's his eyes intriguing me the most. Brown on the surface, but there's a flickering light there, as if he's drowning in his grief and continually fighting to be free. A feeling I know all too well.

"What the hell is a 'zorilla'? You're messing with me

now." Dekken rolls his eyes but the smile remains.

"It's like a skunk, native to Africa. Look it up," I gesture to his phone on the table, feeling smugly certain my years of playing with Aunt Marg have taught me every Scrabble trick there is. Dekken mumbles about there being no internet out here and I nod, looking around the room once more. Of course there wouldn't be, but it doesn't lessen the ball of worry building in my gut at the words 'out here'. Exactly how far from civilisation are we?

Asking him if I could grab some snacks, Dekken nods with ease, letting me venture into the kitchen alone. The fridge is stocked with enough food to hold us here for weeks, from meats to a drawer of vibrantly colored vegetables. My mouth waters thinking about a decent meal, although any notions of a romantic dinner and I'll take my cue to leave. After checking through the drawers, I notice there's not a single knife, grater, peeler, or anything sharp around. Even the forks are pretty blunt.

"What?" The sharp edge to Dekken's tone makes me jump and spin around, but he's nowhere to be seen. I faintly hear the broken rambling filtering through his phone, mixed with his occasional grunts. "Those fuckers," he growls, the harshness of the sound sending a shudder crawling down my spine. "Right, thanks. And don't call me again."

Steeling myself, I fill my arms with Doritos and cookies, returning to our game with a shaky smile. One look of his narrowed eyes says my act isn't fooling anyone.

"Guessing you heard that, huh?" I fold my legs beneath me, nodding with a shrug. Dekken's breath saws in and out, his spine straightening and a calculated look slamming over his features. Jaw clenched and nostrils flaring, he eyes me as if I've slapped his grandma. "Your damn heroes are scouring the country for you, digging into my past. As if they haven't done enough damage already."

My eyes widen. They're looking for me, together? My

mind whirls with all the hidden meanings behind that simple notion. Do they feel obliged to save me or is it more? If they are working together, does that mean Clay has changed his mind? Would Rhys be able to forgive what I said? I feel like the rug has been whipped out from beneath me, my eyes shifting with the same speed my thoughts are.

"And there it is," Dekken snarls, pushing to his feet. "You'd run straight back into their arms, even after Clay specifically stated he doesn't want to be a part of your little ménage fantasy." I don't have time to ask how he knew that as Dekken grips the edge of the coffee table and flips it aside. I shriek, holding my hands up defensively. Through my fingers, I watch Dekken stalk around the room, lashing out at the furniture like a caged animal.

Him like this, I don't know how to deal with. He's so far removed from everything I associate with his personality; bubbly, kind, thoughtful, gentle. It's as if with the change of name has come this whole new person, and I want Kenneth back.

"Hey, it's okay. It's just me and you here, and I haven't fought you once. We can sort this out," I pull myself up and edge forward cautiously. Dekken turns sharply and advances on me so fast, I fall back onto the sofa. Sneering from above, I see the truth of his character flaring to life in his usually dull eyes.

"Do you know you've never looked at me twice? And even when you spent time with me, it's because you were hung up on a guy that left you. He's rejected you twice, yet you still pine for him. What does he have that I don't?!" Dekken's shouting invades my skull, making me wince. Turning, he throws a fist into the wall, leaving a hole in the plasterboard before stomping upstairs.

Silence resumes as he switches off the mic, leaving me alone and repressed once more. I remain glued to the sofa, scared to bolt for the door in case he's right behind me and I wouldn't even know. This new side to him frightens me, and I'm now starting to realize how much trouble I'm in.

After a while, I slink back to the room he showed me earlier, my eyes darting around the entire way. Making it inside without incident, I softly close the door and slump against the wood. Like the rest of the house, in here could use some major updating but it has a bed, dresser, bookshelf and private bathroom. The bag from my trunk sits beneath another locked window, all my clothes and toiletries waiting inside. In any other circumstances, this would be my ideal getaway.

Crossing the room, I sit against the headboard and draw my knees to my chest. Dread of a whole new kind blooms in my chest and a tear escapes my eye. But this one isn't for the loss of a good thing, it's being pulled from the rising worry I might not get a chance to fix it.

My gaze drifts back to the bookshelf over and over, but for the first time, I'm not in the mood. Hiding in fictional escapes won't help me now. I'm at the climax of my own story and I need to figure out the ending. My boys are coming for me, together, so for them I need to stay strong. Prove I'm still the girl they think I am. So although he's scared the shit out of me, Dekken has unknowingly given me something I was lacking – hope.

Dekken

Holding the phone to my ear, I swallow a sob and will my hand to stop shaking. *No, damn it, I don't need Kenneth right now. I need Dekken.*

"I can't do this anymore," I say with all the strength I can muster. In response, I receive the usual verbal abuse about being spineless and a waste. This was my plan, my revenge on Clayton Michaels. At what point did it get so twisted? Being Kenneth was so much easier, I almost settled for letting go of the past and just being him. Clayton even started to consider me as a friend, like Harper did. I could have been happy. But happy doesn't bring Antonio or my uncle back. Sure, nothing would bring them back but acting all "buddy buddy, can I help you with that, here's my lucky pen, milk or sugar," felt like a disgrace to their memories. Even if I did start to idolize Clay in a sense.

"Yeah, I heard you. I'll keep her here until you say otherwise. But not as a prisoner, she's better than that. She's my guest." I hang up before I find myself reprimanded for my tone, knowing I'll pay for it later.

My moods switch faster than I can keep up, and it's scary to me, never mind anybody else. Harper must be terrified right now, not knowing where she is, what's happening around her or who she's really with. I tease her microphone clip between my fingers. I should go to her. Wait, I'm the last person she'll want to see. Maybe she needs a hug. No, fuck off Kenneth, we just mentally discussed that!

A flash of red catches my eye, drawing my attention to my splintered knuckles. Oh no, that won't do. I listen through the door before cracking it open, not wanting to spook Harper if she's milling around. The door to the main bedroom is closed and I creep by unnecessarily, slipping into the bathroom. I gave Harper the en-suite to make sure she didn't feel uncomfortable, and then started professing my love and punching walls. What a gentleman.

Washing off the blood and bits of plasterboard stuck in my hand, I marvel at the bruises already blossoming there. Antonio thought my tolerance for pain was like a magic trick, and it sure served me well growing up in a tough neighborhood. We may have come from the same general area, but Clay's side of town was so far removed from mine, it's not even funny. Calmer, one might say. His streets looked after each other like one big family, mine attacked their neighbors on a daily basis.

I run a hand over my hair, eyeing the fading red in the oval hanging mirror. It's strawberry blond naturally, but I took to dying it the summer before I started at Waversea. The redder the better to match my freckles. Add in the fake glasses and there's Kenny Dockerson. I find it freeing, slipping into his character like a baby powder-lined morph suit. I rambled my every thought, acted on every impulse I had and no one paid any damn attention.

Walking back into the hallway, I hear Harper shuffling around in her room. Stuffing my hands in my jean pockets, I shift from foot to foot, not knowing what to do with myself. I walk to my room, immediately stride back towards the stairs. When in doubt, caffeine it out. Making my way to the lower level, I have a skip in my step all the way to the kitchen before switching on the coffee machine.

Leaning closer, I watch the black liquid pour smoothly into the glass base with an easy smile. I became quite the barista at the café, and no one even noticed my personal experiment to swap out their milk with lactulose, a laxative disguised as a sweet syrup. I had a whole chart drawn up behind the counter and everything, comparing the measure to the time it took for a student to bolt for the bathroom. The same bathroom for which I had the key stashed in my pocket. The record was Ester Griffith, who didn't make it past thirty seconds and shat herself right on the booth seat. In my defense, it was an incredibly slow day and I had some left-over magnesium citrate in my bag.

Huh. It just occurred to me I won't be able to return to Waversea after all this is over. No more science experiments in my breaks, no more midnight walks through the woods in a pig mask. I'll miss the hacking most, since I seem to have a flare for it, but my job is done. I don't hurt people for the fun of it, only those who inadvertently kill my cousin and ruin my life. Except now I'm harboring Harper and...hehe. Harboring Harper. Harbor the Harp as Harper's harborer. Say that five times drunk while doing a naked handstand.

The coffee finishes brewing, and I grab two cups from the rickety old cupboard. Only when I'm halfway through pouring the second do I realize what I'm doing, and place the pot back into its station. I stare into the swirling cup of blackness, my hand flexing towards it and back again. It's fine, I meant what I said. Harper is a guest here until I hear otherwise, and I should treat her as one. But then again, she appeals to the softer side of me and that dick is likely to do something stupid, like let her go.

Lifting the mug, I carry it to the sink, turning back and forth as indecision tears through me. It's just a fucking coffee. But it's so much more. It's a peace offering for the way I acted earlier, letting my jealously get the better of me like that. The way her eyes had lit up as I accidently let it slip Clayton was getting closer killed the last part of hope I had. Not for a relationship, because no one loves the monster and it's what I will always be in her eyes. But when Clay left college last time and then again this morning, she'd clean forgot about him and the tattooed cockwomble who's apparently playing chauffeur and she was just...my friend.

No. No friends, no ties. Revenge is all that matters. Because one way or another, Harper will leave here and never look back and when I'm utterly alone with the walls closing in on me, I'll be able to smile. Clayton Michaels had suffered the way I had, even if just for a week or two. He knew how it felt to lose your entire world in one night. It's the best I can hope for now.

Pouring the coffee down the drain, I throw the cup and it smashes in the sink. Stomping through the sitting room and up the stairs, I catch my reflection as I pass the open bathroom door. "Don't fucking look at me like that," I cry, running the rest of the way back to my temporary room. Slamming the door, I fist my hands and throw my feet down heavily in the most passive aggressive pacing to have ever existed.

This is all her fault! If she wasn't so fucking…her, everything would be easier. I could hate her, hurt her, and use her like the puppet I intended her to be. Not instinctively make her coffee, or stop at the supermarket while she's passed out in the truck to stock up on her blueberry shampoo. *You're not Kenneth, you're not Kenneth.* But then again…being him feels so much better than this. I grab the microphone clip off the bedside table, twiddling it between my fingers again. There's a sense of power to holding her connection to the world in the palm of my hand.

It's a good thing I'm already crazy, because being locked up with her would have bought me a one-way ticket to Nutsville. I'm the prisoner here, and all I want to do is be in her company. We could play some more board games, or maybe she'll read to me. *As if she'll want to be in the same room as you again,* my mind mocks me. I smack my head, trying to dislodge the thoughts descending like a tsunami. *You're nobody, she wouldn't have known your name if it weren't for Clay.*

Taking the assault from my head to the old-style bedframe, I reopen the eased cuts on my knuckles with a roar filled with anguish. It would have been better if she'd never joined Waversea. But, not knowing her would be a worse fate. I couldn't help the infatuation, my need for retribution basically vanishing in favor for watching her. Talking to her, maybe touching her. How could I not fall for her? When I wore Clay's clothes and slept in his bed, took the hugs she intended for him. I know what she wants and what she likes. And now she no doubt hates me, but it'll never be more than how much I hate myself. The loser no one wanted except his older cousin. But now, it's no one.

Rhys

"Eat this." I slide the piled plate across the table to where it stops before Clayton's mopey face. I mean seriously, who comes to an all-you-can-eat-buffet and sits with a tap water? I'm already pissed about the lack of answers I got yesterday while he sulked, but now he's embarrassing me. I return to the buffet spread, loading my own breakfast to match his. Pancakes, eggs, bacon, cinnamon French toast. Everything I need to fill me for another day of interrogating and threatening any fucker who might know where that shitface stalker has taken my girl.

Returning to our booth in the corner, I see Clayton has pushed the plate aside and I move it straight back again. He levels me with a glare as I sit and dive into mine, but as usual I pay him no mind. Still, it doesn't take a genius to notice he's barely eaten, his cheeks are hollowing out and it's only been a few days. As much as I'd like to rescue Harper myself, I've never been her 'savior'. I need him on top form, primed and ready to go.

"I'm not busting my ass to save Harper, for her to kill me when she sees what a state I've let you become. Now eat." I snarl at him with a mouthful of toast before ripping another bite out the bread. Tentatively, like a fucking mouse, he pulls off a section of pancake and nibbles at it.

"I can't keep up with your moods, I never know which side of you I'm going to get." *Yeah, yeah, you and me both.* Between my violent mood swings, the way my foot keeps searching for his in the night and the way I beat him for accepting it in the morning, I can hardly keep up myself.

The lines are becoming too blurred, my self-loathing and need for comfort blending into one big ball of fucked-up outbursts. I'm not even sure Harper would want me if she saw what I've become. And if she doesn't want me, I'm done with this life. She's my one shot, the light at the end of the tunnel. Snub her out and there's nothing left here for me.

I leave it so long, not even I think I'm going to respond to his comment but I can't stop the thoughts from plaguing me. This is what she wanted, us to be a team, a unit. Her protectors, brought together by the damaged parts we've kept hidden until she somehow fixed them all.

"I ...need her back. She levels me out, makes everything seem so easy. When she used to pull away from me before, it was difficult to continue functioning the way I did before she steamrolled into my life. But now...now I'm a fucking mess and I don't know what the fuck I'm doing anymore."

"You don't think I feel the same?" Clayton sneers back, shoving his plate away to lean on the table. His shoulders bunch in a matching white t-shirt to mine. Although he has been mostly subdued and solemn up to this point, there's now a fire raging in his eyes speaking volumes. He's as pissed as me, but he manages to keep it under lock and fucking key. How?

"At least I'm willing to fight for her. What's holding you back?" I watch his features carefully, drinking in the subtle shifts as he reins himself back in with fascination. I won't let myself admire him but damn, what has to happen before I manage self-control of that magnitude? Clayton sighs, reaching over for my coffee and I let him take it.

"When I was locked up, there was a group of guys who always sat together on the bleachers in the yard. They never spoke to anyone except each other, but they were always watching. They preyed on weakness, looking for any hint of vulnerability and cut it out of you. After a while, I noticed the group was growing and those I'd seen disrespecting them were suddenly by their side, silent and gormless. Rumor has it the guards let them run free with some electroshock devices to keep the prisoners in line, and they took turns using them on each other for fun. Fucking psychos if you ask me," Clay breathes out the last bit with a shake to his dirty blond waves.

"Anyway, the answer to your question is I'm not holding back. I've been conditioned to not show my feelings, as I believe you have too. But where I hold onto those poisonous traits, you reject them so much, you explode in random intervals I don't think you even know are coming." I watch him carefully, slowly stretching across the table to slide his plate back beneath his face.

We fall back into silence, me finishing my plate and Clayton almost making it through half of his. I'll take any small win I can get at this point. The waitress pops her head around our booth, clearing our plates and returning with the card machine. Her wide, darting eyes and full smile betray her eagerness to serve our every whim, and looking at the groups of decrepit old men around, I don't blame her. Handing me a receipt with her number scrawled across the bottom, I smirk and reach across to grab Clayton's hand.

"Sorry honey, we're taken," I wiggle my eyebrows. Her blush is overshadowed by Clayton's disgusted outburst, lurching as far away as he can in his seat. I chuckle, making kissy noises at him whilst telling him not to be shy, gaining side glances from everyone around us.

Exiting the diner, Clayton remains several steps behind me as I approach the Ford Raptor. *What a beautiful, fucking beast.* Hopping into the seat and caressing the wheel, I wait for my not-so welcome travel buddy to join me before turning on the engine. The throaty roar bleeding into the air around me is drowned out by Clayton asking what we're going to do now.

It's a great question, and not one I have the answer to. Yesterday, we visited every previous address held on record for

Dekken H. Cornstone, as well as some seedy clubs and back-streets he used to visit regularly. And in return for our efforts, we got nothing. Not a single trace he ever existed. No one recognized his college ID, even his old foster families barely remembered him which is why I call bullshit. I can't imagine the Kenneth who pissed himself when I got a decent jump-scare on him being the kind to have earned all this loyalty through money or fear. It sure as shit isn't through love, that's for certain.

Deciding to ignore Clayton's question, since I don't have an answer, I reach for the gear stick to get us back out there. Surely something will have to give soon, if we keep searching. Before I manage to put this beauty in drive, Clayton's hand lands on my arm and I round my narrowed eyes at him.

"Get. Off. Before I break your wrist." His flared nostrils and clenched jaw mirror mine, a moment of tension passing before he releases my arm on a huff.

"This needs to stop," he gestures to all of me. I roll my eyes towards the window, pretending to be fascinated by a raccoon raiding the dumpster round the back of the diner. This time when he grabs me with a tight grip on my shoulder, I throw my elbow into his gut as he's spinning me round to face him. And there it is again, the beast he keeps caged prowling beneath the surface.

Grabbing for my throat, the honk blares when I shift my knee to boot him in a mess of limbs in the enclosed space. His fist catches me numerous times and I welcome it, relishing the distraction from my thoughts. His meaty hands capture my wrists, attempting to lock them down while he rams a shoulder into my chest. I take the opportunity to lick the side of his face and comment 'kinky,' which has him diving away from me as I knew it would. He should know by now, it's all blurred lines and pleasure through pain with me.

"Ugh, stop doing that! For fuck's sake, we have a common goal here. So leave the bullshit in this truck and stop treating me like a threat. I never thought I'd say it, but I'm on your side,

Wavershit. Let's end this shit between us and get our girl back already."

"So we're doing this?" I raise an eyebrow, pointing between the two of us. I'm sure he's not going to answer, his hesitation to accept being a part of anything alongside me holding him back as always. Not that I can blame him. But, he thrusts his hand out palm up and meets my eye, resignation visible in his blackened stare. And something strange happens.

Something shifts inside my chest. Like the scales of my soul, which have always been tipped towards the festering darkness, have been nudged ever-so slightly in the other direction. Harper found a crack in my façade to wriggle into and inhabit, but Clayton? I've done nothing but bring misery to his life, and he's offering me his friendship. I try not to overthink, and fail miserably, as I gingerly slip my hand into his and clasp it.

"Okay Scum, let's get our girl back."

"This wasn't what I was expecting," I mumble, turning into the parking lot Clayton directed me to. I recognize the building as the care home we found him at last time I was in Detroit, making this two more times than I'd ever wanted to be.

"Well, we don't have any leads or places to go, and it occurred to me whilst talking to Dekken's foster mom yesterday I should drop in on my own. Besides, he visited here too. Maybe the staff will recognize him."

"Ahh, the whole two holes, one cock strategy. I like your thinking." Other than a slight side-eye, Clayton doesn't react and hops out of the cab with me on his heels. The sun is beating down on the green canopies and fully blossomed flowers, like a jungle has burst out of the ground and claimed the building in the center. Trellis' either side of the main door are hidden beneath a network of vines with white flowers dotted throughout. Several of them hang low, forcing me to duck as I pass.

I hang back while Clayton speaks to the old shrill of a receptionist, showing her Kenneth's college ID photo. She doesn't even look at it, grimacing as if Clayton is the shit on the bottom of her shoe and thrusts a sign-in book towards him. He's right on the lead front, yesterday was a complete write-off and we have nowhere else to try.

Following him through the hallways, we reach a door at the end when he pauses. I can see his hesitation and can practically hear the words on his tongue where he asks me to wait out here. It's not that I want to see his mom, but I find myself intrigued once again with his life and how he's managed to overcome challenges I struggle with. What makes him so much better of a man, and if it's as simple as having a mother, I want to know.

"On my best behavior," I vow with an awkward pat on his shoulder. This whole friendship thing will take some getting used to. With a nod, he opens the door and steps inside.

"Jellybean? Is that you?" A slight of a woman jumps out of her armchair as if she's seen a ghost. Her embroidery drops to the floor and she stands on it in her haste to make her way across the room.

"No mom, it's me. Claybake," he mumbles. I ignore his blush, moving around the room to lean against the window for a better view at the pair. "And er...this is my friend, Rhys."

"Nice to meet you, ma'am," I nod, wondering where the fuck that came from. Too many movies, I reckon.

"Oh Clay, you brought one of those high school friends you were telling me about. I always knew you'd be a popular one, like your brother. How's he doing at that fancy college, do you know?" Suddenly, I don't feel like a spectator but an intruder. I knew she was sick, but witnessing the pain in Clayton's eyes as he lies to her is brutal.

"Yeah, he's great. I'm sure he'll visit when he can." Clayton leads his mom back to her armchair, picking up her stitching and gently placing it on the coffee table. Taking the opposite seat, he leans forward to take her hand. "Mom, I want to ask you something, and I need you to focus for a moment, okay?"

Reaching for her mug, the woman smiles sweetly over the rim and I take a second to inspect her. It's clear to see where Clayton gets his coloring, the irises staring back at him so dark, they appear black. Blond waves cover her slender shoulders, the lack of grey suggesting she's younger than I expected. There's almost a regal strength to her posture, and the way she strokes her son's hand with her thumb fascinates me.

"Do you know who this is?" Clayton holds up his phone, no doubt with the image of the red-headed boy we're hunting for displayed on the screen.

"Ahh, little Dekken Cornstone," she smiles and my stance straightens. "Such a sweet boy. Terrible what happened to his family." Clayton shares a look with me before gently removing the mug from her hands and kneeling in front of her. I cross the room and drop into his vacated seat, eager to have our first lead since arriving.

"Take your time mom, but this is important. What can you tell us about Dekken?"

"Well that's easy. I was working in the ER when they brought him in with his cousin. It was the end of my shift and I was dead on my feet, but he was inconsolable so I offered to sit with him. He'd found his cousin in an alley, gunshot to the sternum but he was still alive, just. That young boy fought so hard but he died on the operating table. I broke the news to Dekken." Clayton hangs his head, his breath growing labored. Without thinking, I reach out to place a hand on his shoulder, but catch myself and use it to lift him back up and hiss 'focus' in his ear.

"It wasn't two weeks before I saw him again, he sought me out after his uncle...well, nasty business, that. He begged for my help and I would have brought him home if I could, but we were barely getting by as it was. It was the winter the boiler went and we snuck into the swimming pool after dark to use the showers, remember Claybake?"

Clayton nods solemnly, shifting forward to lay his head on her knees. His mom strokes her fingers through his hair, staring out of the window.

"Even though I'd wanted to, the police came and took him away. I never forgot his strawberry blond hair, his scruffy face and how his bones stuck out too much. But we reconnected, and he's a lovely young man now." Clayton sits upright, asking her a string of questions but her gaze is lost to the gardens outside.

"Mom, please. Do you know where he would stay if he came back to town?" Clayton lifts his phone once more, pushing the image into her eyeline. She focusses, a smile pulling at her lips once more.

"Oh, that's little Dekken Cornstone. Such a sweet boy. Terrible what happened to his family." On a deep sigh, Clayton rubs her forearm and picks up the embroidery, placing it back in her hands. She looks down and gasps with joy, seemingly haven forgotten about the sewn image of two penguins she's nearly completed.

"Take care mom. I love you."

"I love you, Jellybean," she answers vaguely, fully invested in her stitching once more. We exit the room, Clayton pulling the door closed softly with a defeated slump to his shoulders.

"Don't," is all I get before he walks away, leading the way straight back to the truck. I stick my tongue into my cheek, narrowing my eyes at the unhelpful receptionist as I pass. Once back behind the driver's wheel, I stroke the ripped leather and refraining from asking the question burning a hole in my mind. *What the fuck are we going to do now?*

When I can't take the strained silence any longer, I open my mouth but I'm interrupted by the vibrating of Clayton's phone. He pulls it from his pocket, barely glancing at the screen before his whole body stiffens. He throws a fist into my bicep, despite the fact I was already looking, and shows me the display.

Incoming call: Kenneth Dockerson

Harper

"What do you have there?" Dekken's voice flares to life in my head, making me jump out of my skin. I spin, shoving the phone into my back jean pocket. It was stupid really, but I'd seen his unlocked phone left on the sofa when he went to the kitchen and simply acted on impulse. Only when I'd already pressed call did I realize, I wouldn't be able to hear if Clay even answered, but I'd wanted to reach out. For him to know I'm safe...if I am safe?

"I thought...I thought we had an agreement." Dekken's voice sounds small, but the defensive clench of his fists are anything but. I watch the wall slide down over his emotions, the guy that was offering to make some lunch for us both a distant memory. "Harper, give me my phone."

"Dekken, it doesn't have to be like this. We can talk it out, all of us. If you come clean with Clay, I'm sure we could work something-" He lunges at me, forcing a scream through my lips as I attempt to dodge him. Not that there's anywhere to go. He grabs my waist and throws me back towards the staircase. My back slams into the bannister, all the air leaving my lungs on a gasp as pain bursts through my diaphragm. I fall to the ground, struggling to breathe as the phone is removed from my pocket.

I remain as still as my tremors will allow, on my hands and knees waiting for Dekken's next move. After a few minutes, I brave a glance around to find myself alone and slump onto the floor. Focussing on pulling air into my body and exhaling deeply, I manage to slow my erratic heartbeat enough to sit up. Fuck, I don't know what I was thinking except for the need to hear one of their voices. To know what's happening, yet I don't even know if he answered the call.

Water drops onto the open gap at my knee, alerting me to the tears streaming down my face. I went into this kidnapping all wrong. I believed I still had a choice, and allowed myself to be too calm when what I should have been doing was establishing my role at a prisoner. A pissed as hell, badass prisoner who would fight with everything she had to be free.

But no, I went full Belle and empathized with my kidnapper. Now I don't know who holds the power and if it's better to fight or try to reason with him. I stay on the floor, lost to the silence and my thoughts until long after the tears have stopped. What I'm crying for, I'm not exactly sure. A mix of everything, I guess.

I've never regretted my loss of hearing, in fact I've embraced it. In a world where I had no parents or future, I was happy to drift into an alternate reality of my own creation. One built from fantasies of warrior princesses and hero knights, red scaled dragons and the odd sexy vampire lurking in the shadows. But since the day I started at Waversea, reality hit me with a force I didn't see coming. And now I'm here, trapped and pining for two men who may or may not be on their way to me or tearing each other to shreds. *If only I could have heard his voice...*

I push myself onto numb legs, robotically walking back up the stairs after Dekken's outburst, just like yesterday. Spying the safety of my room, the one place he has refused to enter so far, I stop. *I'm the victim in this situation, right?* I shouldn't feel *safe*, or run back to my refuge when things get too difficult to manage. Doing that won't get me out of here, and if the excitement filled me at the thought of contacting my boys is anything to go by, I'm certainly ready to leave.

Holding onto the railing overlooking the living area, I

move forward slowly, keeping the rest of my senses on high alert since I'm one down. The creak of floorboards crunch beneath my socked feet, my heart thumping against my chest. I eye the hatch in the ceiling, wondering if he'd shove me back there if caught snooping.

There's five closed doors on the second level, one being my bedroom and another an unfortunate-colored bathroom, complete with mint green basin and toilet. Along the hallway, I find a strange take on a music room. Leather sofas sits around the edges, with a dusty piano positioned in the middle and nothing else.

Opening the door at the far end, I walk into a hoarder's paradise. Boxes upon boxes are piled high, several scattered around the room filled with paperwork. I peek inside the cardboard box closest to my legs, finding bits of ornaments and collectables that have been left here to waste away. The window in this room isn't covered by a blind, the sun shines upon a pile of long dress covers laid across an armchair. It's as if someone's whole life has been packed into this one room and forgotten about. Miss Della-Rae Taylor's, to be specific, if the name on the paperwork is any indication.

Stepping back into the hallway and closing the door on the life hiding beyond it, I turn to find the last door locked, which is no doubt where Dekken's hiding. Knocking softly on the wood, I ask if he'll let me talk to him. I stand for couple of minutes, shifting foot to foot while wondering if he even heard me. Getting ready to give up, the door is whipped open and Dekken grips my arm, dragging me inside faster than my brain can register. Opening my mouth to protest, I'm thrust into his firm chest and enveloped in his arms. The shudders rolling through his body tell me he's crying, so after a stiff moment, I return his hug and let him.

What the fuck am I doing? So much for fighting my way out of here. A generic aftershave wraps around me, the cotton of his long sleeve shirt brushing against my cheek. His small but solid biceps hold me against him without much room for argument. If he had another violent mood swing right now, he could snap my neck with ease and the thought sends a chill straight to my bones.

Easing myself out of his body but still in his arms, I lead the way over to the bed before thinking better of it and spotting a wide windowsill. Setting Dekken on one side, I sit opposite and lean against the wall.

"I'm sorry, I didn't mean to upset you. I wasn't even trying to escape, I just…"

"Love him?" Dekken supplies for me, having switched on the mic clip on his collar. I nod, unable to hold his intense stare so turn to look out of the window. It looks like such a beautiful day, the warmth seeping through the glass kissing my skin. In the distance, if I look hard enough, I can see the faint spires of civilization, towers or a church maybe?

"Both of them," I finally answer out loud. Dekken's jaw clenches and I quickly try to calm his inner psycho. "I'm just being honest, isn't that what friends do? I wouldn't really know, considering I've never had any." I breathe out a laugh in an attempt to diffuse the situation. Dekken's grunt and long exhale show I didn't manage it.

"Why them? You never even gave me a chance."

"I don't even know who you are Dekken." I whisper. I leave out the fact he's never shown affection towards me more than his usual, creepy ways or I would have gently shut him down a long time ago.

"Neither do I," he admits. His head hangs low and I see him for what he is. A broken man, one who's lost his way and doesn't know how to come back. I begin to ease him with the usual words of everything being okay, but he shakes his head and glances back to me with eyes so sad, I feel my own tears prick in response. "There's something wrong with me, Harper. I don't know what I'm going to do next or how to control it anymore. It's gotten so much worse since I brought you here, and

I'm scared I'm going to hurt you. Or...I'm just scared."

Shuffling forward, I reach out and take Dekken's hands in mine. "You're not going to hurt me," I tell him with more faith than I really feel. I'm not a master at talking to insane people, but if Rhys has taught me anything, it's everyone has their reasons and everyone can be reached. "Dekken, I've listened to your story and I've understood your pain. It's clear you need someone to talk to, although I'd recommend someone professional. Why don't we sort this thing out, together? No one has to get hurt and we'll get you the help you need."

Dekken stares at me for too long, forcing me to hold his gaze. I meant every word, the truth of it plain enough to see in my even breathing. When he does break eye contact, it's to look over at the phone vibrating on the bedside table. The screen flashes on and off with its movements, but it's Dekken's hands tightening on mine drawing my attention. What exactly is he scared of – himself or someone else? The phone rings out, Dekken's head hanging in defeat

"You're right," he whispers into the mic. "I know you are, I got caught up. But I shouldn't..."

"Whoever you're worried about, remember this is your life. You control it, you can fix it and despite everything, I will help you. All you have to do is take the first step, and I'll handle the rest."

"You promise?" His head flies up, the vulnerably shining in his brown eyes pulling at my heartstrings. "Everyone I've ever cared about has left me one way or another, I can't lose anyone else." If I wasn't sure about my plan to get out of here before, I am now. Yeah okay, he's done a lot of shit and most of it was indirectly aimed at me pre-kidnapping. But if I can forgive Rhys for his past, it would be hypocritical for me to turn away someone who clearly wants help. He needs someone to give enough of a fuck to give it to him.

"I promise."

∞∞∞∞

I place my bag by the front door, walking into the kitchen with a lightness to my step. Like returning home after the last day of summer camp and running into the open arms of loved ones, if that's what is waiting for me. Rhys I have no doubt would take me anyway he could, regardless of the harsh words I delivered in an attempt to cut the tie. But Clay...it remains to be seen where I stand with him, but at least I'm going to get the chance to see now.

Dekken is dishing up dinner by the time I reach the kitchen. Apparently it's quite a drive back to Waversea, so we decided on one last, filling meal before hitting the road. Luckily, I'll be an awake and willing passenger this time. My stomach aches as the scents of pasta carbonara reach me, the smokiness of bacon mixed with onion and garlic making my mouth water.

"I didn't know you could cook," I smirk, taking a seat.

"Years of practice looking after myself," he replies easily but there's no venom in his tone. Like me, Dekken has changed into a comfortable tracksuit for the drive. He places the bowls down and sits beside me, allowing us to fall into a comfortable silence. I shouldn't feel relaxed until I'm breathing the fresh air, but the butterflies in my stomach are overpowering my emotions. What will I say to the guys, will anything have changed? The sad truth is if I hadn't been taken, I would have driven home and possibly never seen them again. So after this, I might be thanking Dekken.

I finish in record time, moving across the room to wash the bowl and place it in the rack. Night has fallen behind the closed blinds, the dim overhead light casting shadows across the yellow and orange décor. It's a shame this place has been left to rot considering how large the rooms are, and I'm sure it's isolated enough to draw in a fellow hermit. One who's not in the business of abducting deaf girls and stuffing them in the attic. While waiting for Dekken, I rummage through the cupboards and pull out several bags of chips and biscuits.

"What?" I ask, turning to see his amused expression. "Need snacks for the road." Dekken chuckles, leaving his bowl in the sink and retrieving a bag for me to dump my arm-full of goodies into. Adding in a few bottles of water from the fridge, Dekken takes the bag and walks me to the front door, releasing the two locks before looking back at me.

"You ready?" My smile grows with my nod, Dekken grabbing the bags before yanking the door open. I don't immediately see what makes him halt and tense as I crash into the back of his lanky body, but peeking between his arm and the doorway, I see them.

A fleet of cop cars barely visible in the night, the moon reflected in their windscreens. I can't make out the megaphone-enhanced words through the mic clip, but something is being said which makes Dekken tremble. I try to sidestep him but he holds me back, his grip on my forearm painfully tight. Refusing to hide away any longer, I twist out of his hold and step forward anyway, realizing the severity of the standoff. Not a single siren is on, lines of red light from various snipers pierce the darkness directly onto Dekken's chest.

I don't panic, I don't even think. Relying on base instinct, I step in front of the now-quivering man that has kept me here, and feel the weight of my decision as soon as those red dots land on my body. A thousand words die on my tongue as I open my mouth, the shaky breaths sounding through my head not belonging to me. I promised to get him the help he needs, so here goes nothing.

"Don't shoot!"

Clayton

"What the fuck is she doing?!" Rhys roars from beside me, his hand flying to the door handle until I pin him back into place. His knee hits the steering wheel in an attempt to fight me off, but with my strength and an enclosed space, he was never going to get the upper hand.

"If you run in there shouting, he could hurt her. Let's trust she knows what she's doing, alright?" Rhys stops fighting against me but I keep my arm across him just in case. We arrived at the intersection leading to this deserted lot the same time the police did, thanks to Rhys' PI who traced the phone number and our tip off to the cops. But despite Rhys' begging to run inside and drag Dekken out by his neck, we were unsurprisingly told to wait back and let them do their job.

"She's going to get herself killed," Rhys snarls, his body ridged with tension. One of the cars near the front has switched on their headlights, giving us a clear view of Harper, arms raised and defending Dekken. Fuck's sake, she always did have to see the good in everyone. After a moment, Dekken rests a hand on her shoulder with a low shake of this head. Pushing something into her palm, he gently pushes her towards the porch steps and drops to his knees. The police surge in, their focus on detaining Dekken and it's all Rhys needs to be out of the Ford and running the last stretch of the dirt track.

Hopping out, I jog after him and match his stride with ease. Two female officers are trying to talk to Harper by the time we approach, but even I can see the headlights in her face are making her dazed and confused.

"Hey! She can't hear you," I say too gruffly, my protective streak ruling me. Rhys doesn't give a shit, he barrels through to officers and lifts Harper off her feet with a squeal. Dumping her on the hood of the car, he leans back long enough to check her over for injuries before his tongue is in her mouth. A few moments pass where everyone watches them with raised eyebrows, myself included.

"We'll need her to come to the station and make a formal statement," says the short female cop by my side. I watch the masses pack away their guns and SWAT equipment now there's no longer a threat. Dekken is in the back of the car behind us whilst many of the officers are storming the house.

"Not right now. She's been through an ordeal and he'll crack within minutes. We'll take care of her tonight and bring her in tomorrow." My tone leaves no room for argument, and my patience has officially run out. Sliding my arms around Harper, I pull her away from Rhys' attack on her face and carry her towards the Ford. She doesn't speak, her arms sliding around my neck and burying herself into my t-shirt. For a moment, I wish the walk could have been longer so I could keep her against me, safe and protected where she should be. So much has happened since I told her I couldn't handle this, but it feels like the words are void now. She's ours and we're hers. Nothing else matters anymore.

Sliding into the back seat with her in my arms, I vaguely register Rhys hopping in the other side instead of behind the wheel. The light in the cab goes out, leaving us in complete darkness with our girl still clinging to my neck. Rhys' shoulder and thigh bump mine as we sit side by side, and I shift Harper into the middle so she's straddling both of us. And there we stay. Her fingers draw small patterns on my nape, her head on our joined shoulders and something about it feels right. Only once in a while does my hand stroking her back touch his, but whereas before I would have recoiled, now I take comfort she has both of us to give her the attention she deserves.

I never want this moment to end. I could waste away in this darkened cab, my girl pressed against me and I'd be a happy man. But the world won't wait and there's no rush now we're together again. Reaching up, I flick on the overhead light and ease her back gently.

"Are you okay?" I ask slowly. Her brown curls are limp and knotted, her emerald eyes shimmering with unshed tears betrayed by the wobble in her bottom lip. Reaching out, Harper opens her hand to reveal a microphone clip and attaches to my t-shirt sleeve, the most central point between Rhys and me.

"I'm fine, really. It's just been...a rough few days now I think about it."

"If that fucker has touched a hair on your head, I'm going to break him out of that holding cell, string him up as a human piñata and beat him with a baseball bat until his organs fall out." Rhys seethes, I can't blame him. I feel the same, just not quite as imaginatively. Harper smiles, stroking the stubble he's allowed to grow on his jaw.

"Can we...leave?" She asks, not answering his threat. Sneaking another kiss, Rhys extracts himself and slides out of the cab. After a moment, I realize he isn't getting into the driver's seat and notice the orange flare of a cigarette through the window. Sneaky fucker, he knows there's so much I need to say to Harper, but now I have the chance, no words come out.

"You guys seem cozy, considering I couldn't get you in the same room most the time." Harper smirks but it doesn't fully reach her eyes. There's pain swirling in those green orbs and I put it there.

"Let's just say we've settled our differences, for you." I brush my thumb over her bottom lip and stroke her jaw, marvelling how soft her skin is even after her recent abduction. Harper pulls away from me, her eyes trained on the floor as the first tear falls. "Hey, don't cry. It's all going to be okay now."

"Is it?" Harper swings her gaze back to me and I'm rendered silent by those two words. "If it wasn't for all of this, would you have 'settled your differences' or would I be sitting alone in a heap of cat hair? What about next time you guys fall out? Should I jump off a bridge to make you realize you want me?" The tears fall easily now, her sobs breaking the resolve I didn't think I had left. She falls against me once more, her cries filling the car as I hold her tight. Even if I knew what to say, she wouldn't be able to hear me over her crying so I do the next best thing.

Smoothing shaky thumbs over her cheeks, I lift her face and press my lips against hers. Tentatively at first, the saltiness of her tears branding itself on my soul, then fiercer. I pour my emotion into the melding of our lips, needing her to feel it all the way down to the cracks of her heart which I caused. I'm a fucking idiot for ever thinking I could leave her, that I didn't belong to her the first moment she entered Peterson's lab and chose to sit beside me. Me. The guy everyone avoided so I hid at the back, but she saw me.

From our first meeting, she challenged my bad attitude and started something so powerful, I wouldn't have believed it were possible if I didn't feel it with such passion. I love this girl. No, I fucking worship this girl. She is my queen and I'm her protector, ready to take on the world in her name. And even if I have to share her, she's given me more than I could have ever dreamed of. A place to call home, and it resides right there in her chest.

"Harper, look at me," I manage to finally pull away from her, instantly needing another taste. Her eyes are like daggers to my gut, and I mentally swear those are the last tears she'll ever cry because of me. "I knew the second I took the first step away from you I'd made a mistake. I have been stubborn about it, but I wouldn't have lasted a single day without coming for you. I've hurt you, and I'm so sorry. But this," I knock on the window for the chain-smoking retard outside to join us. Rhys pops the door to rest his forearms on the leather seat, watching us closely.

"This is going to work because we love you. More than you realize, and we'll spend every day proving it to you. Together."

The smile spreading across Harper's face is everything. Her hands link with both of ours and her spark is back in full force, laughter bubbling from her lips.

"Let's get out of here," she giggles and Rhys lets out a whoop.

Harper

The days blur by in a haze of sleeping and questions. I didn't realize how much the whole ordeal had taken out of me until I found myself in a luxurious hotel bed, tangled in the arms of my men. They've given me time to rest, but haven't taken as much as a step away from my side without ensuring the other is there. The old me would have found them overbearing, but not now. I relish each lingering touch and sign of affection like a balm to my wounded pride and heart.

The officer assigned to my case is growing irritated as I still refuse to press charges against Dekken. Maybe this would have been the big break in his career he'd always hoped for, but it doesn't matter to me. I promised to help Dekken and he needs to be in a mental health institution, not a jail cell. Which is why I'm back here once again, listening to the pleading of Officer Mustache and getting the evil eye from his superior.

Rhys reacted the same at first, unable to hide his frustration no matter how hard he tried. But when it came down to it last night, he agreed to back my decision as long as I promised not to have contact with him again. I wasn't in a hurry to see Dekken again anyway and if that's the condition for him to get better, then so be it.

Leaning into Clay's side, I yawn loudly and he calls it a day. This was the cop's last attempt but I've told them from the beginning, I'll only comply if Dekken is offered an insanity plea deal. Rising from the uncomfortable metal chair, I don't bother looking back as we stride through the precinct arm in arm and find the Ford waiting at the base of the outside steps. Rhys slides out from behind the wheel, dragging me into his arms as if it's been weeks since he last saw me, not a few hours. I'll never get enough of his hugs, which he's fully embraced without hesitation now, and wish we could go back to the hotel. But we need to return to reality at some point.

Clay steps in behind, probably noticing the weight behind my sigh. His hands run over my shoulders as he gently eases me away from Rhys and opens the rear door. I slide across the backseat, expecting Clay to jump in beside me like normal but Rhys beats him to it. Throwing Clay the keys, he pulls me into his side and places a kiss on my forehead.

"We don't have to go back yet, if you don't want to," Clay says, after settling himself behind the wheel and adjusting the seat for his large frame. His voice echoes around the cab and into my phone's mic. Keeping it on and in my hand has been the easiest way to hear everyone around the precinct without constantly passing my only microphone clip around or watching the overbearing attempts at sign that make me cringe.

"Yeah, we do," I respond. "It's only a couple of weeks until summer break, and we're all slacking. If I don't push myself to get this degree, I don't know what I'm going to do with my life."

"I'm sure Dean Lawrence would understand if you needed more time. Maybe we could catch up over the summer-"

"Ermmm, absolutely fucking not," Rhys cuts him off. "This will be my first holiday with a reason to have fun, I'm not giving that up for anything." I smirk whilst drawing patterns on his inked forearm with my index finger. I see his dick twitch in his loose sweatpants, my smile widens. Every time I touch him the slightest bit, he's rock hard and raring to go, yet he hasn't made a move on me once. Not even when I crawled into bed in just my underwear after a shower. Both he and Clay have agreed to hold off to make it 'special', even though any time with them both together would be special, but I'm glad for the short reprieve to get my head straight. I want to give them all of me, and I need to be in the right place to do so.

Clay rolls the vehicle forward once we're all buckled in, merging onto the main street with ease. His driving style is calmer than Rhys', seeming to enjoy the ride or maybe the feel of the truck, whereas I would describe Rhys as erratic like usual. He lives in the fast lane, turns without indicating and has a sense of entitlement over everyone else on the road. I get it, Rhys has built up his character as a means to survive, but being his girl-friend means I need to soften his edges, right?

The journey is short, considering the deserted house was only a state away but I still wish Clay could have driven slower, stretched out our return. I snuggle into Rhys in my sweats, my eyelids growing heavy but I don't want to sleep yet. I want to inhale his rich scent, free of cologne, feel the thump of the heart he claimed not to have.

Night has started falling by the time the gothic spires of the dean's halls come into view, right around the same time as the masses of people does. Crowds with signs and cameras filling the main driveway rush towards the truck, forcing Clay to take a sharp turn and use a back entrance. It doesn't help. The crowd chases us, surrounding the vehicle once parked behind my old dorm.

I don't even have the chance to contemplate what hap-pened the last time I was in this very spot, as flashes of cameras beat against the windows like the firing end of a gun. Rhys tries to shield me with his body, but they are coming from all sides so instead he plucks the phone from my hand and switches off the mic. With a wobbly smile, he pushes his way out of the door and barks orders for everyone to back up, I presume, judging by the crowd's sudden lurch away. Offering his hand, I take it and allow him to pull me out of the truck.

Clay is in front of me in an instant, using his body to shove a path through the people closing in on us once more. I keep my head down for the most part, and each occasional glimpse I brave up, I see banners and signs with my name splayed across from people I've never even seen before. Reporters thrust microphones into my face, as if any fully hearing person would be able to hear them over the noise I imagine is being made.

Eventually, at an incredibly slow pace, we make it inside my dorm halls. I look around the stairwell, suddenly noticing I'm not where I expected and give Rhys a questioning look.

"*His place is even worse,*" Clay mouths for me. Ushering me up the stairs before the main door is broken in, we close in on my dorm as the door swings open. A flurry of pink pajamas barrels into me, the familiar scent of bubble-gum dousing my senses. Reaching up, Addy slips my spare set of receivers over my ears before cradling my face in her hands.

"I've missed you so much!" her squeal makes me flinch. I smile, despite the tug of guilt I seem to feel at the tears welling in her eyes. I didn't ask to be kidnapped, but I didn't really fight it either and she must have been so worried. They all were, while I was being selfish.

"I was only gone a week," I try to brush off. The four of us enter the dorm, Addy pulling me onto her bed and the boys sitting on mine opposite. A moment passes where we are all clearly thinking, 'now what?' until Clay pushes his hand into his jeans pocket.

"Here." He tries to give Rhys the keys to the Ford back, but Rhys shrugs.

"Nah, keep 'em."

"Is this the part where you tell me I have to drive it back to the rental place in Michigan so you can steal time with Harper?" Rhys' eyes burn into mine, a mischievous smile pulling at his lips showing he's contemplating it. But in the next second, it's gone and he returns his carefree gaze back to Clay beside him.

"I didn't rent it, I bought it. But I've got my Porsche back now so I've no need for a truck. You do though, considering I told the officer to scrap your orange hunk of shit after they finished with it." A vein pops in Clay's temple briefly as I watch the pair with fascination, until he realizes he has the keys to a brand-new Ford Raptor in his possession.

"So I start a bromance with you and you give me a car?"

"You're a reflection of me now *Claybake*, you have to look the part." I swear I see a smirk grace Clay's face at the pet name, the two turning back to face my confused expression. It's like that weird feeling one would get from seeing their divorced parents suddenly getting on after years of fighting and bitching. Creepy and unnerving but definitely for the best.

"We can wait it out in here and sneak back to mine when the Harpies grow bored. That's what they're calling themselves all over the app," Rhys explains with an amused roll of his eyes. I try to return his smile, but it's all so much. The sudden rush of fans, the cameras, the reporters are no doubt publishing about my life story across every website and paper, even the boys getting along like old friends. It's what I want, but everything is changing so quickly after my week of quiet, my head is spinning.

"Maybe I could...I mean, I want to go to yours. But I just..."

"Need some space?" Clay supplies, his face the picture of understanding. I nod shyly, leaning into Addy's arms further.

"I want a bit of normality back before we rush into the three of us being...a throuple? There's no urgency now, right?" The boys stand together, making their way over to me. Rhys pulls me up first, spinning me so my back is leaning against his front and Clay's chest pressed against my cheek.

"No rush, Babygirl," he whispers against my receiver. They each take a turn kissing me with tender longing before saying goodbye and leaving. The dorm seems larger without their united presence, but my heart feels heavier. I want to run after them and beg them to stay, but I know I need some time to process everything. Now I'm not worried about being stalked, I can be a normal college girl again. Besides, the start of a relationship should be the most exciting part, and I want to enjoy it for as long as possible.

"Well, it seems we have a lot to talk about." Addy giggles from her bed, her eyes dancing with mischief. I pull off my hoodie, slip out of the sweatpants and drag my bra out of my t-shirt sleeve.

"No talk, just sleep," I say, sliding beneath the duvet with her.

∞∞∞∞

I wake to an obnoxiously wide smile, full of Addy's straight teeth shining in my face. Ugh, I have not missed how chirpy she is in the mornings. The smell of coffee hits me next, and I drag myself upright with a hand over my eyes. Outstretching the other one, I demand she gives it to me and feel the weight of a travel mug being placed in my hand. I drink at least half before removing the hand from my eyes, reveling in the heavenly hazelnut latte as Addy waits for me on the other side of my blurred vision.

"Come on, lazy bones. I'm dying to see what's inside," She signs to me, before turning to retrieve a box from the desk and placing on the bed. It's cardboard and plain, but I sense something ominous going on here.

"Where did it come from?" I sign back lazily with one hand.

"It was on the doorstep," she beams. When I don't move other than to raise an eyebrow, Addy sighs dramatically and opens it for me while I watch. Inside lays my stuff. First she pulls out my '#antisocial' t-shirt, followed by my leather jacket, ripped jeans and leather biker boots. Oh god, I'd totally forgotten about my boots having spent the last week slumming around in tracksuits and trainers. Alongside were my toiletries, hairbrush and make-up bag that were left in the truck, there's a note.

You asked for normal. Get dressed and get to class. Don't be late.

Picking my phone up off the bedside table, I see that I am indeed, running late. Vaulting out of the bed, I shove my coffee into Addy's hands and quickly dress. The grin doesn't leave her face as she watches me brush my hair fiercely enough to bruise my scalp, and I hold my middle finger up at her in the mirror's reflection. Running to brush my teeth, I shove on my jacket and shoes to find her waiting for me by the door.

"*Breakfast?*" she winks, and I have the sudden suspicion she wasn't so eager to see what was in the box, because she's in on whatever this is. But I'm going to release the reins and let it happen, because no two days with Addy or my boys are the same and I'm ready to see what today brings.

Rhys

Harper breezes in, the image of the girl I first met. As if one night with Addy has rejuvenated her, there's a confidence to her stride and strength to her posture whilst striding into the lab. She doesn't falter seeing me at the first desk and Clayton hiding at the back, both of us with an empty stool by our side. The new biochemistry teacher approaches her, a beaming smile in place despite Harper being late.

"Ahh, Harper Addams, I presume?" The woman is enthusiastic, to say the least. Her dirty blonde hair falls to her shoulders in crazed waves which match the wild set to her blue eyes, the kind that screams mad scientist. "I'm Professor Madisetti, but call me Liz. Master Waversea has requested for you to be his lab-partner for the rest of the semester, but I don't take orders from him so sit where you like."

I raise my eyebrow, not half as pissed as the old me would have been at the professor's insolence. Harper definitely approves, high fiving her before sliding her phone onto the front desk. Walking past me, she sticks her tongue out and I gnash my teeth at her playfully. I glance back to see her take a seat beside Clayton, as I'd planned. Well, for the most part.

Returning to her introduction of herself, Liz's voice fills the front of the room, but I'm too focused on Harper to pay attention. I'd fallen asleep with my phone in my hand last night, scrolling through the app and putting people claiming to be Harpies back in their place. For this 'normal' day to go to plan, I can't have students gawking or following my girl around. I can't take all the credit, since Clayton was the mastermind behind the idea, but I'll be the one to see it through.

Everyone around me pulls out their laptops or notepads, taking notes now the lesson has officially begun. 'Equilibrium concentrations', oh the joys. I studied this and most of the other curriculum's topics when I was a preteen, driven by specialized tutors when I thought I had a future worth living for. But the more aggressive my father's beatings became over the following years, the more I was determined to do the exact opposite of what he wanted.

Slouching over the table, I keep my eyes fixed on the clock hanging above the door, watching the minutes tick down until I can pull Harper into me again. I'll never grow bored of her blueberry shampoo or soft skin pressed against my chest. If I had my way, she'd never leave, but I know how important getting a degree is to her so if I have to sit this far away to keep myself from distracting her, so be it because not being in the same room isn't an option. She's like a drug I'm addicted to and have no intention of letting go.

Liz is scribbling 'tid-bits', as she calls them, over the smart board when something hits me in the back. I twist to see a sea of paper airplanes scattered across the floor in obvious failed attempts, and raise an eyebrow at the sniggering pair at the back of the room.

"*You're supposed to be learning,*" I mouth and then frown at myself. Fuck, who have I become? Swooping down, I gather the airplanes before Liz turns back around, feigning total innocence when she eyes me skeptically. Every time she back turns, I spin on my stool to fire the aeroplanes, hitting several other students on the way and receiving a face full in return.

"Master Waversea," I turn to see Liz leaning over my desk. "Care to enlighten us how we will find the concentration of each species when the reaction comes to equilibrium?" I look over her shoulder to the slides on the board, pulling from my fragmented memories for the days I spent in the home-version of a classroom made just for me.

"Well, given that we have the delta G and initial concentration of glucose one-phosphate, we'll make an ICE chart to assess the initial change in equilibrium by tracking the path of the calculation."

The class is silent behind me and the taste of the words on my tongue are vile. Ugh, I don't think I've ever been so disgusted with myself and that's saying something. Liz returns to the front, sifting through papers for some hand-outs which she presses on my desk with the instruction to 'take one, pass the rest back'. Counting through the stack, I find the copy that will reach Harper and scribble a note on it before complying. Only Susanne-Shit-For-Brains drops them across the floor and Whore-To-All-Harlow gets my kinky message, giving me a suggestive wiggle with her eyebrows. *No thank you.*

The rest of the days goes mostly the same, between stealing kisses from Harper's lips at the lockers and snarling at anyone who gets too close to her at lunch, I sit through each dull lecture until my brain is ready to implode. Where do they even find these professors? At the national suicide convention and their rehabilitation is to spread the misery?

Harper was right though, we haven't had the chance to enjoy the blossoming of our relationship. Other than the worry over her safety, I've been a cock like usual. But I want this, to feel the butterflies when she walks into a room looking badass as ever, the jokes and laughter I never thought would be mine. So even though I'm bordering driving the ballpoint pen in my hand into my ears, I know I'll be here again tomorrow. And the next day, and the next, because it's where she'll be.

The last lecture of the day finally finishes, Vickers dismissing the class with her frail tone. Someone needs to convince her to retire, if not for my sanity than for the sake of her cats when she keels over on the desk. Waiting for everyone else to leave first, I throw my empty backpack over my shoulder and stand in time to intercept Harper.

"Hey beautiful, what you up to later?" I throw in a wink to make her smile, and can't contain the flurry of excitement building in me when she does. I reach for her, but Clayton's arm winding around her middle beats me to it. I roll my eyes and fist my hands, knowing I've been hogging her every chance I get but who can blame me, I'm a selfish prick and she's fucking beautiful.

"I don't know, I'll see where the wind takes me," she replies coyly. *Yeah, right.*

"Well let's hope it blows you to the gymnasium, and then you can blow me in the shower." Her giggle fills the room as I walk away, unable to be that close and not have her bared to me. My blue balls have turned glacial, but I know when I finally get her at my mercy again, it'll be so worth it.

The pair follow me all the way to the gymnasium, since Clayton has practice like I do and we both know ultimately Harper goes where we go. The team were already on the court when we entered, but I still take my time getting Harper seated and sneaking a fiery kiss before heading off to change. Clayton catches up with me in the locker room, pulling his kit out of his gym bag and starts to strip.

"I'm pleasantly surprised by your restraint today," he comments as I pull out the shorts pressed and folded in my locker.

"Don't fucking patronise me. I meant what I said last night, I'll do whatever it takes to make Harper happy. It's all I have to live for." When he doesn't respond, I turn to find him leaning against Coach's office window, waiting for me. His eyes are watching me too closely, so I finish dressing and storm out of the room ahead of him. Harper eyes me curiously as I step onto the court and I force myself to relax my bunched shoulders.

Coach jumps up from the side bench, ready to get practice started now I've arrived. Barking orders for us to warm up, I fall into line but my eyes are fixed on Harper. She has her laptop open on her knees, no doubt working on the assignments we were given today. Looking over the screen, her green eyes captivate me briefly before she looks away and the connection is broken.

With her close and safe, I'm able to commit to the practice drills and for once, actually enjoy myself. I run the length of the court, dropping into a set of push-ups before running to repeat the same on the other side. My muscles burn deliciously, my body begging to be pushed to its limit. It's been too long since I've had a physical outlet, of any kind.

The majority of practice is focused on routine drills, passing the ball down a line, running through defensive techniques the sophomores showed us last time they took over. No one seems to care or even notice Clay and I have had a few weeks out. If anything, the group feels more in tune with each other but that's probably my doing. Since I've stopped being so angry at the world, I'm coming to realize how much my mood affected not just myself but everyone around me.

The rest of the team clasp hands and head off in various directions, but I'm not done yet. Nudging Clayton with my shoulder, I steal the ball from his grip and duck around him, dribbling up the court. He's on me like a whippet and I'm the sexy-ass, tattooed rabbit hopping up to shoot a clear basket. We run back and forth, scoring and shoving each other until I turn and almost trip over the feisty brunette I find there with the ball in her hand.

"Oh Babygirl, I've got way too much pent-up energy for you to be handling my balls." Ignoring my statement, Harper passes to Clayton and runs around me, clearly having chosen his side. Bring it on. Not holding back anymore, I intercept Clayton and steal the ball, ducking low and spinning on my heel to head back towards my net. Attempting to shoot, Clayton barrels into me and knocks us both to the ground as Harper takes the ball. I shove him off me, running after her and whipping her off her feet before she makes it to the ARC line.

"That's cheating!" she squeals, kicking wildly when I refuse to put her down.

"My game, my rules," I say into her receiver after nudging her hair aside with my cheek. Keeping a firm hold on her waist, I plant her down and spin her to repeat myself whilst she reads my lips. Clayton steps in behind her on instinct, blocking the light from her face with his bulky frame.

Between our heaving chests and her glistening eyes staring at me, the energy around us suddenly shifts into something more potent. The adrenaline crackles through my veins like electricity, my hand trailing from her arm to the softest part of her neck, and higher to drag my thumb across her lower lip. Seeing my inked skin caressing her flesh does something to me, my carnal side coming to the surface and refusing to be denied.

"We agreed not yet," Clayton's hand catches my wrist as I start to wind her hair around my fist to pin her in place. I resist the urge to snarl at him like an animal, the lust filling my head making my vision blur slightly.

"We also agreed not to make decisions without her, so what do you think Babygirl? Are you done with playing normal yet, because the three of us are anything but." Upon hearing my words, even Clayton's grip lessens on me, his hands moving to rub gentle circles on her shoulders. Harper tries to resist, but her eyes flutter closed and she leans into his chest, dragging me forward to cage her between our bodies.

"I...we have a lot to figure out in terms of....dynamics," her voice is husky. Contradicting her words, Harper's fingers slip beneath my jersey and her nails lightly scrape over my sweat-slickened abs. "But a little fun wouldn't hurt," she smirks.

I don't need any more encouragement to yank her into my arms and march us into the locker room. Clayton barks at the last straggler to fuck off as I sit Harper on the bench, my mouth instantly finding hers. My tongue shoves its way inside and my fingers hastily remove her jacket and drag her t-shirt off. I'm so lost to her soft moans as I rub her nipples through her bra,

I forget it isn't just me and her until Clayton's hand lands on my shoulder.

"You got to taste her last time, it's my turn." I pull away from Harper to stand at my full height and bump my chest into his. When he doesn't immediately back down, I shove at him for real this time but he doesn't budge. Fucker.

My fists clench and my breathing feels constricted, like I can't take a full breath as a fog of sex-fueled rage descends over me. I'm trying so fucking hard to be the man Harper wants me to be, but when I'm this close to spreading my girl open and taking what I need, I can't be rational. I either need to be pleasuring her or punching a hole in something, preferably her creamy pussy with my dick but failing that, Clayton's determined face with my bloody fist.

"I have to make sure my girl is pleasured properly, so it's best I do it," I grind out through my teeth. Clay's humorless laugh fills the space, his stance cockier than I've ever seen it.

"Our girl, asshole. And I'm more than capable to have her screaming my name and forgetting yours. Grab a notepad, you should take notes." Reaching out to pat me, I smack his arm around and raise my fist when Harper's voice travels to me from a distance.

"Not making decisions for me lasted longer than I expected." Turning to search for her, the shower flaring to life draws my attention to her lithe, naked body standing between the cascades of water. Oh my fuckery. Her faded pink curls straighten as they grow wet, the glint of her nipple piercing catching the light. My eyes trail the length of her pale skin and the red patches seeping through her from the heat of the water.

A beat passes where Clayton and I remain frozen in place, before we rush to strip off and join her. Clayton beats me to it, not wasting time with foreplay as he skids to his knees on the tile and throws her leg over his shoulder. I growl in frustration until Harper's hand wraps around my rock-hard cock. Her gasp at Clayton's assault between her legs is music to be my ears, my dick jolting as her pleasure adds to my own. Her tight grip on his blond waves is a direct contrast to the gentle stokes she's teasing my dick with, running her thumb over the piercing there.

I try to close my eyes, or look anywhere else, but my gaze keeps drifting to where my previous enemy is feasting on her like a buffet. It's strangely hot, seeing her grind herself against his face and listening to her whimper without being directly involved. Her breath quickens, as do her thrusts on my cock and I grasp her glorious tits. Drawing a nipple into my mouth, she strokes me faster with a vice-like grip that's bordering painful. But I thrive on pain and there's no greater pleasure than a jerking-off I'll still be throbbing for days.

My balls tighten with her rising cries, the locker room filled with the sounds of my girl starting to come apart for her men. I move my assault onto her other nipple, feeling the tremble of her impending orgasm shudder through her. I vaguely hear the door opening beneath all the noise, turning my head to see Coach halt wide-eyed in the doorway. As if he couldn't hear what was going on, slimy fuckface. Seeing my glare, he quickly backtracks and leaves us – not that Harper even noticed.

She falls apart at the same time I do, my cum squirting over her hip and sliding down her thigh. I stifle the noise that leaves me by burying my teeth into her shoulder. Her strangled moans fade out, her hand catching my jaw and dragging me in for a savage kiss that has me hardening again in her hand. I could go continuously for this girl and she would never lose her appeal to me. Pulling himself up, Clayton takes her mouth as soon as mine has vacated it, her juices still evident on his lips. Yeah, I'm hard again.

Harper

It was two whole days before I bumped into Klara, which is two days longer than I'd expected. Stepping out of the bathroom cubicle, I halt to see her crying into Renee's shoulder, not having realized they were in here. Ducking behind my hair, I sneakily reach up to turn my receivers on while they're not looking. Klara's high-pitched whine makes me wince at first, but I straighten my spine and waltz over to the basin.

"I hope you're happy with yourself," Renee snaps at me. I raise my eyebrow in her direction, Klara facing away as she continues to sob.

"What did I do?" I ask, not bothering with the hand dryer and flicking the water in their direction.

"Isn't it obvious?" Klara squeals, spinning to face me. Her face is red and blotchy, her eyes puffy. I notice she's dressed conservatively in a black dress that covers her from neck to knees. A long cardigan, tights and black pumps swallow the rest of her, as if she's going to a funeral. "I've put on three pounds, and now I'm too heavy for the top of the pyramid and I can only wear black!" She bursts into tears again and hides her face, Renee still glaring at me over her shoulder.

"I'm going to regret asking this, but is three pounds *really* a big deal?"

"It's a huge deal!" Klara explodes in a ball of flailing arms and a shrieky voice. "As cheer captain, I have to abide by the rules I set as much as anyone else, and with my Rhysie gallivanting across country and putting himself in harm's way looking for you, I've not been able to stop stress eating. Why did you have to come into my life and mess everything up?!" I will myself to take a deep breath, wondering if it would be kinder to walk away than hurt her feelings any more than they clearly are, but this one-sided rivalry needs to meet its swift end. I'm done playing around.

"Okay well, first off – it's hilarious your own rule has come back to bite you in your over-inflated ass. And secondly," I step closer the same time Renee does, sandwiching Klara between us. "Rhys isn't yours, never was and never will be. Get over it and move on because this is growing beyond pathetic."

I allow myself a moment to drink in her shocked expression and wobbling chin, wondering if this is the same feeling Rhys gets when he puts someone in their place. My instincts want to fight that notion, to prove I'm not that kind of girl but the words have already left my mouth. Leaving the pair behind, I exit the bathroom and find my men on either side of me in an instant.

"Do we have to go to Vickers lecture? Her voice has me bordering suicide," Rhys groans from beside me. I glance at the bags under his eyes and slump to his posture, taking his hand in mine. He's been in every lesson so far this week, not particularly listening but there in person which has shocked everyone, including me.

"Yeah, we do," I smile sweetly. "This is the last week of lessons and finishing assignments, then all the end of year celebrations begin. You can do this." Tugging him inside the lecture hall, the bony woman with crazed gray curls eyes us until we take our seats. I've put a stop to us sitting separately since the appeal was lost as soon as we ran out of scrap paper to throw at Rhys.

"And besides," Clay leans across me, "Huxley told me about this tradition the Shadowed Souls have where they-"

"Master Waversea?" a sharp voice cuts over us. I look to

see a trio of police officers in full uniform making their way over to us from a side door Vickers must have let them enter through. They're all stacked and I'm sure they feature in the precinct's calendar shoots, but scowls twist their handsome faces and all eyes are narrowed at Rhys.

"Harper isn't answering anymore questions, she's been through-"

"We're not here for her. You're coming with us." Their words leave no room for argument, and Rhys spots the same time I do, the extra figure who steps out from the open doorway. Phillip Waversea glares at his son across the room, ignoring the other students who are filtering inside completely unaware of the monster in their midst. I try to hold onto Rhys' hand as he stands, but there's not much I could have done even if he didn't release me.

Rhys has barely straightened before one of the officers has grabbed his arm and drags him away. I will him to look back, but he doesn't. His father stands aside as they pass, sneering at me before closing the side door. Having settled realizing something is going on, the students around us begin whispering to each other until Vickers claps her hands and starts the lesson.

"It's going to be okay," Clay murmurs beside me, pulling me into his side but I refuse. I can't let Clay comfort me when I don't know where that door leads to or what they are doing to Rhys. What if the cops are crooked and are hurting him? Why's his dad here? I fiddle with the toggle on my hoodie until I'm shaking with worry.

"I can't sit here any longer." My words were meant for Clay, but seeing the entire class spin to look at me and Vickers stops mid-sentence, it was louder. Shooting upright, I grab my unpacked bag and walk out of the hall. First I round the building, looking for where that door would come out with no avail, then I head for the Dean's offices. Surely any official conversations would happen there, unless it's strictly unofficial and that's what I'm worried about.

He doesn't announce himself but I sense the instant Clay takes up stride behind me. Only as I pass the central fountain does he whip around to halt me.

"Harper, you can't walk into an interrogation. Let the police get whatever they came here for." It's what the police came for worrying me. Tears swim in my eyes as I try to barge past him but his hands on my arms are like vises, keeping me stuck in place. When I give up fighting him, I slump into his chest and exhale a shaky breath. "It's okay, he'll be fine."

"You don't know that." I mumble. As far as I know, Rhys hasn't filled Clay in on his past, and it's not my place to either. But it's still hard to swallow the rising worry when I'm the only one feeling it. Would Clay be so calm, with his hands stroking my back tenderly, if he knew?

"Let's go to the cafeteria, we can sit by the window and watch for when he leaves, okay?" I allow Clay to lead me away, my eyes scanning every window for a glimpse of Rhys as we pass. I only part from the safety of Clay's body to rush to a recently vacated seat by the window, dropping into the seat and fixing my eyes on the arched doorway across the courtyard. On the edges of my vision, I notice the students who still stare a little too long and look like they want to approach me, but one narrowed glare has them all returning to their lunch.

A takeaway coffee cup in pushed into my hands, stopping me from picking at my cuticle beds. Clay's foot hooks mine beneath the table and he sits back for our wait. This is why I fell in love with Clayton. He knows exactly what I need without me having to ask, appreciates how I prefer the world from a silent perspective and most importantly, he's always here. It's easy to be overshadowed by Rhys' character, but Clay is the one I need to lean against more times than not. The thought, however, makes me frown.

"What's wrong?" he asks, and I eye those around who have started to look at me with awe again. One kidnapping and I'm a walking attraction it seems. So instead of answering out loud, I sign slowly enough for Clayton to keep up.

"*I hope you know, I am always here for you too. If you ever need me.*" I wonder if he's kept up with practicing, and his wide smile confirms it.

"*We're all in this together,*" he signs back. I reach out to take his hand in mine, lifting my coffee to my lips and focusing my gaze out the window. *Come on Rhys, show me you're okay.*

Its two coffees and a bear claw later when Rhys finally emerges, and I jump out of my seat. Slinging my backpack over my shoulder and dragging Clay away from the muffin he was picking at, we reach the doorway to find Rhys has already disappeared. I round the cafeteria, wondering if he would go to my dorm or his house when Clay answers for me.

"His place," is all he needs to say. We take off to the edge of campus, crossing the main road and eyeing the house at the end. I haven't been back here since the night of the party, the one where I ripped Rhys' heart out and stomped on it in my last act of kindness towards him. If you love them, let them go, right? Except it's too late for now, and nothing will hold me back from my men anymore.

The house is dark inside when we approach, the front door unusually locked. I peer inside and knock on the glass, calling his name but I don't hear a response. Clay mentions the gymnasium but I shake my head, sensing Rhys would want to be alone. Wandering around the house, I pass the garage and walk into the back garden. Rhys is leaning over the porch railing, a cigarette resting on a split lip.

"Shit, Rhys. What did they do to you?" I run up the porch steps, cradling his face but he pulls away. Turning his back to me, I can't hear his reply but Clay signs it to me from below the railing.

"*He did it to himself.*" Narrowing my eyes, I pull my receivers out of my pocket and snap them on almost angrily, needing to hear what he is going to tell me – whether he likes it or not. When I try to turn Rhys around and he shrugs away from me again, I lose it. Stomping around him, I yank the cigarette from his mouth and throw it down, crushing it beneath my boot. And when Rhys reaches for the pack in his pocket, I snatch that too and throw it into the jacuzzi. At least this gets a reaction, changing his bored expression to one of anger. Good, because I've been sitting around for hours worrying and I won't be shrugged off without so much as an explanation.

"Can't you give me time to process my thoughts?!" he growls, getting close to my face. I shove him back a step, standing my ground. He jolts forward as if to attack me, forcing my fist to snap out and send his face wheeling sideways. The hint of a smile I see there tells me I've played into his standard punishment bullshit so I fold my arms and refuse to let him goad me again.

"Either fight me, fuck me or leave Babygirl. That's all I'm good for anyway."

"Whatever they said to you, don't shut me out. We're beyond this self-loathing bullshit now." He raises his eyebrow in a way suggesting we're not, and I roll my eyes. Marching over to the porch swing, I stretch my hand out for Clay to join me. "Okay, do whatever Rhys. Process your thoughts. Clay and I will be right here, waiting. Maybe kissing, definitely touching. My clit has been throbbing for days and I'd die for a large, calloused hand to-"

"They think I had something to do with your kidnapping," Rhys blurts out. Crossing the porch, Rhys shoves his way in between us and pulls me into his side.

"I don't understand. What part do they think you played when Dekken-"

"Took you to an abandoned house which is my birth mother's name, apparently. Della-Mae something. I've never even heard the name before." Rhys melts against me, burying his head in my chest with a groan. I share a concerned look with Clay, realizing he was the one who came to the police interviews with me while Rhys went off defacing property or something.

He wasn't able to deal with the details so I spared him from sitting through them.

"But your father…" I mumble, at a loss for words.

"Sat across the room beside the cops and blamed me too. I swear I didn't have anything to do with this Harper." Looking up, his piercing blue eyes captivate mine. Haunted yet desperately pleading for me to believe him, as if I won't anyway.

"Of course you didn't." I stroke his recently shaved face, his jaw smooth and strong above the masses of tattoos lingering underneath. The conversation drops away, leaving the three of us in our bubble against the world. Rhys has never had people to rely on or bring him out of his moods without the need for violence before, and I imagine this is the first time of many. Even when Rhys kicks up his feet and lies them across Clay's lap, he doesn't react and I continue to slide my fingers through Rhys' hair.

"So many things don't make sense. We can't keep you safe if we don't know what we're fighting." Rhys says after a while, his mind still working through what I can't be bothered to think about anymore. I want to move on with my life and enjoy the little things, without some elusive darkness always looming over me. I glance at Clay whose brow is also furrowed, the need to protect me present as ever. I see the moment a revelation washes over his face, his dark eyes flicking to mine.

"Actually, I think I might know what, or rather who, we're fighting. And this runs much deeper than we previously assumed."

Clayton

I pick up Harper's backpack and ask Rhys for his keys, leading the way inside. Unbeknown to Harper, I've been staying here since I'm sure every inch of my old dorm room will be bugged and Rhys threatened to go on a geek mauling if I didn't. Rifling through the bag, I pull out Harper's pencil case and trusted pack of post-it notes she always has spares of. I scribble words and stick them out in a brain map across the kitchen island until I realize Harper is yet to walk inside. Rhys notices too, having headed straight for a bottle of whiskey on the counter, and turns back to face her.

"We won't bite Babygirl, unless you want us to?" he smirks, but the sadness in her eyes makes me pause.

"I'm sorry, it's...weird. The last time we were all here..." I frown in the direction she's facing, staring at the front door. Damn, I hadn't even considered what it might be like for her to come back to the place I fucked everything up, sending a stab of guilt through my gut. Abandoning my task, I walk over to drag her into my arms.

"There's no words that can take back my actions from that night, but for what it's worth I'm sorry. To both of you. I've been fending for myself for so long, I don't think I wanted to be a part of a team as much as I didn't deserve to be. But I was wrong, and this," I lift her face to look at me, "is so, so right." I take a moment to indulge in the softness of her lips, pressing my mouth against hers in an unhurried caress. She tastes his coffee, sugar and something uniquely Harper, but I'd describe it as the taste of strength. When I manage to release her, I'm greeted with a wide smile on the other side of my vision and lead her back towards the island.

"Okay so, here's what we know." I point to the circle of post-it notes, using pencils to link them to a central one with Dekken's name on it. "The hog-hazing, the library stalking, the attack in the labs involving your receivers, the fake screenname, my locker, the phone taps, the sex tape, the fire, and the kidnapping." Writing another name, I slap it over Dekken's and step back to let Harper and Rhys see. *'Phillip Waversea.'*

"I mean...I'm all for blaming that fucker for everything. But we already know who is responsible for all of these things." Rhys pours out three measures of whiskey and slides the glasses across to us.

"Hear me out. I was with Harper during her questioning at the station and heard it all, which has had me thinking." I pull up a stool, beckoning Harper to sit in my lap once I've settled myself on it. "You mentioned Dekken was afraid of someone, said he wasn't calling the shots since the sex tape?" She nods.

"Only since the sex tape, apparently," she points over to the note.

"Exactly. Daddy dearest was here that day for the governors meeting, and maybe he tracked the recording back to Dekken, who would have spilled everything he'd overhead us saying about destroying Phillip's reputation. He didn't seem too impressed about with you at his weird dinner party either, so maybe he masterminded the whole kidnapping in an attempt to get you away from his golden boy who's going to take over the college one day." Rhys watches us closely but doesn't interject, although Harper is shaking her head.

"The kidnapping seemed like Dekken's idea. It was rash and he said he panicked because I was leaving. But then...he said he wasn't allowed to let me go either..."

"It seems unlikely Dekken stumbled across a neglected

house in the middle of nowhere, belonging to Rhys' mom by accident. He must have been guided there by the very man that just sat and accused his son of doing it. Maybe Dekken thinks Phillip only got involved on the day of the meeting, but what if he's been pulling the strings for far longer?"

"Like how?"

"Dekken being my roommate for one, or how he entered the college on a fake name without an issue. Then there's the disciplinaries for sneaking into the labs and killing the rats that were never taken further." Harper and I look at Rhys together, waiting for some kind of response. His focus is on swirling the amber liquid in his glass, before downing and refilling it to repeat the same. Sliding from my knees, Harper walks around the island to remove the glass from his hand.

"What are you thinking?"

"What am I thinking?" he scoffs, pacing away before walking straight back with a flap of his arms. "I'm thinking my dad tried to take my girlfriend from me and the only place he could think to put her was in the abandoned home of a mother I've never known. Not to mention the money and resources he has at his disposal. If he decides to pin this on me, there's no defending myself. I'll be someone's shower bitch by the end of the week." Harper cups his jaw, bringing his attention back to her. "And you ruined my cigarettes."

Harper giggles, pulling Rhys by the arms until she's backing up to me again. Lifting her waist, I plant her into my lap, as I presume she wanted, and push her hair to one side as she drags Rhys in to kiss her. I can feel the tension rolling from him in waves, even with Harper separating us but my attention is quickly turned to her ass. Whether knowingly or not, she's rolling her hips across my cargo-contained dick as I fight a groan.

Harper's back arches in her tank top, my fingers itching to explore her skin. To explore every smooth inch until my touch is burned into her. I've been holding back as much as I can, trying to live up to the chivalrous part I play in this trio, but she's making it so difficult right now. Kissing along her shoulder, my lips drag up the length of her neck until she's moaning softly into Rhys' mouth.

"I think it's time this happened," Harper breathes between kisses.

"Right now?" Rhys asks, his t-shirt hitting the floor in the next second. Harper nods, reaching back to stroke my nape, but the last functioning part of my brain not centered on my throbbing dick sees this for what it really is, a distraction.

"I've had enough of all this serious bullshit. I want to take control and feel something else than like I'm losing myself again." Her words confirm my suspicions, and I gently slide her hand from me to place a kiss on the back of it.

"No."

"No?" The pair of them shift to face me, Rhys' hand freezing on the fly of his jeans.

"That's what I said, no. Not like this. You can't find yourself through us or bury your head in-"

"Ball sacks?" Rhys chimes in with a pained look. I slide my arms around Harper when she tries to pull away, my eyes locking on hers.

"I was going to say, the sand. I promise when this happens, it will be everything you want because we'll be giving ourselves over to your pleasure. You need to be ready to do the same." Seeing Harper's disappointed pout makes me smile because she has no idea how hard it is to deny her on a daily basis, but it's what is right. Sliding my eyes to Rhys, I raise an eyebrow at him. "Besides, all or nothing, right? That was your idea."

"Wait," Harper elbows out of my hold and hops down to face us both. "You're saying I can only have sex with both of you, together? Every time?" I mirror Rhys' smirk at her wide eyes, although his is completely predatory. Sensing he's about to pounce at her words, I scoop his t-shirt off the floor and shove it into his chest. Growling at me, he tugs it back on and approaches Harper with a softer edge to his features.

"Not every time, but the other needs to know, agree or be in the room. No sneaking off behind locked doors," he throws a narrowed glare back at me, before stroking his knuckles across her cheek.

"Exactly, and right now, I don't agree." Crossing my arms, I lean against the island whilst fully aware my erection is trying to burst through my pants.

"Is your mission in life to cock-block me? 'Cause you're doing a fantastic fucking job," he mumbles without taking his eyes from her. "At least say you'll stay here tonight? Actually, every night. I'm done with us being separate and you know I can't stand the quiet." Harper smiles, leaning into his touch with a small laugh.

"Ironic, considering I relish it." She stretches her hand out to me without looking and I stride forward to take it. "I'll stay if you will?" Rhys pulls away with his smile back in place, filling her in on our new living arrangement. Harper's shocked expression passes between us, giving me the chance to drink in her natural beauty once more. From her brunette waves to emerald green eyes, her short stature yet vast mental strength, there's no doubt this girl was made for me. Well, us apparently.

"Yeah, it's been a blast sitting in Rhys' armchair until he falls asleep each night. He's been so clingy since we got back so please do come stay here, if only to let me get some proper sleep." Harper giggles, pulling us both in closer for a big squeeze before ushering us towards the kitchen.

"I'm sure I can be persuaded with some dinner," she smirks and smacks us both on the butt. I reach for an apron I find lying around, ready to play out this fantasy when Rhys snatches it from me. Doing one better, he strips off completely before donning the apron and I have to watch his pale, untattooed ass cheeks swan around the kitchen. Fantastic.

Harper

The library is surprisingly empty considering final dissertations are due by this weekend, but maybe that's because I'm the one lagging. Campus is buzzing with talk of parties and summer plans, and then there's the three of us. Even the self-proclaimed king of campus twiddling a pencil beside me is feeling a little flat. After the revelation about his mom, Rhys hasn't had his usual spark and it's killing me inside. Sure, it's been blissful sleeping between him and Clay each night, but without his cocky confidence and intense energy, the dynamic hasn't been the same between us. I'm drowning in the sexual tension and fighting to break whatever sense of honor these two are clinging on to.

Typing on my laptop, I lean across Rhys to check a reference in the textbook open before him and slide my hand inside his thigh. He tenses immediately and Clay eyes me suspiciously across the table. I shoot him an innocent smile and return to my work. Hooking my foot under each of theirs, I drag my hoodie over my head and fan myself dramatically. It's not even hot in here, but my tank top grabs their attention as planned. Clay taps the top of my screen with his pen and returns to his own, making me roll my eyes. Damn him and his iron will. I'd question if he had a dick if I hadn't seen it, felt it, been stretched by it every glorious inch by in-.

"Whatever you're thinking, stop it before I bend you across this very table," Rhys dives on me like the predator I knew was still lurking beneath the surface. His slender hands lock onto my shoulders, his face hovering so close to mine we're sharing the same breath. Flicking my tongue out, I catch his lips and smile at his responding growl. I can hear Clay protesting, but can't see him so I'll pretend my receivers aren't working. Rhys' fingers ease to a gentle caress, brushing his thumbs over my collar bone delicately. I push my chest into him, trying to coax him into acting on his words but he's not having it. This chivalrous bullshit needs to do one.

A hand grabs my arm, dragging me from my seat. I frown at Clay as he pulls me through the tables and towards the bookshelves. Looking back for Rhys, I see him still in his chair staring after me longingly. I don't resist but I do shrug his hold down to my hand as we reach the base of the stairs which leads to the second floor where the printers live. Of course, Golden Boy brought me on an errand to fetch his work in an attempt to draw me away from Rhys. I grit my teeth, not wanting to cause friction between the three of us but Rhys' cockblocking comment comes to mind.

There's no one else here, the few central tables empty and line of printers abandoned. Clay doesn't stop until he pulls me to the photocopier at the far end, spinning me by the waist so abruptly, I shriek. His hand clamps over my mouth, his strained whisper sounding beside my receiver.

"Do you enjoy playing with fire Harper? Rhys is barely holding it together. I have to look at your sexy curves every day and feel your ass pressed against me every night. I was raised to be a gentleman but you're making it so. Fucking. Hard." Clay grinds against me to show me just how hard, his solid erection and words making me wet with ease. I grind back against him, pulling a groan from his lips. I fight against his hold, needing to free my mouth to tell him to act on it already. I don't need a gentleman, I need to feel so many things, with dirty topping the list right now.

Pushing me forward, I find myself trapped between the

photocopier and Clay's body, his heat seeping into my back. His large hand moves from my mouth to stroke a path across my jaw and down my neck. Grabbing my breast roughly, I throw my head back against his shoulder on a sigh. *Finally.*

"I thought you weren't allowed me without Rhys' approval" I mock and then mentally slap myself for arguing this. Dominating Clay is hot as fuck. He grunts and pulls out his phone, holding it in front of me so I can watch his typing.

'I'm working out Harper's frustrations, don't bother us.'

"Happy now?" he asks, but doesn't give me a chance to answer. Yanking my jeans and panties down enough to pin my knees together, Clay slaps my ass and the sound echoes around the domed ceiling. Dipping his fingers between my thighs, he groans at the wetness he finds there. I push myself back against him, craving him, needing him. I ache to be sated, to be taken and used by the men who plague my dreams with incredible threesomes and my waking days with equally filthy fantasises.

Clay bends me over the photocopier, forcing me to tiptoe in order to keep my balance. His hands explore my ass, kneading me roughly enough to sting yet nowhere near hard enough. I wriggle impatiently, earning myself another spank. His long fingers part me leisurely, slipping through my juices to circle my clit and back again. His movements are unhurried but stoke the fire within me as fiercely as if he was taking me right here and right now. I bite my lip and groan when those same digits slide into my eager channel.

"I need more," I whine like a desperate slut.

"Tough shit," is his only reply. With a hand holding my nape firmly in place, Clay pumps his fingers into me steadily. With my legs restricted by my jeans, I am helpless but to take it. His fingers curl, caressing my g-spot before a third is added. Each time my moans fill the domed ceiling and my body tingles with the impending orgasm I need, he pulls out of me and uses his thumb to circle my clit. I curse and squirm, biting his thumb when he tries to silence me once more.

"You're making it impossible to be honorable," he growls beside my receiver, his fingers entering me once more.

"Then stop. I don't want it."

"But you deserve it, and that's why you chose me." This time round, his fingers plunge into me relentlessly. He doesn't slow or tease anymore, allowing the climax to build into an inferno which quickly consumes me. My walls clamp down on him, although he never slows. Not even when tremors rake through my entire body and my knees threaten to give out. Wave after wave of pleasure crashes through me, all of the built-up sexual frustration from the past few weeks taking its toll on me. Even once they ease, I rest my cheek against the photo-copier's cool surface, panting.

Clay's hands don't leave my skin, stroking sweet circles around the globes of my ass cheeks. Pulling my panties up, he lifts my torso upright to lean against him as he re-buttons my jeans.

"I'm starting to really hate you." I mutter.

"Nah Angel, quite the opposite I think. You're falling for me harder than ever. At least, that's what your sweet pussy is telling me." I scowl at myself, hating how my body continues to betray me. Even though we've professed our love to each other, the three of us are still relatively new and working out the kinks. A part of me still wants to pretend I'm not completely hopeless when it comes to these guys, but I can't lie to myself.

We remain plastered together until I find the energy to stand on my own again, stepping out of Clay's strong hold. I rub my thighs together, relishing the tenderness there. Clay's smirk is too smug, causing me to roll my eyes. When did he get so... Rhys-like?

Throwing his arm over my shoulder, I let Clay lead me back to the stairs and down like the prize he's just won over. The few students milling about peek around the bookshelves or throw me some serious side-eye, obviously having heard me. I ignore most, throw the middle finger at a few and saunter back to the table where Rhys is waiting.

That's right. This poor, naïve, deaf girl has two of the hottest guys on campus fawning over her, and I didn't need my hearing or to whore myself out to do it. Amazing what you can do when you take a step back long enough to see the bigger picture. The one where the stoically silent jock has suffered too much heartache to let someone in easily, or the classic bully everyone is ready to write off, who has never known love.

Rhys doesn't notice my approach, and as I look over his shoulder, I can see why. Working on his own laptop, one I've rarely seen open, his fingers are flying at lightning speed to write his dissertation. He doesn't even need to stop to check references, quoting scientists as if he's done this multiple times before. When I lay a hand gently on his shoulder, his laptop is closed and he's before me in a heartbeat.

"Feeling better?" Rhys' lips brush my jaw, sending a shiver down my spine.

"For now." I reply, my face tilting but his moves back before our lips can meet. Rhys must see the disappointment in my eyes, since his face softens, and he brushes my hair behind my ear.

"Soon, Babygirl. But the Caveman's right, there's no rush. We want everything to be perfect for you." You're perfect for me, I think, but manage to hold it in. For some reason, I think Rhys isn't ready to hear it as much as I want to say it. Because once it's out there, he'll have to come to terms with the fact I'll stand by his actions from here on out. Everything he does will be a reflection on me and the type of person I am now, not that I'm worried. Because if there's one thing Rhys Waversea hasn't had in life, it's someone to rely on.

Rhys

Fuck yes, this is happening. I'm done for the afternoon, it's the hottest day of the year and I need some time out from life. I can't sit through another damn lecture or feel Harper's curves pressed into me one more night without losing my mind.

Squeezing a dollop of my $1000 a bottle 'Golden Glow' sunscreen, I smother my arms, neck and chest before laying back on my cashmere blanket. I've already altered my skin enough for one lifetime, I refuse to let the sun turn me into a walking leathery cock before I turn thirty. Besides, Harper won't want a peely mealy when she's choking on my dick later. Pushing my earbuds in and sunglasses on, I rest my head on my hands and sigh.

The sun beats down on me like an old friend, flooding my system and banishing the shadows lurking there. After the stress I've been through lately, a day in my own back yard is exactly what I need. I've been so focused on making sure Harper is okay, I haven't spent the time to make sure I'm okay. So while she's studying inside with Clayton, or I hope that's what they're doing, I'm going to do just that. My thoughts whisk away with the music filling my head, leaving me blissfully empty. Every so often, the faintest breeze brushes over me as I drift further into my mental reprieve.

Reaching for my ice-cold beer, my hand pats the grass until I'm forced to look for it. Not seeing the bottle where I left it, I sit upright and push my sunglasses onto my head. The woodland in front of me is still, as is the lawn around me. Looking back towards the house, I see Harper and Clayton duck down behind the kitchen counter because they are slow and obvious as fuck. If I didn't have my music playing, I'd have heard their sniggers approaching. So much for studying.

"Very funny! I'll have two beers put back in its place!" I shout, returning my sunglasses to shield my eyes and lay back in my reclined position. It's not long before a shadow casts over my face and I smirk, cracking an eyelid. Harper leans over me, her eyes roaming my body as I watch her secretly from behind my shades. Her soft hands land on my chest, stroking through the sunscreen in leisurely circles. Biting my lip, I try to remain still for her to continue the exploration of my body, sliding lower towards my waistband. With a faint kiss on my lips, she disappears and I look towards the house to watch her dash back inside.

Shaking my head, I curse her for making me rock hard while I sunbathe. My eyes grow heavy once more, my mind now plagued with images of Harper straddling me in a bikini. Song after song plays into my ears, my body going slack as I seep further into the blanket, whisked away on a half-conscious dream. I don't resist, especially considering I don't get any action in real life, allowing myself to be pulled into oblivion.

Harper's leaning over me, her chest rubbing against mine. I can practically feel the brush of her hair tickling my skin through the fog of my dream. She licks her lips seductively, like the sexiest mirage to have ever been imagined. Her nipple piercing shows through the thin material of her baby blue bikini, her back arching as I reach to stroke it with my thumb. My mouth waters to taste her, to have her tongue plunge into my mouth.

Dozing in and out of reality, my fingers twitch and my cock is throbbing. I'm stuck between wanting to hunt Harper down and take her without abandon, and wanting to lay here to watch the fantasy play out. I can't wait to be inside her again, 'cause fuck knows I've had this dream so many times I know what's coming next and it's not me. Harper is suddenly naked, all of our clothes having vanished and as I look between us, her pussy is glistening. *Glistening* with wetness for me.

I groan audibly, the noise rumbling through my throat. Harper must have been lingering close again and have heard me because a real hand touches my side. I suck in a breath at the feather-light touch, needing more. Her hair tickles my arm, something wet running over my chest. My body is tuned to her touch as the music continues to leak into my head. I refuse to open my eyes, allowing my dream to blur into real life and heighten the tingling feeling rolling through me.

"Come back for more, Babygirl?" I ask. I had a feeling she would from the mischievous glint to her eyes earlier. She can't resist touching my bare skin. Scraping her nails against my abdomen, I hiss through my teeth. We've played this game before; she's teasing me and if I touch her, she'll stop. I hated it at first but it's grown on me, like a sexy lesson in obedience and I'll happily be her plaything because the gratification at the end is so much sweeter.

Palming my own dick, which doesn't break her rules, Harper continues to claw at me until I'm sure I'm bleeding, just how I like it. Moaning through my music, I scrunch my eyes closed when I feel the roughness of her tongue drag across my stomach towards my belly button. Kinky. And when she bites me....holy, ow. *Wait, fuck that hurts!*

Jerking upright, I throw my sunglasses aside to see a set of beady black eyes locked on mine. A hairy mass is frozen on my lap in the form of a fucking raccoon with crumbs around his nose and mouth. Similar crumbs are all over my body, adding to my confusion. Pulling my headphones out, I yell at the furred fucker to get lost and that's when the sounds of laughter hit me.

"Where you just jacking off to that raccoon?" Garrett shouts as I jump up, still hard as stone in my swim shorts. "We stopped by for a BBQ but if you'd prefer to molest a squirrel, we can turn away." The whole set of Shadowed Souls are on my back porch, half dying in a fit of hysterics and half genuinely concerned. The blond takes a photo on his phone and I can imagine PETA flattening my door any minute.

"What- erm, no. Obviously not, I was..." Harper appears at that moment, slipping through two of the guys dressed in chino shorts and vests. "Harper! What the fuck is this?!" I shout, pointing at the crap stuck all over my body. A vein pulses in my head, a strange sense of humiliation smacking into me. Harper pulls an empty cupcake wrapper out from behind her back, her eyes streaming with tears as she clutches her side from laughing too. *My god, I'm gonna kill her. I'm gonna fuck her, then I'm gonna kill her.*

Harper

"Only you would get excited to spend a free period back in the lab where we sit for an hour every day," Rhys moans as he trails into the room from behind. He's back in his bad mood again since the raccoon incident, but when I saw the critter steal his beer, what else was I supposed to do? Cover him in cake crumbs, obviously. The campus nurse cleared him for rabies so it's all good.

Crossing the room, I smile at Liz who is rearranging the contents of yet another cupboard. She's been arranging the room the way she likes it as often as possible, and now it barely seems like Peterson was ever here. The walls are covered with brightly colored posters, displaying images and facts from chemical reactions to atoms. Her desk is bursting with color in the form of highlighters, post-its, a stationary organizer and the most random assortment of personal belongings. There's even a seven-foot bunting swooping from one side of the room to the other with the periodic elements on each flag. The woman's as crazy as her blonde hair that can't pick a direction, but I can tell she'll quickly become my favorite professor.

Shrugging off my backpack, I empty out the contents and power up my laptop as Clay copies me across the table. With lectures nearly over and this being the last week to hand in assignments, Liz said we're welcome to use the labs to make up for the time I lost. Rhys kicks another stool closer, the skid across the floor making me wince. He knows he doesn't have to be here, but doesn't seem to know what else to do with himself lately than follow me around like a lost puppy. Since the interrogation with his father, he's been solemn and quiet, and I hate it.

"Here," I turn my laptop to face him. "Why don't you annotate what I say and do? It'll make it easier for me to write my final dissertation and we'll get out of here quicker. You think about what we can do after." His blue eyes darken to let me know exactly what he'd like to do, and I'd let him if it were just the two of us. But it's not, and Clay wants our first time to be special. I think he is building himself up to the thought of sharing me with Rhys, even though their blossoming bromance is helping, but I'm getting impatient. Wandering hands and pining kisses won't cut it for much longer.

Clay and I busy ourselves hunting for the equipment we need while Rhys cracks his neck and rolls his shoulders, making note-taking seem like an Olympic sport. He chews on his lip ring, his eyes following my every movement in my skin-tight jeans and crop top beneath my leather jacket. I don't need to check as his stare draws heat across my body, my movements enjoying the attention a little too much.

Placing down the microscope and test tube rack, I bend over beside him to collect my hair into a high ponytail and take far too long doing so. A sharp sting lashes across the back of my thighs, making my yelp and spin around but it's not Rhys holding the ruler. Clay raises an eyebrow at me and strides away.

"We have work to do," his voice calls back as I rub the spot just below the curve of my ass. Grumbling, I gently remove the bundled vials of rat's blood we acquired from the veterinary labs and place them in the wooden rack. Then, I add a sample of each onto separate glass slides and label them so we can finish the experiment Clay and I started weeks ago.

"Come on then, you speak and I'll type," Rhys says. The switch in their moods was a novelty at first, seeing new sides come to light, but sometimes it's plain confusing. I throw him a smirk and roll my eyes.

"Fine. If you open the spreadsheet on my desktop, you'll find the list of patients Clay and I analyzed. The files we found in the library gave us details on their enzymes, blood sugars, vitamin levels and mineral deficiencies. We've gone as far as we can with the paperwork, now we're going to replicate some of their traits in rat's blood and look for similarities as to why they may have been admitted to the hospital in the first place."

For the next forty minutes, Rhys types while I comment out loud on the various experiments we try. Clay hands me vials and test tubes on command, double testing everything I do to make sure I don't miss anything. Adding microscopic amounts of sugar and vitamins, we manage to mimic the blood traits of the patients, but it's still no use. We can't find any comparisons between these seven people who were admitted in the 80's for the same symptoms.

"So, we've got absolutely nowhere," I huff out. Dropping into a nearby stool, I rest my cheek against my fist. It's not like I was expecting some kind of scientific breakthrough, but at this stage I have a whole essay to write with only a bunch of failed tests to report on, and no time to start fresh with on a new subject matter.

"What were you expecting to find?" Rhys shrugs, standing to stretch. "Two college students in a small-time lab aren't going to be able to replicate the biomarkers for rheumatoid arthritis in rat's blood." I sit up straight, frowning.

"What? How did you...I mean, there's no way you could know that." I'm practically growling by the end, taking in Rhys' usual carefree expression while he's watched me waste my time.

"It's in your spreadsheet, Babygirl. Blood test results for the 'RH levels', referring to their rheumatoid factor. You've also commented about the x-rays noting joint damage and each was given an MRI, which would have been used to test for the severity of the condition." Clay has joined my side to stare at Rhys, his posture tense. Either not noticing or caring, Rhys shrugs once more and closes my laptop. "I'm starving. I'll grab us lunch."

We watch him stride away in silence, neither knowing what to say. Resisting the urge to sweep the vials and equipment onto the floor, I take a deep breath and start to clean them away. Clay is halfway through helping me when Liz asks if he can help her carry some boxes to the Dean's offices. His dark eyes swing to me beneath furrowed brows.

"Oh, just go already. I'll be fine." He hovers beside me for another moment so I ignore him, washing the vials until he's stalked away. I know he'll rush anyway, but this is the first moment I've had alone all week. The silence descends on me like a physical weight, whether from relief or nerves I'm not sure. I open my laptop, seeing that Rhys has been writing my essay for me instead of noting down my words. Damn him.

Packing it away and wiping down the surface, movement catches the corner of my eye but I flinch when it's not either of my boys I find there. What I thought was one person, a tall girl with a Cheshire-cat sized smile, quickly multiplies as others step out from behind her. Students of both genders swarm around me until I lose sight of the classroom, their wide smiles filling my vision.

"Can I help you?" I ask when no one speaks. Goosebumps line my skin and I wrap my jacket around myself defensively.

"We wanted to say hi and that we think you're so brave," a girl with long black plaits in front of me mouths, but no sound came out. I eye her curiously when a hand gently clasps my shoulder, making me flinch. Being turned, I hear the hushed whispers being passed around about not spooking the deaf girl. When face the guy who touched me, he also mouths his words slowly without making a sound.

"The way you talked Kenneth into letting you go was amazing. Is it true he kept you locked away and all you could drink was from a bucket of your own pee?" What the fuck? I narrow my eyes evilly and step back, only to bump into someone as the group closes in around me. My eyes dart around, now noticing the matching shiny pin each one is wearing on their classic Waversea jackets. With a crowned woman's head and the body of a bird, I realize who these people must be. They're my Harpies.

"No, it's not true," I finally find my voice and stand straighter. "Kenneth, or Dekken as he should be known as, has been through things you could only imagine and I'd appreciate it if you stopped spreading such rumors. He's going to get the help he needs, but to be blunt, it's not any of your business." Instead of backing away as I'd hoped, the crowd nod enthusiastically. A blonde I recognize from Addy's dance group clicks her fingers in my face for my attention, *bad fucking idea*, and starts mouthing at me again but I'm not paying attention. The conversation happening behind me is much more interesting.

"I told you not to ask her that! We don't get many chances to talk to her alone."

"Yeah, what the fuck Ryan? She won't open up to us if she's on edge, and that reporter said he'd only pay us for a decent story."

"I heard TMZ will give us $100 for a photo." Multiple hands grab me in the next second, spinning me for a flash to burst into my vision and leaving me seeing spots. I shout, trying to shove my way free until a hand grabs mine and holds me in place. I fight against it, blinking rapidly to look up at Clay's face. Fuck, he's pissed.

"You all have five seconds to get the fuck out of my sight before heads start rolling," his deep tone courses through me with a shudder. The crowd scatters instantly and I go to take a step into Clay's body but his crushingly tight grip holds me in place. His free arm whips out to grab a guy by his top knot, yanking him backwards. I try to get Clay's attention but he's too focused on the skinny dude with patchy stubble. "Delete it, now," he barks, gesturing to the phone still in the guy's hand.

Releasing him once he's complied, the rest of the crowd disappears out of the door in a flurry of hushed whispers. I guess they got the story they came for. Clay's chest in heaving, his stance unwavering as I step in front of him.

"Hey, what's gotten into you?" I ask. When he doesn't relax or look at me, I smack him in the chest. "First the library and now this. I'm not complaining but you're usually my calm one," I blurt out without thinking. It does catch his attention though, his black irises landing on me with an intensity that surprises me. His hand finally realizes mine and I fight a whimper, holding it to my chest. Our stare-off continues and I try not to fidget, suddenly unsure of how to soothe this side of Clay.

Without a better idea, I step forward slowly and lean against his chest. His arms wrap around me instantly, holding me so close, I can only inhale his manly scent. His lips graze my forehead the same time the tension drains from his body, our embrace turning more intimate.

"This is all my fault, and I don't know how to handle it," he says against my receiver after a while. I try to step back but he won't let me. "It's bad enough I couldn't protect you from Dekken before, and it seems I still can't. All I want for you is the easy life you came here for, but apparently it won't happen as long as I'm in it." This time I shove my way free from his hold enough to stare at his strongly angled face.

"So be it, because you're not going anywhere." His small smile is enough to ease the vise around my heart. I've never asked for anything except for my boys to be themselves and I'll take care of the rest. Tiptoeing, I press my lips against Clay's for a moment of the sweetness he provides me with plenty to spare. But that's okay, I'll carry Clay when he needs me to. Slipping my hand into his once more, we turn together and stop suddenly at the sight of Rhys leaning back in the professor's chair, feet on the desk and over halfway through his baguette.

"What, don't I get a show with my lunch?"

Clayton

Even with Huxley's tip-off at our last counseling session, I wasn't fully prepared for the tannoy announcement. The Shadowed Souls aren't just known for their notoriously messy end of year parties, but also for the huge scavenger hunt they use to give out the invites. They've even managed to blag for the board to let anyone who wants to participate out of class, stating the games boost character development through a healthy dose of competition. Apparently Garrett has an obsession with the game Cluedo, forcing his boyfriend to play it over and over.

"My fellow students," Garrett's falsely humble voice leaks from the speakers in the corner of Vickers' lecture hall. "The time has come for you to prove your worth. Our end of year party is sooner than you think, and The Shadowed Souls only want the best of the best in attendance. If you're ready for your mental and physical strength to be put to the test, get yourself to the gymnasium in the next twenty minutes to receive your first clue. However, if you can't hack it, don't bother trying. Our parties are only for the strong of stomach."

Half the class jump up and rush for the door while the other half look disgusted by the idea. I suppose that's normal for the science geeks, but I imagine most of the college is trampling through hallways and piling out of doors right about now. Using my cargo-clad thighs to push myself up, I extend a hand to a horrified looking Harper.

"But I haven't finished..." She points feebly at her laptop, pouting her bottom lip. Leaning over her, I drag the word document into an email to Liz and click send before she can protest any further. Across the other side of the room, Rhys watches me closely but also doesn't make a move. Taking her hand in mine, I hold Harper's gaze and run my thumb in small circles.

"We both know you finished your dissertation days ago and no amount of proofreading will make it any better. It's done, so now it's time to enjoy yourself." Her small smile sparks my own, this time allowing me to pull her up. I bite my bottom lip the way I have each time I've looked at her today. She's wearing a cute pair of denim shorts that poke out from beneath Rhys' white vest, the low cut and wide arm holes exposing her black bra and lickable cleavage. Walking past the row of chairs, I grab a fistful of Rhys' polo shirt collar and drag him to his feet. "You too, sour puss. Let's go."

Rhys shrugs out of my hold and follows, grumbling about me taking over as leader but we all know once he's back to his regular self, he'll be overshadowing me again. I might as well seize the chance to shine and let Harper see there's so much more to me than a mopey, righteous asshole.

"Can't you ask your buddy Hux to tell you when and where the party is?" Rhys asks, coming level with us and takes Harper's free hand.

"Where's the fun in that?" I retort, keeping to myself I tried and he said I have to earn my invite like everyone else. But that's fine, we could all use the distraction and I find myself oddly excited. Leaving the lecture hall, I see I was right about students running like a stampede towards the exit. Being a head over everyone else, I notice a gap coming and pull Harper into it with a whoop. We're forced into a run and her giggle reaching my ears soothes any reservations I may have had. We're doing this.

The gymnasium is flooded with bodies trying to get in, the doors ahead closed. Not content to wait around with everyone else, the three of us slip out of the crowd and creep our way around the side of the building. Several people notice and start to follow, bound to set off a chain reaction so at the next alcove in the brick's structure, I haul Harper against my chest and begin to kiss her neck. Rhys catches on quickly, stepping into her body to capture her mouth with his until the others grumble and stalk away.

Making it round the back of the gym without any more followers, I crack the unlocked door to the locker room and let Harper and Rhys pass inside before entering myself.

"What took you so long?" Huxley's smirk-filled tone fills the space. He walks towards me and clasps my hand before nodding to Rhys. Settling his brown eyes on Harper, he searches her face before pulling her in for an unexpected hug. I've spoke openly and honestly to Hux during our sessions, which have gone way beyond his need for extra credit now. He is doing it for me. Which makes him the one person who knows the extent of my feelings for Harper and how she's saved me from myself.

Leading the way into the center of the room, Hux points towards my closed locker. "Don't say I don't look out for you," he comments before continuing on and exiting into the main gym. Harper makes a beeline for my locker, rifling through the contents and I take the opportunity to catch Rhys' attention.

"Hey," I mumble. Not to talk behind Harper's back, but to have a moment without the fake bravado he's been putting on all week for her benefit. "You okay man?" His dead eyes slide to me lazily, the smile he never used to be without a distant memory unless Harper is involved. I'm going to hazard a guess what happened with his dad is what's eating at him, but it's not my business. Still, I'm not naïve enough to pretend I don't care – the tiniest, iddy bitty, miniscule amount.

"No," he breathes after a while. Harper turns and I watch the way his eyes soften and lips twitch upwards on instinct. He steps forward, winding his arm around her shoulders. "What we got, Babygirl?"

"The only thing in there other than Clay's gym stuff is

this." Harper shows us some kind of gadget with a USB cable and a single button on the front, but without plugging it in, it's hard to know what the shiny black box is for. We share a confused look as an uproar of sound bursts to life beyond the internal door. Figuring the game has begun, I rush to empty out my gym bag and put the device inside before moving towards the door. Harper steps between Rhys and I with a confident nod, her spine straight as I push through the door.

Her hand latches onto my wrist instantly, the noise level doubling. People are rushing and shouting, seemingly in search for something between the rows of bleachers. The three of us run into the masses, looking for any sign of the Shadowed Souls but I can't see a single one of them amongst the chaos. Heading towards the stairs separating the orange benches, I kneel to look below them like everyone else is doing.

"What are we looking for?" Harper's hand rests on my back as I stand, her body pressed against mine.

"We'll know it when we see it, I'm sure." I'm not sure, but fuck it. Taking her hand, we all hunt high and low. Shouts from all around fill the air, people screaming they 'found one', but what one is remains a mystery as they bolt for the main door. Harper is army crawling beneath the bleachers, looking in the places I can't quite manage.

Reaching the top of the stairs, I see Klara down on the court, moving through the crowd with her posse at her back and propositioning others for help. I grimace, determined to not let her near Harper or get an invite if I can help it. I'm all for letting Harper fight her own battles, but she's still mine to protect – from everyone. Rhys stands shoulder to shoulder with me, grunting when his line of sight follows mine. Pulling out his phone, he pins a message to the top of the college app, offering to double whatever Klara offers in exchange for sending her in the opposite direction.

I open my mouth to say something along the lines of 'nice one' or 'good job' or equally as awkward, but I'm saved the embarrassment when Harper pops up at the far end of the row. Instead of shouting, she signs to me but the smile across her face could only be a successful one.

"*Found it!*" Nudging Rhys, we run to greet her and she sneakily slips it out the back of her skimpy shorts. Our faces are reflected in a plain CD, held safely in a plastic case. I spin for Harper to slide it into my backpack and we make a hasty exit through the locker room once more. Leaving out back, we watch the floods of people darting across campus towards the computer labs.

"Huxley must have left us an external drive," I lean to whisper by Harper's receiver. "Whose laptop is closest?"

"Mine's back in Vickers room," Harper moves in that direction but Rhys holds her back with a shake of his head. Striding in front, Rhys reaches the base of the hill beneath the gymnasium and walks into the nearest building, leaving us to follow him into the history block.

"Rhys Waversea needs a laptop," he yells into the empty hallway. I laugh when the thuds of opening doors drowns me out, quickly accompanied by the thunder of footfalls. Laptop bags are held out from all directions and Rhys picks one randomly, ignoring the exaggerated swoon from the redhead who offered it to him. "That's all, you can all fuck off now."

The hallway clears again within an instant, even the redhead making herself scarce. Crouching against the lockers in his full grey tracksuit, Rhys raises an eyebrow at me expectantly. Oh right, yeah. I hand him the CD and drive, before Harper and I join him on the floor. The small, blue circle on the screen has all of our focus, spinning continuously for a whole minute before finally loading.

"Why not use USB's? They would have been much trickier to find." Harper comments, her foot tapping impatiently.

"But much easier to use," Rhys replies. "Only the third floor of the computer block houses computers old enough to have CD drives installed. My father was adamant Waversea moved with the times and upgraded all software for the latest tech. No expense spared on the board's funds." The image on the screen finally loads to display a fully black screen with white text.

'I have seas without water, coast without sand, towns without people, mountains without land. What am I?'

"Fucking deluded?" Rhys supplies. Harper giggles, lifting the laptop onto her crossed legs instead to study the words. We pass a few ideas between us, trying to use our knowledge of science to consider minerals and atoms but Rhys beats us to it with a snap of his fingers.

"You're being too literal. It's a map, like the one hanging in the Dean's central lobby," he rolls his eyes like it's obvious. Neither of us comment on the fact Rhys has been letting his inner geek shine through lately, and we won't, but it's good to know there's more to him than arrogance and ink. Removing the disk and drive, Rhys stands first and pulls Harper up, slipping his free hand into her back pocket. I close the laptop and leave it tucked against the locker, hoping redhead finds it before someone else does.

The area outside is considerably quieter now, the call of gulls passing through a cloudless, blue sky. A few stragglers are dragging their feet, looks of defeat claiming their faces until one of the girls notices Rhys is spinning the CD around his index finger.

"Hey! Rhys has one of the shiny frisbee thingies!" She rushes forward on a gasp, bringing the rest of the loiterers with her. Her huge eyes stand out against a delicate face framed by golden hair, her clothes obnoxiously colorful. "I can trade with you! I can write your essays all of next year or...or...clean out your Jacuzzi?" The smile that grows on Rhys' mouth is pure evil, his lip ring glinting in the light.

"Yeah? Go on then, fetch." Rhys curls his wrist inwards

and flings the 'shiny frisbee' an impressive distance. The small group flee, shoving and tripping over each other as we turn and leave. We break into a run, knowing we won't have long before others figure out the riddle. Luckily, the computing block is across campus and once we reach the central courtyard, it's still fairly empty. Harper's ass looks amazing in her tiny shorts, and it doesn't go unnoticed Rhys has fallen back to appreciate the view as well.

"Stop staring at my ass!" Harper calls back, looking over her shoulder with a sly smile. "Winning first, then I'll let you get close to ogle later." And damn if that sentence didn't make me sprint faster.

Harper

Looking at the large oak tree, I hold my hand up to shield my eyes from the midday sun. A red dot on the campus map lead us here, ahead of everyone else it seems but I know we won't keep our advantage for long.

"Can you see anything?" I call. Clay and Rhys are nearly at the top now, searching through the branches for who knows what. I'd been skeptical at first, but this scavenger hunt is proving to be exactly what we all needed. A distraction. So even though I prefer the type of puzzle that comes in a paper format, like a Sudoku or a good brain teaser, I'm starting to enjoy myself. The competition is exhilarating, but it won't be for much longer if they don't hurry the hell up. Rhys drops down a moment later, the ink on his neck and arms glistening through a sheen of sweat.

"There's nothing," he grumbles. I imagine if Rhys had set up this hunt, he'd be loving life with linked fingers and a mocking 'muhaha', but alas as a competitor, he's wound tighter than a jack-in-the-box. "We're chasing our own asses here for some pointless party while Jolly Roger up there is blabbing about this being the best day we've ever had." Rhys kicks the tree trunk and slouches against it, arms crossed.

"Are you done?" I raise an eyebrow. Closing the gap between us, I rest my cheek on his chest and his arms wind around me automatically. I mimic the rise and fall of his chest in my breathing, stealing a moment of serenity amongst the madness.

"Clay's just trying to lift our spirits, you know. Like you usually do. Let's humor him for today. He'll probably go back to his broody shit tomorrow and...I'll miss him like this. He deserves to be carefree for a change." Rhys strokes my hair until I look into his crystal blue eyes.

"Yeah, okay. I hear you. And for the record, he won't go back. We won't let him." My eyes widen at this, my chance to respond stolen by Clay thumping to the ground with the same lack of news. This time when I look around at our surroundings, Rhys is right by my side, hunting with me.

We're on the far north side of campus, the tree beside a gated entrance for the botanical gardens. The terrain is gravelled, the oak's branches hang low like clenched fingers reaching for the sun.

"What if we're wrong? What if it's in there?" I point towards the gardens. Rows of blossoming flowers and growing veg lead towards a domed greenhouse in the distance. Fuck, this next clue could be anywhere.

"We're not wrong," Rhys answers. "The map is so overly animated, the oak tree takes up the whole corner and the sticker was specifically-"

"On the base of the trunk!" I spin around and drop to my knees, sifting through the overgrown grass covering the bottom of the tree. Hands bump mine as Clay and Rhys join me, shuffling around the bark until Clay calls out.

"Here! I've got it." I push his fingers aside to see the set of coordinates carved into the wood. They're small enough to miss, but there's no denying what the numbers are intended for. Rhys is already on it, pulling his phone out of Clay's backpack and jumping onto Google Maps.

"It's a car park on Carter Street. We'd better get going, I can hear the others coming. Quick, scratch off the numbers."

"No!" Clay and I jump together, planting ourselves between Rhys and the tree. As much as I'm enjoying being on top, no pun intended (right now), I doubt the Shadowed Souls would appreciate a party with no guests. Besides, the trunk has already been defaced enough for the sake of this scavenger hunt. Rolling his eyes, Rhys grabs my hand and pulls me after him, racing away from the oncoming crowd. He wasn't kidding, there's a fuckton of bodies scrambling up the pathway behind us.

"I bet most of them are just following the few actually playing along," Clay half-shouts as he catches up to us. We cut through various buildings, taking shortcuts across campus until we near the forest that will lead us to Rhys' house. Neither of the guys falter in their steps, knowing the exact route through the woodlands until we spill onto Rhys' back yard and make a bee line for the Ford.

Clay doesn't stop as we roll past the car park, spotting a truck advertising 'Sal's Supermarket' right where the coordinates said it would be. Gunning it to the other side of town, I have the window open and a smile plastered across my face. The wind whips my hair around wildly, the sun kissing my forearm as I rest my chin on it. I wish I could bottle this feeling and label it 'the college pastimes I've been waiting for'.

Rhys is up front with Clay, the pair chatting easily. There will still be rough times ahead but for one moment I can see the type of life I could only dream about each night since I arrived at Waversea. One I never expected to become a reality and almost lost everything for.

The supermarket is a huge, double storey store housing everything from groceries to clothing and electricals. Like a one stop shop for all your basic needs. The front is branded with the double S logo on every spare inch of the windowed exterior. Bold, white letters spelling out the name sit against a navy background above the wide entrance. Clay slides into a parking space with empty bays either side, but doesn't move to get out.

"What are you waiting for?"

"Look," is all he says. I return my gaze to the open car window, hunting for what he clearly saw. Further down from the entrance, past long lines of shopping carts, twin booths have been set up side by side. A topless man sits behind each booth, the one on the left ripped with pecs firm enough to see from here. On the right is a man similar to that of a sumo wrestler, his brow glistening with sweat and sugar coating his lips from the doughnut box in front of him. Above them both is a cardboard sign, the painted writing instantly recognizable to me.

'Kissing Toll. Pick right and grab your invite.
Pick wrong and move along."

"This has Addy's name all over it. The Shadowed Souls must have dragged her in to help," I smirk to myself. Moving to get out the car, Clay beats me to it with the central locking, keeping me trapped inside.

"You're not kissing anyone for a party invite," he grumbles. Rhys nods along with Clay's words, neither turning to look at me. *Oh, for fuck's sake.*

"Who said I was going to do it? I've had fantasies like this and I just wanted a front row seat. Pucker up buttercup, this one's all yours." I pat Clay's shoulder and hoist myself up onto the window ledge, spinning and jumping out before either can catch me. I make it three whole cars closer to the store when a pair of slender, inked arms lift me off my feet, which is much further than I'd expected.

"I'll do it," Rhys growls at me and I'm unable to contain my laughter. He jolts me against him again, gnashing his teeth beside my receiver in what I presume was meant to be a threat, but I find it hot as hell. "We're doing this for Clay, right?" Rhys pulls me into a crouch beside a car, blocking us from view. Clay squats too, his hand latching onto my arm despite the way I'm locked against Rhys' body.

"What are we waiting for?" I ask at the same time as they both shush me aggressively. Jeez, competition really brings out the worst in both of them. Leaning around the back of the vehicle, I see what must have been too far out of range for my receivers to pick up. The other competitors. First to approach the booths is a group of girls, rushing straight for the hunky man. Their giggles fill the air, the tallest in the middle leaning across the booth for her skirt to flash her hot pink G-string to the world.

Pulling back and seemingly fairly pleased with herself, the man behind the booth shrugs and shoos the group away. Seeing their error, the next cluster of guys head for Sergeant Sweaty instead. Seeing them hesitate over who will kiss him is the funniest thing I've seen all day, as are the rounds of rock, paper, scissors they use to make the decision. The loser creeps forward hesitantly, rounding the booth to plant a quick peck on the guy's cheek, much to everyone's loud disgust. Again, the rounder man shakes his head and the group stalk away.

And that's when I see it. Smiling to myself, I feel the moment Rhys' arms slacken around my middle and bolt for it. Even though there's only a few cars separating me from the store front, the boys would have caught me easily if I hadn't caught them off guard. There's loads of people approaching now, most looking confused about what to do next until I slip through the middle.

Between the two booths, set back against the window-pane, is a tiny replica stall with a blue French bulldog sat patiently behind it. He cocks his head at me, his tail beginning to wag as I kneel to scratch behind his large, pointed ears. A black bowtie has been attached to his collar next to a folded piece of paper, but I have to pay the toll first. Leaning down to smush his wrinkly face and kiss his wet nose, he showers me with licks from the soft pad of his tongue.

I block out the excited murmurs which break out behind me, sneaking a peek at the typed text inside the paper and leaving it there for the next person. This pup is about to receive the most kisses he's ever had in one day. Although from the obedient way he was waiting, maybe he's used to being part of the Shadowed Souls hunts. Striding back to a relieved-looking Rhys and smirking Clay, we jog back to the truck to hit our final destination, or should I say, our first.

"I should have known," Clay chuckles as we enter the gymnasium once again. The group of sophomores who set up today's games are sitting in the front row of the bleachers, along with the blonde cheerleader who first showed me around and Addy. Spotting us, the group begin to cheer and clap.

"It's about time!" the one I know as Garrett hollers. Rolling my eyes, I focus on the last challenge waiting in front of us. A rope hanging from the ceiling with a bell at the top. The height may seem daunting to most, but my men race for it like a fairground ride. Clay reaches it first, but Rhys throws himself to grab on higher and kicks Clay's hands away. Figuring I'm not needed for this part, I head over to sit beside Addy and watch.

Rhys climbs with all the grace of a leopard, hoisting himself upwards without faltering. Well, until Clay begins to shake and yank the rope side to side from the bottom. Curses fill the gymnasium but there's mirth to Rhys' tone, the ring of the bell sounding less than a minute later. Sliding back down, Rhys dives onto Clay with punches to his biceps. By the time the pair join us, they are both smiling and bumping shoulders.

"Interesting," Garrett remarks, reminding Rhys he has spectators. Crossing his arms, his pierced eyebrow rises as he tries to be serious again.

"Come on then, where's the fucking party invite?"

"Oh yeah, that." Garrett leans back, spreading his legs wide enough to press against his boyfriend and Huxley. "Party's at our place on Saturday, after the graduation ceremony."

"That's it?!" Rhys narrows his eyes and clenches his jaw when Garrett yawns in response. Crowds of students burst through the main doors, clambering over each other to reach the rope first. Winking at Addy, I slip from the bench and pull Rhys away before he kills someone, with Clay right behind me.

"That can't be it," he moans as we exit through the back of the locker room.

"Hey, we won, right?" Rhys nods but the look of annoyance has yet to leave his face. I know what will wipe it clean off though. "And now I'm all sweaty, hungry and tired, so someone is going to have to wash, feed and snuggle me." Like I'd expected, his face lights up instantly and Clay pulls me under his arm, promising to hold me to that too. *Damn, how did I get so lucky?*

Rhys

I hate people. Deep down, I genuinely despise the entire human race, myself included, bar one person. Almost two, but only because our late-night Call of Duty games are growing on me. It's like having a brother I suppose, some irritating fucker that's always around and crushing on my girl. Except I don't think brothers usually chug back whiskey at stupid o'clock in the morning and discuss drunk how they're going to double team the sleeping beauty upstairs when the time is right. Or maybe they do, I wouldn't know.

Harper had fallen asleep last night spread across mine and Clayton's laps, leaving us to watch the chick flick she chose without her. I was bored out the other side of my face, but I kinda liked it. I don't usually take the time to just…be. My mind temporarily shut off, my entire focus on sifting Harper's silky through my fingers.

I've come to the conclusion having a girlfriend is a lot like owning a cat. As long as she's fed and stroked when needed, she'll stay loyal. When pissed off though, she'll probably knock all the shit off the counter and leave a dead bird on my doorstep. I should probably hire a bodyguard for Klara, but then again I really don't give a shit what happens to her.

My mind drifts until another body bumps into me. *Where was I? Oh yeah, I fucking hate people.* More specifically in this moment, the hordes of black robes and square hats gunning for the central courtyard alongside their family members. Ugh, don't even get me started on families. I can't stand walking on the same ground as the sniffling dads ahead, or breathing the same oxygen as the overbearing mom next to me, wiping her son's cheek with a licked thumb. Disgusting. Yet still, I find myself oddly curious with the exchange.

I may be a first year, but I've been dragged to these graduation ceremonies for years. Another one of my father's attempts to show me what success looks like, from a man who inherited his wealth. The hypocrite who insisted I had to prove my worth to our family name when he hasn't. And once again I'm surrounded by the mothers kissing their oh-so-amazing sons, remembering why I loathed those visits so much.

The courtyard is packed with bodies, all shuffling towards the hundreds of chairs set up in rows from the Dean's offices to the library. In the centre, a walkway has been left which veers around the central fountain. A sea of proud fathers can be seen through the cafeteria windows, toasting with the free champagne to their parental achievement. Congratulations, you forced your child to endure years of stress and an unimaginable amount of pressure, only for them to be thrown into the world jobless and riddled with debt. What a fantastic day to celebrate.

Dropping into a chair on the back row, I slouch down despite being too far from the erected podium which will act as today's stage to be spotted. I'd also made the clever decision to wear all black, from my sneakers and skinny jeans to the baggy hoodie with the front pocket. This way, I can hide how I'm destroying my cuticle beds without people confusing it for nerves, when in reality, I just really need a fucking cigarette.

The college board marches onto the podium in a line, filling the seven chairs waiting for them, signaling for the visitors to take their seats too. The lousy college anthem begins to blare through various erected speakers, forcing me to pull up my hood to cover my ears. I know I'm not supposed to think it, but my brain has no filter. Harper's way of living is ideal and after this, I might hunt for the nearest screwdriver to impale into my eardrums. The graduates parade through the central aisle, directed onward by a class marshal until they are finally seated. Only then does my father appear with the local mayor by his side, setting off the first of many, *many* speeches.

Fuck. My. Life. I don't need a screwdriver, my brain is about to explode through my ears and blood will seep from my eyes any moment. This is taking far too long and I need to get back to my girl before she misses me too much. No doubt Clayton is 'dealing with her needs' again; a task I can't do because we all know I won't be able to control myself. I need to feel her skin against mine, the point where our flesh meets and to have her convulsing around my cock. The tightrope I've been walking on out of respect for the new relationship the three of us have is about to snap. After I've done what's needed today, I'm not holding back any longer. Harper's mine and she needs to know it in every part of her being. Specifically, nine inches deep in between her thighs.

The valedictorian has finally finished his speech, and kudos to him it was rather inspirational to those who are lucky enough to have aspirations. Now begins the long line of graduates queuing for their brief moment on the stage to shake hands with my father and receive their diplomas. Yeah I think I'm done with this. Pushing to my feet, I make a beeline for the main hall where I know my father will be heading next to put on an act for potential future investors. I plan on intercepting him before that and getting the answers I'm more than due.

"Rhys! Wait!" I turn my head back to see the Brent twins chasing after me in their robes but I don't break my stride. Only when they run ahead and block the hall's entrance am I forced to stop, gritting my teeth. The pair are identical, from their straight, mousey-brown hair to their deep blue eyes. Both beautiful, but after being signed to two modelling agencies since the time they were seven, they know it.

"What?" I bark when they don't immediately speak.

126

"We didn't expect to see you here," the left one answers. I never bothered learning their names, despite the monthly sessions where they fought over who would suck my cock first. I do know one of them doesn't have a gag reflex, but I couldn't tell which one it was so I'd flip a coin each time. I'm fair like that.

"We're leaving Waversea on Monday," Righty continues. "How about we hook up after the party tonight for one last-"

"Nah, I'm good." I cut her off. Their matching pathetic pouts make me want to rip my own dick off for ever putting it in either of these stuck-up brats, but that was the old me. The new one only yearns for one girl, and she definitely needs my dick attached.

"Is this because of the deaf girl? You must see that-" Lefty's voice trails off when I step forward to glower in her face. She swallows thickly and a visible shudder rolls through her as my voice sounds gravellier than I'd expected.

"Is this the part where you tell me she's not good enough for me. 'Cause you can save it. You may have entertained me for a while, but neither of you can begin to compare to Harper." I'd expected the pair of them to bolt, but instead I watch the confident tilt to Lefty's eyebrow.

"Actually, I was going to say you're not good enough for her. I read about the articles about her, how she put her own safety over Kenneth's mental health. She's amazing, and we all know you like rough, hot sex with almost-strangers. It suits us fine because once we've left here, we'll forget all about you. Everyone will. But there's no need to ruin her when you've got so many other offers."

I stand frozen long after the twins have side stepped me and walked away, my mind reeling. It's one thing to have doubts, but to hear them voiced from the last person you'd expect has shaken me. Does everyone think that? Are they all watching and gossiping, waiting for the moment I fuck it up with Harper so they can all point and say, 'I told you so'? I shake my head, scowling at myself. Everything used to be so simple when I only allowed myself to feel one emotion. Hate. Not that I'm going back to that, but at some point soon I'll need to re-evaluate exactly who I am and what I stand for. Because I can't fully give myself to Harper if I don't have those answers.

"I'm going to hazard a guess you're waiting for me," a dull tone reaches my ears. Pulling my hood down, I turn to face my father. His blue eyes are blank, his face looking drawn in a crisp, black suit. So much for the element of surprise.

"We need to talk."

"Not here we don't. I'm busy." He barges past me and I let him, knowing threats won't work. The only thing my father cares about is his reputation. Following him inside, I briefly take in Addy's handiwork on the hall. The girl has an eye for detail, and even though she's spent most evenings this week at my house telling Harper about her grand ideas, I must admit it looks much better than I anticipated.

Black material covers every hint of wood paneling and window, as well as draping outwards from the center of the ceiling. The usual hanging bulbs are encased in open silver cages, the metallic grey replicated through the vases of sprayed lilies, candle center pieces on each table and the serving trays spread across a wide buffet. A fountain formed of tiered champagne glasses sits on the opposite side of the room. In true Waversea style, classy with no expense spared.

Heading straight for the masses of canapés, I shove the meticulously placed trays aside and lift one altogether so I can hop onto the table. With the tray on my lap and legs swinging, I help myself until the potential investors flood in. I don't know where my father has gone, but he'll find me soon enough. A woman, roughly in her sixties, with stretched skin and fake tits saunters her way towards me with a coy smile.

"Fried mushroom and risotto balls?" I offer her the tray with a wink. "Or for the meagre price of a blank cheque, you could have my father's balls in your mouth by the end of the evening." Snatching her hand back and acting disgusted, although we both know the twinkle in her eyes said otherwise, she stomps over to my father as he re-enters from backstage, re-adjusting his tie. Scumbag.

"That's enough Rhys," he says as he approaches me. "Let's go talk."

"Nah, not right now. I'm busy," I mock his words from earlier. His hand wraps around my arm, yanking me from the table with more strength than one would expect. It occurs to me, as his grip digs into my bicep, this is the first time my father has physically touched me since the last time he beat me, a week prior to me starting college. I haven't considered before the freedom I was granted in my plan to destroy him, the thought seeping in as I twist away from him.

"Your fly is still undone," I comment and chuckle as his steps falter. The sharp sting of a smack blooms at the back of my head, making me laugh louder. Several faces turn our way while I'm led backstage, and I flip off every single one with a smirk.

Rich people see life through rose-tinted glasses, and if they want to view me as a monster I will happily oblige. No one in this room would step in if my father decided to pull out his knuckle dusters and lay into me right here, right now. Many would place bets, some may question why I didn't bother fighting back sooner. The simple truth is I believed I deserved it and accepted it, allowing the pain to fuel my anger. But not anymore.

Stepping into a room the drama students use for costume changes, I only hesitate for a millisecond before closing the door behind me. Rails of outfits line the walls either side of me, with a few curtained cubicles at the back for privacy. My father shrugs out of his suit jacket and rolls up his white sleeves in a move I've seen a thousand times before.

"Out with it. What do you want now?" he huffs like I'm an insolent child wasting his time. I narrow my eyes, desperately wanting to be out of here as memories creep back in, but I can't leave until I got what I came for.

"I want answers. Actually, after the shit you pulled with the police, you owe me answers." I straighten my spine, not that he looks my way.

"I don't owe you anything."

"Yeah, you do. Not only do I think you fucked with Dekken and put Harper in danger, but you also tried to pin it all on me. Is that why you asked me to mentor her? To make your story more plausible?" My father rests against a low table with a single sewing machine at the far end by the wall, clapping slowly. I clench my jaw. He is the only person in the world who has the power to make me feel this insignificant this quickly, and I have no idea how to break that hold.

"You think you've got it all sussed out, but you're the issue here and, somehow, are still of no use to me." He chuckles with a shake of his head, but he's the only one who gets the joke. His words aren't new to me, but his relaxed, no-shits-given attitude is and it unnerves me. "I thought you had promise until you met *her*. Alas, the one time you didn't do the opposite as you were told and it's for something as serious as this."

"What the fuck are you talking about?" I blurt out, earning myself a scowl for my language. I leave the safety of the door, stepping closer and folding my arms.

"This is what you were born for. You were supposed to be my solution, but I knew at a young age you weren't the son I needed. You were too weak so I changed tactic. I molded you into the man I needed, until that deaf charity case reversed all my hard work, so I had to find an alternative."

"An alternative as in Dekken? What could he have done that I couldn't?" I let the remark about Harper slide, adding it to the tally of things I will hurt him for. As soon as I understand what I'm up against. "No more mind games, tell me what's going on."

"We're poor." He states, leaving those two words in the air as if they answer everything. Nothing else is said for a while, until my father huffs again and kicks across a chair for me to sit on.

"That's ridiculous. We're the richest family in the state, everyone knows that." I fill the silence when I can't bear it anymore.

"We were the richest family, once upon a time. But my father, grandfather, and many before lived beyond their means. They took out unfathomable loans, using the college as collateral. Everything is tied to this damn place," he looks around and that's when I see it. Pure disgust for the legacy he'd claimed to love.

"Why the big secret? You've never shown anything but love for the college. You conditioned me to go here." I push through the haze clouding over in my mind, the nauseous feeling of my world being tipped upside down sinking in.

"I was a few years older than you are now when my parents died, fresh out of this place. Joint suicide, you know? They knowingly left me with debts you wouldn't believe, forcing me to take on the stress they couldn't handle. So I started researching a way out, and I thought you would be it." He pauses to sigh, his eyes never meeting mine. "There's a loophole. If I close the college, I'll be liable for every cent owed. I could even face jail time. But if the investors were to make the decision to shut the college, the debts will be expunged. I set it all up for you. You just needed to be your usual, disappointing self and we'd have been free."

I slide down in my chair, all previous worries of an unprovoked attack forgotten. He wants out. My father *wants* me to tear this place down, and what's worse is he's been using me this entire time. He forced me to hate him, counted on me to go against his wishes and if it hadn't been for Harper, I would have.

"Why did you tell me all of this? You didn't need to drag Harper into your backwards scheme, or Dekken for that matter." I scrub a hand over my face, everything clicking into place in my mind. In asking me to protect the scholarship kids, he intended for me to run them out. Instead of mentoring Harper,

I was meant to get rid of her. And when I did neither of those things, he used Dekken to do it instead. What a fucking idiot I am.

"I'd presumed being raised by only me, you'd have been different. But even since you were a toddler, you were too soft. You cried all the time, were scared of your own shadow, called out in the night for a mother you'd never known. I knew then you weren't cut out for this, but I still tried to fix you. Sadly, there's no cure for being born pathetic." Checking his Rolex, my father grabs his jacket and strides towards the door.

A thousand insults, curses and threats fill my mind, but as he walks out, I don't move. My body is numb, my breathing shallow. Like I've been transported back to the little boy hiding under his bed, never understanding what I did wrong. My father has always had the power to strip me back and reduce me to nothing.

I hear music and people chatting beyond the open door, the party in full swing now. The party I should be crashing, but instead I retreat further into the room. Behind the tatty curtain of a changing cubicle, I slump to the floor. And hide. And cry.

Harper

"Hey, I was getting worried. Everything okay?" I bound up to Rhys as soon as he steps through the door. He ducks his head into the crook of my neck, but not before I see the puffiness of his eyes. His father's a bastard for sure, but if I find out he laid a finger on Rhys, I'll go after him myself. I try to get Rhys to look at me but he mutters I look beautiful and heads upstairs.

"I'll go," Clay says, appearing from the kitchen. "You have another visitor anyway." I turn to see Addy walking up the porch steps, a huge smile plastered on her face. Her pink hair has been brightened again, tickling her shoulders in wild flicks. Her dress is a long sleeve top in silver glitter, reaching just past her ass with a low V-neck which should be scandalous. Only matched with a pair of silver heels, she looks smoking hot.

"Am I underdressed? Or...overdressed?" I frown at my own party outfit. Black heels with high waisted PVC trousers and a lacy bralette on top. My hair is loose in curls and I've only applied minimal make-up.

"Are you kidding me? Shut your face, you are gorgeous! I'd do you," she winks and walks past me. Addy makes herself at home, pulling a bottle of wine out of the cupboard and fetching two glasses. I pause at the bottom of the stairs, wondering if the boys are okay. To be honest, they could be killing each other since my receivers don't reach that far and Addy wouldn't bat an eyelid, but I'll leave them to talk or fight it out. For now.

"Come on babe, stop frowning. You'll be a prune before

you know it. Besides, we're celebrating." I accept the wine glass Addy is holding out for me, quirking my eyebrow for her to spit it out already. "Remember the children's camp I told you I volunteered at? Well I spoke to my friend who handles the volunteer placements there and I got us in! We leave on Monday!" Her jumpy squeal is cut short by my concerned look. I don't want to quell her excitement, but I've been looking forward to spending some free time with the guys and exploring our relationship.

"Oh, you banana," Addy throws a tea towel at me. "The camp has a sports regime and I told them about all about your basketball bosses. All four of us got in!" This time, I squeal too. Addy clinks her glass with mine and we drink to summer fun.

"What's going on down here?" Rhys walks up behind me, a direct opposite to the man who entered the house a short while ago. His hair is styled back, his face smells like a collection of products from his extensive skin clear routine and he's donned a slim fitting shirt and jeans. Clay is right behind him with a cheeky smile in his usual white tee and cargo pants, gorgeous as usual.

"Addy's got us into a summer camp." I lean into Rhys to finish my drink, feeling him tense beneath me. Noticing Clay and Addy have fallen into a conversation, I turn in Rhys' arms and plant the kiss I've been waiting to give him on his lips. "I would love to have this experience with you, but if you aren't comfortable with it, we don't have to go."

"We'll talk about it later. There's a lot we need to discuss," Rhys murmurs by my ear. I don't like the sound of that, but tonight is the Shadowed Souls party and I've been buzzing about this all day. Even when Clay physically restrained me from chasing Rhys out the door. Yes we do need to talk later, and at the top of the agenda is reminding these guys we are a team. Not three individuals anymore and I won't be railroaded into sitting aside every time they have something to deal with. I've been alone enough in my life, so no more. The glass in my hand is refilled by Clay, then gives one to Rhys and proposes a toast.

"To the end of an eventful first year."

"And to the party of the century. Let's get shit-faced!" Addy adds. Hell yeah, I'll drink to that.

***

Ho. Ly. Shit. The Shadowed Souls frat house resembles a mini mansion. The porch is supported by thick, white columns, and the dozens of windows are illuminated by colored strobe lights bouncing around inside and out. But that's not what gets my attention. There's people – everywhere. On the roof, hanging out of windows, covering every inch of the front lawn and porch so I can't see the front door. Some clever shits have tied a hammock high up between the central pillars, which I watch dubiously as I pass underneath.

With my boys acting as bodyguards either side of me and Addy in front like a yappy chihuahua, we push our way inside. Thankfully, I have forgone my receivers tonight, each of the boys having a brand-new microphone clip attached to their tops, thanks to Rhys, but those are both off right now too. My implants are practically vibrating anyway with the heavy bass of music passing from the floor and through my body, so I definitely don't need the weeklong migraine tonight would cause if I could hear it.

Addy signs way above her head that we need shots, carving a path towards the back of the house for the kitchen. I keep my eyes trained on the feet around me, struggling to put one foot in front of the other with people crashing into the boys at my sides and knocking me off balance. Yeah, that's why, because it has nothing to do with the bottle and a half of wine we've already had prior to arriving. Lifting a whole tray of shots, Addy sways her hips to the imaginary beat and leads us outside.

Out here is even worse, with the added element of a swimming pool. On the right side of the decking is a DJ booth facing out onto the backyard, which has literally hundreds of people crammed into. It's more like a festival than a frat party, inflatable balls being passed back and forth over the crowd's raised hands.

Noticing an open spot against the far railing, I tap Addy's arm to grab her attention but she's currently eyeing the giant pink flamingo in the center of the pool. Klara is bone dry in a tiny white bikini with a cocktail in her hand and sunglasses on, despite the sun setting hours ago. On our way past, Addy stabs her heel into the flamingo's neck before I'm able to stop her, but the flailing cheerleader sinking fast is too hilarious not to enjoy.

"*This is such a perfect end to the year, I could cry!*" Addy signs the moment she's set the tray down on the railing.

"*Don't do that. Your make-up is on point tonight,*" I reply as Clay nestles in behind me. His fingers trace patterns over the exposed section of my abdomen, raising goosebumps all over.

"*As if it's not every night,*" Addy throws back and I can practically hear her scoff in my head. Downing the shot she hands me, I instinctively reach out to grab Rhys by the belt, pulling him closer. My fingers dip beneath his waistband, brushing against the piercing on his already-hard dick. I don't need an explanation, as the heat I find reflected in his eyes is more than enough. His jaw is taut, his grip rounding on my inner thigh tight enough to bruise. He's barely holding on to his control, and I don't want him to.

"*You're so lucky, I kind of hate you,*" Addy signs with a wink, betraying her own words. Slipping into the crowd, her fuchsia hair disappears instantly. Rhys steps in front of me, caging me in until I can't see the party anymore. I should be social and enjoy it while I can, but my body is screaming to turn around and take these guys straight back home. Clay's hand creeps up to my neck, twisting my jaw to watch his lips move.

"*I'm going to find Huxley and show my face, because with you looking like that, we won't be here long.*" He drags me into a kiss intensifying the need building inside me. *Fuck yes, this is happening tonight.* Striding away, I ignore the cold I suddenly feel at my back and focus on Rhys. He's chewing his lip ring, his hands roaming my shoulders but I don't miss the seriousness of his expression. It's not all from lust, there's a haunted darkness to his blue eyes making me feel uneasy.

"Are you okay?" I ask, slipping my arms around his neck. He ducks my gaze once again, walking me backwards with his hands on my hips.

"*No talking, let's dance,*" his lips say. Removing one of my arms from the back of his neck, he gently places my hand on the speaker I'm now standing next to for the beat to roll through me. It's not a slow song and the noise level must be horrible for him, but Rhys hoists me against him and grinds slowly. Every hard inch of him presses into my abdomen, his lips claiming mine in an attempt to distract both of us from his troubles. I'll allow him tonight to forget about whatever is disturbing him, but tomorrow we will hash it out.

Song after song moves through me, Rhys' body an anchor to the tipsy desire robbing me of all sense. I can't tell where I end and he begins, our hands exploring each other as much as our clothes will permit. At some point, either I or Rhys unbuttoned his shirt but I can't remember who. All I know is the abs hidden beneath his tattoos are now marred with scratches and my lips feel bruised.

I barely register another set of hands winding around me until Rhys pulls away and I'm still being held. I spin into Clay's hard chest, his loose blond waves tickling my face as he leans down. But it's his smile dazzling me. Wide and unapologetic, Clay's smile lights up his whole face as if he's gazing at the most precious thing in the world. Warmth fills me, the need to let him know I feel the same riding me hard. But in this moment, even if I could form a coherent sentence, words don't seem enough.

Taking my hand, Clay pulls me towards the house and I reach back to link fingers with Rhys, needing to know he's with me. I only wobble slightly when Clay doesn't take me towards the front door as expected, but leads me to the wide staircase instead. My eyes widen as we ascend, the reassuring smile he gives over his shoulder not helping the pounding of my heart. We're doing this here? Right now? What if I'm a lousy lay when I'm drunk, what if I prove to not be enough for them, what if I can't handle both at the same time? It hits me how much is riding on this, and now I'm wondering why I've been so pushy for it to happen.

There aren't many people on the second floor, other than the odd couple making out against a wall. Clay leads us to a door at the end of the hall, one suspiciously empty and has a lock which he bolts after we've entered. It's a simplistic room compared to the rest of the house, the lack of personal belongings showing it's fairly unused.

"*I couldn't wait any longer,*" Clay answers my questioning look. Switching on his mic clip, he sets it on the bedside table before turning to me. Pure hunger is shining is his bottomless, black irises, and it looks like I'm his next meal. I step back as he advances, my back bumping into Rhys as I'm closed in. Fuck, I know I've been all dirty talk and flirty looks, but I don't know if I can do this. No time to back out now.

Clay's mouth captures mine, his tongue sliding inside to dance with mine. He takes like whiskey and power, the heady combination filling my senses. Hands cover my body, my clothing being peeled off until I'm fully naked in only my heels. Clay breaks our kiss to remove his t-shirt while I sink my nails into Rhys' thighs for reinforcement, finding them bare too. His cock pushes against my ass insistently, causing a lump to form in my throat.

"I...I don't know if I can do...all of this," I gesture to the bed, insecurities finding me in my tipsy state. Rhys turns me slowly, his hands cupping the side of my face.

"We won't do anything you're not ready for. All we want is your pleasure and happiness." My eyes roam his strikingly blue eyes, fixed jawline and the tattooed demons lurking underneath. Where Clay is classically gorgeous, although he really should smile more, Rhys has a savage beauty I understand. His pain lives just below the surface, threatening to swallow him whole but somehow, he manages to keep a carefree façade in place. He's found a way to let me in and I have to prove I'm capable of being the light he desperately needs.

"I love you." My statement seems to catch him off guard, even though I thought he already knew of my feelings. Apparently not. Taking the lead myself this time, I push Rhys to sit on the edge of the bed and straddle him. My lips cover his as he pins my head in place with fistfuls of my hair. There's a harshness to his kiss, more so than downstairs, as if he needs me to know he feels the same.

Clay's large hands lift me to my feet, forcing a growl from Rhys as we're interrupted, but it doesn't last long. Holding me against him, Clay lifts my leg and plants it over Rhys' shoulder, much to both of our surprise. When neither of us move, Clay's fingers splay my pussy, holding me open as he guides Rhys' face into me with a grip on his hair. And it's is the hottest damn thing I have ever seen. Ever.

Rhys' tongue does wicked things to me while I rely on Clay's hold to keep me upright. He alternates between sucking my clit, running the pad of his tongue over my opening leisurely and spearing it inside of me. With Clay kneading my breasts and sucking on my neck, I'm lost to the sensations rapidly consuming my entire being. I'm a slave to their touch, a captive to their intentions, and I don't want to be freed.

Remaining as the self-appointed ringleader, Clay peels me away from Rhys and orders him to move further up the bed, right as I'm on the verge of a soul shattering orgasm. I groan in protest until the blunt head of his cock slides between my ass cheeks, rubbing into the slippery wetness waiting there. I arch my back, needing him more than I need my next breath.

"I don't have a condom," Clay snarls suddenly, his movements halting.

"Implant," I tap my arm. "Get in me. Now." No more words are needed, Clay's large hand on my nape forcing me over Rhys as he fills me in one slick move. I can't swallow my gasp, needing a moment to adjust to the sudden intrusion but Clay doesn't give it to me. His hands cover my ass, holding me in place while he takes me without abandon. My hand wraps around the base of Rhys' shaft, our eyes locked as Clay's thrusts drive against my g-spot, calling for my climax instantly. The sound of skin hitting skin and his balls smacking against my clit heighten the intoxicating feeling I'm drowning in, sending me over the edge.

I can't help the moans escaping my mouth, leaving my throat raw as wave after wave crashes through my body. Clay refuses to slow, despite how tight I've become, drawing out my pleasure for what seems like hours. When I don't think I can stand any longer, Clay eases his pace (about damn time). One by one, he pops my knees onto the edge of the bed, taking me in long, languid strokes as I finally turn my attention to Rhys' cock.

The piercing is winking at me in the artificial light, waiting patiently for me to run my tongue over the metallic balls. His hands sink into my scalp and I pull back with a wide grin. We've played this game before, putting Rhys' control to the test until he's put his hands behind his head. I lick him slowly, my nails teasing his balls and teeth grazing his shaft while I watch his every reaction. Eyes scrunched, his teeth sink into his bottom lip. Call me sadistic but I love him like this. More so because I know no one else has had him this way.

It's Clay who breaks first, wrapping my hair around his hand and pushing my head all the way down Rhys' cock. In none of my many fantasies was this how our threesome played out, with Clay calling the shots over Rhys and I, and it's hot as fuck. The more sides I see to him, the harder I fall and dominant Clay has just made me plummet. His hand bobs my head in time with his dick invading my tight channel, deep and impossibly hard. Rhys' groans match the volume of mine, both of us at Clay's mercy.

"I won't last at this rate," Rhys grits out. Clay slaps my ass, causing me to yelp, and releases my hair instantly. Nestled deep inside me, he takes the time to unbuckle each of my heels and remove them before pulling out. Turning me by the shoulders and pushing me down onto the bed, I come face-to-face with the monster-sized dick that was inside me.

"Want to see how good you taste, Angel?" My eyes flick to Clay's as he guides me back and lowers me directly onto Rhys. So. Fucking. Hot. The pleasurable pull of Rhys' piercing tugs inside me, making my eyes roll back. Clay's dick brushes against my lips like a kiss, making me smile before I take him deep into my throat. Rhys grinds beneath me, coaxing another orgasm to build but in all honesty, I'm not sure if the last one even stopped. This is nothing like what I'd expected, and so much better. There's no clear divide or turn taking while the other watches. We are one entity, united and equal and it feels so damn good.

Clayton

I pull into a parking bay, switch off the truck's engine and slump back in my seat. I can't stop yawning and my eyes are itchy, but it was so worth it. Last night was beyond mind-blowing. This morning however, not so much. Hungover Harper is like a fluffy bear cub who has missed a meal, super cute when grumpy but you know not to poke her with a stick, no pun intended. And unfortunately, Rhys did poke, super no pun intended.

To give her credit, Harper waited until we'd finished breakfast, a morning feast for all provided by Axel, and returned to Rhys' before she laid into him with her questions. I knew it was coming and tried to escape earlier, but Rhys yanked me onto the kitchen stool before I managed it. I'd already heard about the conversion with his dad, but listening to it again allowed me to take it in fully.

Phillip Waversea isn't just a terrible father, but a fraudulent scumbag and that's putting it politely. What kind of man manipulates his son, through physical and psychological harm for his own financial gain? Yet Rhys insists there's no concrete evidence to do anything about it. It's all hearsay and Rhys' word against his father's, which he's right in presuming no one would take seriously. The well-spoken, self-proclaimed billionaire would always win over his troubled, tattooed son who only Harper has seen the good in. Even I would have struggled to believe it merely weeks ago.

None of that is the reason I'm here though. I'd been

meaning to make this visit for a while, but with us leaving for summer camp tomorrow, now is my last chance. Sliding out of the truck with my backpack, I make a beeline for the red brick building in front of me. 'Langton State Mental Hospital' is displayed over the single door entrance, the whole structure simple and discreet.

I step into the main lobby, finding a small waiting area to my right and glass-contained counter to my left. I don't know what I was expecting, but the cheery man I see there wasn't it. Maybe a uniformed guard with a gun strapped to his chest, or orderlies in blue scrubs with a syringe at the ready. Instead, the receptionist's attire is relaxed, in a rock band t-shirt and jeans, his coffee-colored hair flowing down past the table and out of sight. Ahh, I get it now. This is more of a zen, own-your-peace, rehab program center.

"I'm here to visit Dekken Cornstone," I say while approaching. The man, whose nametag labels him as Bert, quickly masks his surprise with a smile, asking me to fill out a stack of forms. I borrow his pen and lean on the side of the counter since I'm the only visitor who has shown up today. That should be a sign in itself.

"You'll be the first visitor Dekken has had. Do you know him well?" I grunt in response, my eyes fixed on the questionnaire before me. "He's such a kind and gentle kid. It'll be good for him to have a friend to talk to."

"Well I'll talk to him, but on account of him stalking and kidnapping my girlfriend, I don't think I'll be much of a friend." The man is rendered silent at this, accepting the forms back and gesturing for me to take a seat. Crossing my ankles, I pull out my paperback copy of The Da Vinci Code, expecting a long wait to be cleared to enter the facility. Harper proposed a mini book club for her, Addy and I to have fully in sign language to help me practice. Although, I wonder if she's secretly missing out on the study sessions we used to have, where people wanted to be her friend because they liked her instead of for a magazine feature.

"Mr Michaels?" My name is called merely a few pages in, Bert asking me to follow him. Reaching a set of lockers at the rear of the room, he turns to hand me a token. "We don't allow visitors to take any personal belongings into the institution. Can never be too careful, you know." With a shrug, I dump my bag and phone inside, locking it and pocketing the key. Satisfied, Bert knocks on the door next to us for a large security guard to step through with a handheld metal detector. Having given me a once over, I'm permitted entry.

The security guard leads me along a corridor on the outskirts of the building, only white walls and shut doors visible to me. I can't imagine what the inside must look like, but I reckon it's not the padded cells and straight-jackets I envisioned. The staffing seems minimal, the atmosphere too calm. Everything that should put me at ease but really doesn't. Reaching a set of double doors at the end, I'm ushered inside and told to make myself comfortable.

Once again, the room is eerily empty. Rows of low, cushioned seats are separated by coffee tables, a closed shutter at the back from a kitchen hatch. Inspirational quotes fill the walls, speaking of the greatest journeys beginning with small steps and so on. Rounding the chairs slowly, I settle for one right in the middle and lower myself into it. And that's when the real wait begins. Alternating between drumming my fingers on my jeans and picking at a rogue thread on the bottom of my white tee, the yawns return. If only I had my book this time, I'd have been halfway through by now.

Finally, a door opens and I sit upright, realizing I'd slouched all the way down. A woman steps through first, a clipboard in one hand and her other on Dekken's shoulder. There's no cuffs or restraints, just the regular red-haired boy I knew walking towards me shyly. His head remains ducked while the woman introduces herself as a counselor and moves to sit in a nearby seat. I rest my elbows on my knees, watching Dekken get comfortable opposite me.

"I didn't expect to see you again," he mutters. Everything I wanted to say has fled my mind, my curiosity getting the better of me.

"Why is it so quiet here?" Dekken shares a look with his counselor, seeming happy to have a distraction from the worry eating at him.

"Oh well, this is a facility specifically for criminals, but since I haven't been tried yet, I'm in a holding section of the building. This side is for those in custody, but there's only a handful of us so not many visitors come. People tend to disown their friends and family when they hurt them."

"Except for Harper," I add for him. His whole face lights up, a smile claiming his features and banishing the nerves recently present there.

"How is she?" Dekken scoots forward in his seat, allowing me to see him properly at last. The artificial light reflects off a fading bruise around his left eye and a slit healing in his lip. He's lost weight, which makes him almost skeletal in an oversized grey sweatshirt and tracksuit bottoms. In his excitement to hear about Harper, Dekken props his face between his hands, allowing his sleeves to slip over a matching set of bandages on his wrists. I didn't want to feel bad for him, but stooping as low as self-harm tugs at my masculine pride.

"She's great," I answer to distract us both, "aside from being worried for you. Rhys had to hold her back from coming with me today, but it's important we hash this out once and for all." Dekken stiffens at this, recoiling back into his seat and raises his knees up to his chest.

"If you're here to ask who was helping me, I can't tell you-"

"No, no. I already know everything. What I want is for all of us to be able to move on from this, you included, and it starts today. You didn't hurt Harper when you could have and she cares for you, so I owe it to her to try." The counselor watches us both intently from the side-lines, making notes on her clipboard. I'm basically doing her job for her here, but it's easy enough to pretend she isn't there. Dekken returns to sitting before me, like a snail crawling out of his shell now he doesn't sense a threat.

"I suppose you want an explanation but I don't really have one. I hated you, I wanted to ruin your life. But when I met you properly, I was so desperate for you to like me, and your mom has always been so kind to me. And then Harper showed up. Everything got so muddled, I got confused." Throwing his face into his hands, I eye his paler red hair with interest. Clearly the shade I am accustomed to was dyed, another part of the façade that made Kenneth.

"Take me back to the beginning. I know you were grieving, but why did you focus all of your anger on me and not the gang member causing all of this?" Dragging his hands down his face, Dekken's wide eyes dart around as if he's never considered that before.

"I-I came to all of your hearings. I heard you confess your guilt for Antonio's death, despite only being charged with robbery. You admitted it!" Sensing the shift in his mood that Harper warned me about, I lift my hands, palms facing forward and speak calmly. Even the counselor seems ready to intervene, but this all started with me and I intend to settle it.

"Feeling responsible and being guilty are two different things. I didn't raise the alarm or pull the trigger that killed your cousin. Just like I didn't ask for my brother to run into that alley and take the bullet intended for me. We both lost people we loved that night, and we've both suffered for it. The difference is my grief was beaten out of me behind bars while yours was left to fester."

Dekken stares at a spot on the table between us for so long, I fear I've broken him. My words are the truth, but I might have rewritten the way he's seen the events that led him to do terrible things. Possibly causing him to finally see I'm innocent of the crimes he thinks I committed, and how unprovoked his actions were. Sensing we are done here, I rise from my seat slowly.

"Believe me, Dekken, I understand acting rashly through heartache more than anyone, but I'm not the one responsible and I think you know that now. I'm sorry for the pain you've had to deal with alone, and if I'd known, I would have helped you sooner. But I'm glad Harper managed to get through to you." With a nod, I move to leave when Dekken's small voice stops me.

"But...what do I do now?" I turn my head with a raised eyebrow.

"What do you mean?"

"Without the anger and grief, I don't know what to do with myself. So what am I supposed to do now?" I drop back into my seat, sitting forward to stare straight into his brown eyes.

"Live, Dekken. Be thankful for each day. Remember the girl who saw through your pain and put herself in front of a sniper for you, how she fought to make sure you were cared for properly. But most of all, live for both Antonio and yourself. Once you get better, you can be whoever you like. You're free now."

The first tear falls onto his freckled cheek as Dekken stretches his hand out in offering. I can see how much he needs this, how important this moment will be for his recovery, so even though it'll take me a long time yet to forgive him for putting Harper in danger, I round the table and pull Dekken in for a hug. He squeezes me tightly, sobbing into my t-shirt like a child. I may be the one to lose a brother, but Dekken lost all the family he'd known. The ones to keep him on the right path, to help him when times got rough. So I'll take that baton. I'll make sure Dekken gets help and has the fresh start he needs. Patting his back, I pull away with the first smile I've had since arriving.

"And make sure you write to Harper," I order whilst clasping his shoulder. Striding away from Dekken, a feeling of relief expands in my chest. This visit wasn't only for his benefit, and the heavy weight of guilt has finally been lifted from my shoulders. I just hope Dekken feels the same.

Harper

A generic pop song bursts to life in my head, making me flinch so hard I nearly slipped over in the shower. Leaning my forehead against the glass cubicle, I focus on willing my heart to climb back up my body and slow to a normal pace. That damn girl is going to kill me one of these days. Switching off the faucet and wrapping myself in a towel, Clay pokes his head around the door a moment later.

"Addy's here," his mouth says through the music blaring around my skull.

"Yeah, no shit, and she has my phone. I nearly shat out my heart." Clay's eyebrows knit together as I pass, in hunt of the Fuchsia Fuckwit. Finding her lounging on Rhys' bed, I ignore the flare of jealously that hits me unexpectedly and I snatch the magazine from her hands.

"Oh, hey there," Addy smirks, looking over my wet hair and towel combo. "Is it my birthday?" I roll up the magazine and smack her with it until she gets off the mattress, noticing my phone on the pillow so I switch on the mic app instead.

"It's all fun and games until I fall and break my legs in the shower," I try to shout at her but I can't help the smile growing across my face. Damn her. She's batting her eyelashes innocently at me in a cute outdoorsy outfit, khaki shorts, a black vest and walking boots.

"I thought you'd like some music since you didn't have any company in there," Addy wiggles her eyebrows. Heading into Rhys' dresser, I dive into the drawers he's given to me and fish out a similar outfit to Addy's, except with full length pants. Excitement bubbles inside me as I dress beneath my towel and tuck my phone into the side of my bra before joining Addy's side.

"Why does Rhys need dress shoes for a summer camp? He knows it's out in the woodlands, right?" I peer into Rhys' duffel bag on the edge of the bed, my smile falling as I see the smart clothes packed in there.

"Maybe he's having an identity crisis. I'll go ask him." After Rhys told me everything that went down with his dad yesterday morning, we'd spent most the day relaxing on the porch swing. His head on my lap and my fingers stroking his hair, enjoying the beautifully sunny day in peaceful silence. I didn't want to badger him for what was going through his mind, but I bet finding out he isn't as rich as he's grown up believing must be unsettling to say the least.

Drying the ends of my hair with the towel as I go, I eventually come across Rhys and Clay together in the home gym. And what a sight it is. Rhys is on the running machine while Clay squats with a weight bar across his shoulders, both gloriously shirtless and lined with a sheen of sweat. My butt cheek throbs on instinct as if the spank Clay delivered to me the other night has been imprinted on my soul, a shiver of anticipation rolling through my body. If only Addy wasn't right behind me...

"You need to re-evaluate your packing choices," she barges past as I linger in the doorway. "Think more jerseys and sneakers than suits." She walks up to the TV Rhys was watching and switches it off, the size of her balls making me chuckle. Rhys isn't impressed with Addy, as usual, hopping off the treadmill and gesturing for Clay to take her out. Both wink at me as they leave, Rhys holding his hand out for me to join him on the weight bench. Pulling me into his lap, I unashamedly run my fingers over his inked chest.

"I'm not going to camp." I straighten as his words find my

phone's receiver.

"Wait, what? Where are you going instead?" I stand to put some distance between us, needing my body to stop yearning for his long enough to think straight.

"Babygirl, I really don't do kids. And I've been thinking... I wanna find my mom." My heart calls for me to comfort the way Rhys ducks his head, almost seeming ashamed of having feelings. But with the time to leave fast approaching, I realize he's left it too late for such things on purpose.

"You were just going to leave? We spent all day together yesterday and you couldn't find one moment to tell me this? Do I mean so little to you I couldn't get a proper goodbye?" I don't need anyone to tell me I'm being beyond selfish, especially when I know how hard it is for Rhys to open up, but I can't help feeling hurt. A small voice in the back of my head has been wondering how long it'd be before Rhys pulled away, if the novelty of the three of us would wear off for him. Well, here it is, and he wasn't even going to say goodbye.

"Are you kidding me?" Rhys' words are muffled as he spins me from my mental berating and pins me against the closest wall. His jaw is clenched and nostrils flared, but all I see in his blue eyes is misery. "It's because of how much I love you, I couldn't face you. All day yesterday I tried to find the courage, but I can't deny you. The thought of leaving you makes it hard to breathe."

"Then don't," I plead. "You agreed we'd be a team now, you don't need to be alone anymore. Just give me two weeks of camp and then we've got the whole summer together. I'll come with you wherever the journey takes us." My voice quivers, betraying the depth of my words. A better girlfriend might be able to step aside, let Rhys find his mom and come back when he's ready, but not me. In such a short space of time, I've become consumed by affection, devotion, and fear. A soul-deep fear it could all be snatched away any moment.

"Okay Babygirl, I go where you go. I'm all yours." Rhys'

mouth presses against mine, sealing the promise in his words. I pull his body closer, allowing him to fill my senses with everything he is. Misunderstood, strong, damaged, beautiful. Rhys wears his tattoos like armor, only allowing people to see what he wants them too. But with me, his barriers are down and I can peer straight into his being. Cupping my face in his hands, Rhys reluctantly pulls away from me with a smile that doesn't reach his eyes. "You'll need to help me repack then."

∞∞∞

"-And this is where you'll be staying." Wendy, the camp leader, stops outside a quaint wooden cabin, turning back to us with a wide smile. She's a tall blonde in her late forties and the proud owner of the two Dobermans I was licked to death by in the main reception whilst receiving my info pack. Addy's arm has been linked through mine for the entire hike from the parking lot, the boys at my back. Pinecones litter the ground, the sun breaking through thick cloud to shine on the clearing.

The camp is much bigger than I anticipated with two distinct sides separated by a huge, circular lake. We are currently on the Northern side, where the cabins, mess hall and calmer recreational activities take place. Across the lake, there's everything a sports fan could want, from a soccer and cricket pitch, basketball court and even a putting green. Not to mention the kayaking and water sports which the lake is used for. The whole camp is encased by a forest, far from civilization.

"Oh, forgive me," Wendy steps into our way as we all move towards the cabin as a unit. "This is the female's accommodation. The facilities for men are further down by the canoe shed." I don't need to look behind me to feel Rhys tense, his voice filtering into my receivers a moment later.

"We can't even share a room now?" His arm winds around my front protectively and I lean into his body, despite how hot and sticky the short hike has made me. Rhys has been in a grumpy mood all day, and Addy didn't help by calling him Mr Grumpy Gills and quoting 'Finding Nemo' during the whole lengthy drive here.

"It'll be fine. It's just for sleeping, you'll barely notice I'm not there."

"I'll definitely notice," he grumbles.

"Come on, I'll let you be the big spoon this time," Clay puts his arm around Rhys' shoulders. Shoving him off, Rhys stomps away with his duffle bag in hand and I share a thankful look with Clay for trying.

Once the boys have disappeared from view, Wendy shows us inside the cabin. Several girls have arrived already and are unpacking between the two long rows of bunk beds. A few of them rush over to Addy, clearly knowing her from previous years of volunteering, while I continue the tour. At the far end, the space opens out into a small kitchenette with dining table big enough for eight. Behind an opposite door, I see a communal shower room and bathrooms.

"Meals are provided three times a day in the employee's mess hall and should you need anything such as extra bedding, pop down to reception and ask. Most of our volunteers and staff know at least some basic sign, if you don't always want to wear your receivers." Wendy looks to me with warmth and understanding in her blue eyes, making me feel at home even though I just got here. She heads out the back door, showing me a view of the grounds below from the porch. Addy re-joins me, her brown eyes twinkling with a joy I feel as well. I'm not one for big displays of emotion, but even I can admit I'm giddy with excitement to be a part of something. To start living at last.

"Take some time to get settled in, go for a walk if you'd like," Wendy offers. "We're having a BBQ down by the lake for the volunteers this evening, before the kiddies arrive tomorrow. You're both welcome to bring your partners if you'd like to join us." The woman's smile falters when Addy and I share a confused look and burst into laughter.

"I'm curious as to which one you think is mine," Addy muses. "Neither of those hotties are mine. They're her boyfriends." Apparently Addy's voice was loud enough for the others to hear, as I'm soon ambushed with questions and the odd 'congratulations' from the curtain twitchers staying here. But I can't deny it feels good to have people envy me for once, instead of pitying me for the shitty hand I've been dealt in life. Thankfully, Addy pulls me out of the small crowd and picks out a bunk for us, acting as my guard dog while I unpack. One outfit change later, I'm back in Clay's arms with Rhys taking up the rear, his fingertips skimming the edge of my summer dress against my thighs.

"What?" Rhys questions when I stop his hand from reaching any higher. "I didn't agree to two weeks of abstaining from you so you'd better start grovelling." I roll my eyes at him, biting back a retort about him being bribed to come. I know I should have let Rhys go, although I'd hoped once he got here, he might start to enjoy it. But now I'm sensing his discomfort, I realize I was being selfish.

"I'll make it up for you every day for the rest summer," I turn to plant a kiss on his lips.

"Twice a day, for the rest of the year." His smirk appears, putting me at ease instantly. I lean back into Clay, pulling Rhys with me until I'm the filling of this sexy sandwich.

"Um, guys?" Clay leans in to speak by my ear. "You're forgetting I have needs too, and we have an audience." I still at this, looking towards the lake where indeed, almost everyone is watching us with unconcealed surprise. Amongst the volunteers present, the employees can be told apart by their army green polo shirts and caps. I feel my face redden and slip out from between my men, taking their hands in mine.

Striding towards the fallen logs placed in a rectangle, we sit between the girls from my cabin and strike up a general conversation about camp life. They soon pick their mouths off the floor, recalling stories of typical youthful pranks, helping injured wild animals and even a hurricane one year.

"Have you had a chance to check out your rota yet?" a petite brunette asks from across the fire pit a few of the employees are lighting.

"Briefly. It's pretty full on, isn't it? I'm worried I won't know what to do." Understatement of the century. My rota varies from cabin carnival and junkyard wars, to ninja warrior and water balloon fights. Somehow Addy got the science-based activities, like exploding volcanos and tie-dying, but maybe it's a work-through-the-ranks type deal.

"Oh, don't worry about that! Each activity has a staff member to lead it, you're just there as an extra pair of hands. We get a range of kids from rough backgrounds and those with disabilities. Just be kind and understanding and you'll do great!" I smile, feeling more relaxed now. Addy walks over in a similar dress to mine, her tattooed sleeves on full show, to hand me a beer.

"Food's ready boys," she says, dropping in Clay's space once he's moved. I should hate the way she bosses my guys around, but it's refreshing to have someone confident enough to not be scared of them. Rhys can be off-putting at the best of times and Clay has practiced his emotionless expression for years. But Addy doesn't take shit from anyone, least of all me and that's why she's been the ideal roommate. I'd have hidden from life a hundred times over if she'd let me.

"I'm so lucky I found you," I say, clinking bottles with hers.

"Not as lucky as I am," Addy pulls me in for a half-hug. "My life's been far more entertaining since you stepped into it."

Rhys

In the three days we've been at Camp Everwood, I've discovered something. I'm a fucking idiot. For years, I've been so focused on ridding my dad of his legacy and wealth, I haven't spared a thought about my life afterwards. Or considered a future for myself at all, even though I haven't succeeded yet. And being here has proven to me, the future is beyond fucked.

"Are you sure you don't want to tag along?" Harper asks me for the fourth time. I smile, pulling her into my lap for a brief kiss. I can feel the heat of glares hit me from all around the mess hall, but I won't be rushed. Harper is my salvation in this world, and I'm already parted from her more than I can handle. Lifting her back to her feet, she runs a hand through my hair before half-skipping towards the exit with Clayton by her side.

Returning to my lunch, I push the mashed potato around my plate with the fork. The food isn't awful by any means, but I can't help that my palette has been conditioned for the finer tastes in life. Ones which I won't be enjoying anymore now I know the truth. I'm poor with no prospects and nothing to offer to the one girl who'll see any worth in me. Irony sucks. I used to feel invincible, but now I have someone worthy of the world and I can no longer give it to her.

The staff and volunteers take their lunch breaks on a rota of those eating with the kids in a separate hall and those taking them outside for some free rec time. I am in neither of those categories. In fact, I'm not doing much around here except moping and being the recipient of multiple scowls.

The volunteers are pretty evenly split between the paid college students looking to boost their resume and elderly do-gooders with nothing else to do with their retirement. I knew I wouldn't be bonding with pensioners anytime soon, but I'm not used to being completely ignored by people my own age. Usually, guys and girls alike are falling over themselves to please me, fooling themselves to thinking they are part of my inner circle, but not here. Here I've had a crash course in being an outsider.

Pushing to my feet, I walk away from my plate and towards the open doors. A pair of girls in the corner are signing to each other about me being an asshole, clearly thinking I'm oblivious to their conversation. It's odd how I'm always classed as the judgemental one, when the entire world takes a single look at my tattoos and writes me off as a shallow dickhead. They're not wrong, but still. Not even Harper knows how sharp my mind is, my brain logging the movements of her hands as she practices with Clay across the dinner table most nights.

Stepping outside, I pull the collar of my denim jacket closer to my neck. The brightness of this morning seems to be fleeting, stormy rainclouds rolling in fast. Without a destination in mind, I shove my hands into my pockets and stroll into the surrounding forest. Twigs crack littering the ground beneath my sneakers, birds flocking from overhead as if they can sense the monster walking amongst them. It's only when I pass a sign for the 'Cub's Clearing' do I realize my unplanned walk has led me straight back to my girl like a siren.

I hear the group before I see them, and even from this distance, its Harper's laugh I pick out. She doesn't laugh enough. Not when the sound is so beautiful, I want to play it into my ear on a loop just to get through each day. Approaching the edge of the treeline, I lean against a trunk set back in the shadows to watch.

There's to be some sort of circus show this evening in

the lodge they use for nightly discos. Addy's troop have been on decoration duty, while Harper is helping the kids practice their 'acts'. Even some of the volunteers have signed up to perform some simple acrobatics or juggling. At least I presume that's why Clay is throwing small, defenseless children high into the air and is surrounded by others asking to be next. Who knew he was so good with kids?

I'd briefly thought about offering to be the Tattooed Man, but I don't think demons and skulls are preferable when the audience is mostly under twelve. I wouldn't feel comfortable having my life choices under a spotlight anyway. I've always seen myself as a survivor, but recent events are making me think I'm more of a deluded, inked self-harmer.

Harper is across the clearing, helping a girl in a wheelchair spin hula hoops on her arms. Both of their smiles are infectious, so I hop up into the tree, not wanting to be caught grinning like some hungry predator. Yeah, watching from amongst the foliage is much better.

Evelyn, another little girl, barrels into Harper's side, knocking her onto the forest floor with a throaty laugh. Evelyn doesn't care, planting herself in Harper's lap for a cuddle and only turning back when she wants to sign something. Addy had introduced the pair on her first night here, and they've been almost inseparable since.

There's around twenty kids in each group session, this one with two male members of staff and four volunteers. On one side of the clearing, spongy mats have been laid out for gymnastics, aka crab crawling and somersaults. Between spinning plastic plates on a wooden stick and taking turns on a unicycle with a volunteer's help, I notice a young boy on all fours, roaring like a lion and leaping through a hoop. I didn't think camps like this existed outside of movies, and I wonder how different I would have been if I'd had the chance to play like this.

The session is rounding to close, even before the rain begins to fall. Clay sheds his coat for the girl in the wheelchair, pushing her along the woodland path on the off-roading wheels worthy of a small quad bike. Harper's right behind him, Evelyn hanging off one arm and a box of equipment in the other. I move to follow when the two staff members catch my attention, hanging back to have a cigarette. Watching the pair walk beneath the cover of the trees, their smoke drifts to me and invades my nostrils. *Holy nicotine.* I collapse against the branch at my back, some of the tension seeping from my bones.

"That new girl is hot as shit," one of the voices floats to me. And the tension is back tenfold.

"Yeah, she is. Too bad she's always got a bodyguard hanging around. If not one of those douchebags, then Addy would have our nuts for getting too close. You'd think her pussy is some kind of gold mine with the way they act."

"I can handle Addy. Rumor has it Harper needs two at a time to be sated. I say we sneak over to the female's cabin after dark-" Launching myself from the branch, I land on a crouch and uppercut the guy speaking in one swift movement.

"You go anywhere near that cabin, I'll tie you to this tree by your tiny dick and beat you for hours with a baseball bat." I sneer at the bastard who's fallen against the trunk, too focused on him spitting out blood to notice his friend's fist until it connects with my face. My head wheels sideways and red curtains my vision. Throwing punches wildly, the two of them descend on me, but they're no match for my years of fighting.

Bending low, I tackle the taller one to the ground and the hop up to face the other. He's of a similar age to me, skinny with a top knot. Ugh, I hate him already. Ducking below his next wide fist, I sweep his legs out too. Dropping down, I let my inner monster take over for a while and alleviate the stress I've been feeling. Noses crunch beneath my knuckles, blood flying onto the woodland floor. I have to commend the way they both fight back, a boot smashing into my jaw.

Next thing I know, Clayton is yanking me to my feet and shoving me away. I remain in a fighting stance, the lines between friend and foe blurring as he helps the employees. He tells them to get lost but they don't move, peering around Clayton with smirks. Funny how brave they are now there's a six-foot wall of muscle separating us.

"Are you trying to get us all kicked out of here?!" Clayton snarls at me, his features hard as stone. He hasn't looked at me like that for a long time, and I suddenly hate it. I'm not that bully anymore, they deserved it.

"You didn't hear what they said about propositioning Harper!" I yell, my fists finally releasing.

"Then let them." Clayton shrugs. My mouth drops open and my shoulders go slack. Has he lost his fucking mind? Rage takes over, my skin feeling too tight as I fight against scratching it all off or killing Clayton where he stands. I opt for punching the nearest tree trunk instead, relishing the pain splintering through my forearm. *Wow, taking my anger out on nature, what a cunt.*

"You can't be fucking serious," I spit out. The two fuckers behind him are jeering, calling me a psychopath but I tune them out. My full attention is centered on the blonde I recently considered something akin to a companion. Clayton closes the gap between us, gripping my shoulders tightly.

"Rhys, she's a beautiful girl. Guys are going to hit on her. The difference is I know she'll put them in their place, don't you?" His question catches me off guard, my head starting to spin. Never mind Harper being my first girlfriend, I've never put my trust in anyone before. Sure, she'd hold her own but how long will I be enough for her until she starts looking for something more. Because there's a whole planet full of better men out there than me.

"Stop overthinking," Clay gives me a rough shake. "She *loves* you. Do you know how hard it is for me to admit that? But I also know you give her something I can't, so I have to suck it up and share the most incredible girl I've ever known with you." I nod along with Clayton, until the dickhead behind him pipes up again.

"If she were my girl, she wouldn't need anyone else. Clearly neither of you are good enough for her."

"Get the fuck out of here before I finish the job he started." Clayton hisses, refusing to release me. The pair stride away laughing, thinking they've won but this isn't over. Clayton won't always be around to save them, and they're as good as marked.

"Forget about them," Clayton says, clearly reading my thoughts again. I'm like an open book when it comes to him and I hate it. I can't stand people seeing the real me I want to keep hidden, the one my father knows is weak and undeserving. "We can't be with her all the time, and you can't beat up every guy who finds her attractive. Take the compliment." Shrugging out of Clayton's hold, I pace in a circle to come straight back to stand in front of him.

"Don't you ever worry we're gonna hold her back?" I mutter. From what, I'm not sure in this moment. Life experiences, worthy partners. All of it. The slight hang of Clayton's head is the only indication he's not as confident about this as he's pretending to be, which equally eases and unnerves me.

"All the time," he admits. "But she chose us. Hell, she fought for us even if it meant she'd lose us both. It's our job and privilege to live up to that." I nod slowly on a deep exhale. Punching his bicep lightly, Clayton scoffs at the blood splatter I leave on his white sleeve.

"Why'd you have to be so fucking right all the time?" I smirk, starting to lead the way back to our girl. Right after I find a first aid kit and sort myself out, although I don't think a band aid is going to cut it this time.

Harper

Circling the stick around the drum, I twist a huge ball of cotton candy and pass it over to the boy patiently waiting for me to get the hang of this machine. He thanks me politely and I press my hand over my heart, turning to face my helper, Vivien.

"They're all so sweet," I gush.

"Only when they want to be," she cocks an eyebrow at me, returning to her own cylinder. The circus night is so much better than I expected, which isn't meant as an insult, but I didn't think the camp would go this big. Then again, Addy was involved in the planning. She could pull a party out of $10 and a stack of cardboard. Either side of the pathway is a long row of stalls, ranging from food kiosks to funfair games. I'm based next to the ticket booth, where one of the employees, Tom, is dressed like a ringleader and doing a great job at selling tickets for the main show taking place shortly. The children can exchange the camp bucks they've been earning all week for a ticket, with each one receiving a free balloon animal from Tom's beautiful assistant, aka his wife. They're an older couple who have worked here every summer for the past sixteen years.

Dishing out round after round of cotton candy, my face is beginning to hurt from smiling when arms wrap around my body tightly. I flinch at first, until a nose nuzzles into my hair in a Rhys-like fashion.

"You smell so good," he groans beside my receiver. I know how much he loves my blueberry shampoo, which is why I'm always stocked up with the stuff. I try to look back, wondering if he walked straight out of the woods behind me but he won't let me budge. "I've missed you so much."

"I saw you at lunch," I giggle. Resting my head against his, Vivien takes the next mini customer for me.

"Too long," Rhys grunts like a caveman. I twist in his arms forcefully, despite the fight he puts up about it.

"Well, you could always help-" my words fade as I get a clear sight at his face. "Oh my god, Rhys. What happened?! We're at a camp for disabled and vulnerable children. How the hell did you get this?" I try to stroke the purple bruise lining his jaw but he jerks away from my touch. His eyes are fixed in the other direction, and as I follow his gaze I see why. Chris and Jack, the staff members I was working alongside earlier, are walking past with matching nose bandages and black eyes. They scowl at me as if I'm the problem, which only leads me to ask Rhys more questions.

"They deserved it," is the only response I get. The affectionate, lovesick man I had a moment ago has slipped away, but I refuse to let him sidestep me. "They threatened you, okay? I had to put them back in their place." Rhys grits out, and that's the first time he's ever lied to me. I can see it clearly in his blue eyes refusing to meet mine. But why, after everything we've been through, would he lie to me now? I'm calling bullshit on something, but until I find out what exactly, I'll play along with Rhys' story.

"Then I need to thank you. Will you let me kiss it better?" I see his small smirk, so even though Rhys remains half turned away from me, I press against him and trail feather light kisses along his jaw. I know from the look out the other two, Rhys' hand will also be messed up, so I raise it to my lips next. "I know your intentions were honorable," I lie, "but please walk away the next time. I don't care what people say about me and if I do, I can stick up for myself."

"I know you can," Rhys sighs, pulling me into him. Pushing up on my tiptoes, I wind my arms around Rhys' neck and see Clay walking towards us. Without alerting Rhys, I lazily sign 'what happened' with one hand and let Clay fill me in. Ahh, I knew it. Jealousy won't be an easy feat for Rhys to overcome, it took him long even to stop thinking of me as a possession. But I need to make sure he doesn't harm anyone else, for everyone's sakes. Just not tonight.

"Come on, my shift has ended. Let's go have some fun." Shedding the pinstriped apron and handing it to Holly, the volunteer who has come to relieve me, I link fingers with Rhys' unharmed hand. Clay joins my other side silently, while Rhys makes a subtle remark about the cut of the khaki shorts I'm wearing.

"Don't start with me or I'll add to your bruises," I warn him with a raised eyebrow. And there it is – the man I know. Full smirk, heated eyes, the sly nod that says challenge accepted. We walk the length of the path, stopping every so often to watch the kids pull tickets from the raffle pot or fish a rubber duck from a paddling pool of water. It's humbling being in a place where everyone is accepted, no matter the ailments they struggle with.

A boy with Spiderman braces on his legs rides a unicycle through the center of the crowd with a volunteer supporting him on either side, his laughter tearing through the background noise and pricking the back of my eyes with tears. Each and every one of these kids already has something the three of us didn't until we found each other; the feeling of acceptance.

Nearing the end of the path, I see a basketball hoop with a spiral of stuffed teddies tied to the pole. There's a long queue waiting for a turn, the next in line being Evelyn. Spotting me, her little face lights up and she signs for help. Unlike me, Evelyn was born unable to hear into a fully hearing family, but she's still immersed in the deaf community. She attends a special school and spends her summer here, her confidence evident in the masses of friends she has.

"I've got it," Clay reassures me, jogging over to Evelyn as her turn is up. Instead of taking the ball from the volunteer as I expected, Clay hoists Evelyn onto his shoulders, passing the ball up to her. She giggles loudly, stretching high to drop the ball into the net. Clay cheers for her, victory dancing with his shoulders so Evelyn is bumped around, laughing and clutching onto his hair. Once she's back on her feet, the volunteer signs to ask which teddy she'd like, and of course, she picks the pink dolphin twice her size.

Bouncing past, Evelyn waves at me and goes in search of her key worker. There's one key worker for every six children, unless their disability requires one-on-one care. Rhys' hand has remained tightly squeezing mine the entire time, and even when Clay sweeps me up, he doesn't release me. The kiss Clay intended to be brief lingers, our breaths mingling and eyes growing heated. Putting me down, Clay leads me and my tagalong towards the woods. The music seeping through speakers and excited chatter falls away, my heart kicking up a beat.

The instant the darkness cloaks around us, hands grab onto my body. My hair is twisted high on my head, both sets of lips finding my neck in what can only be a pre-planned move. I imagine the guys have spent each night in their cabin discussing strategies to make the most of two sets of hands. Fingers trail across my abdomen and brush over my crop top, my nipples tightening at the faint touch. I lean into them, a growing need I've been ignoring now desperate to be sated.

A mouth covers mine, my tongue pushing inside immediately. The metal of Rhys' lip piercing brushes against the corner of my lips, his hand around my neck pushing me back a step into Clay's hard body. Solid erections press into me from both sides, my thong growing wet in my tight jeans. My crop top is lifted, the cool air kissing my chest a moment before Rhys ducks his head to do the same. I can't fight the groan that escapes me as he latches onto my nipple, fingers fumbling to unbutton my pants.

"Wait," Clay freezes, "I think I hear someone crying." I stiffen too, drawing Rhys off me but not before he latches down in a frustrated bite. I hiss through my teeth, calling him a bastard while covering myself. Listening as intently as my receivers will allow, it takes me a moment to pick up on the small, whimpering sound through the trees.

Ignoring Rhys' protests, I switch on my phone's torch and move further into the forest. I find her quickly, huddled behind a trunk with her knees pulled up to her chest. She's a girl of around eight or nine, with mousey brown hair in a long plait other than the fringe covering her forehead. I kneel in the dirt, placing my phone down and gently take her hands in mine. Her dark eyes flick up to me, her porcelain-like face recognizable now.

"Hey, Maisy right?" She sniffs and nods, her eyes darting around at the two men behind me. I hadn't worked with her personally, but I've seen her on the edge of the nightly discos, usually with a pair of ear defenders on. "Was it too loud for you?" On her next nod, I ask the guys to go fetch Tara, her key worker and her ear defenders, but mostly I sensed Maisy would rather they weren't both gawking at her.

"I don't like loud noises either," I say, nestling in beside her. She doesn't make eye contact with me much but leans into my side, her body shivering slightly. My phone torch lights the woods around us, casting shadows that may freak her out, but I still don't put my arm around her. From what I've seen, Tara is careful not to touch Maisy and I figure there has to be a reason, possibly a male-related one judging by the way her little body has eased since the guys left.

"I know the world can be a scary place, and sometimes the noises are the worst part. I've been deaf for seven years now. I have these implants, see," I shift my hair aside for Maisy to look at my receivers, explaining how it all works. I remain still as her little fingers trace over the metallic disc beneath the skin behind my hair. "I only just started wearing my receivers all the time recently. Before that, I preferred the silence."

"I like the quiet," her voice is so small, I briefly wonder if I imagined it. I stare at the top of her brunette head until her eyes flick to mine.

"The quiet can be nice," I agree. "But there's some sounds I love. Like running water. There's something so pure about it. And laughter makes me smile. What about you?"

"I dunno," Maisy ducks her head into my arm again. I lift it slowly, allowing her to curl into me before I lower it across her back. "I don't like thunder."

"Thunder can be a scary one. But how about the rain? I don't know why but I love hearing the rain fall, even though it gets loud sometimes. It's not a bad loud," I trail off, wondering if I'm even making any sense.

"It's a good loud." I smile at Maisy, sharing a moment of bonding before the footfalls grow closer. Tara crouches, observing us closely before asking Maisy a ton of questions she refuses to answer. I hold up a hand to silence Tara, turning my attention back to Maisy.

"I think the show will start soon. Would you like to come watch it with us?" Maisy smiles shyly at me although her attention is acutely aware of the others around us. Rhys hands me the ear defenders, which I slip over her head and gently pull her to her feet. Allowing the guys to go first, we stroll out of the woodlands as everyone else is heading for the main cabin. I fall into step to follow when Wendy comes bustling up the path towards us.

"Oh, there you are!" Her cheeks are red, her blonde hair whipping around her as she skids to a halt. "Jack, one of our acts for the show, had to pull out after getting into a scrap with a volunteer. We need someone to fill in and everyone was raving about our very own Strong Man from this afternoon's practice." Her blue eyes fall on Clay and I burst out laughing. He's shaking his head and backing away until Rhys shoves him forward a step, a wide smile gracing his face too. Fuck yes, this is happening and

I'm recording the whole thing.

Clayton

If I wasn't set against stepping out in front of a crowd before, upon seeing my 'costume' I sure as shit am now. The offensive garment is shoved into my hands by a beaming Addy, who rushes off before I can curse at her. Staff, volunteers and children are bustling around everywhere, all already dressed for their parts and having a last-minute practice of their acts. Beyond the thin door separating us from the manmade 'arena', I hear the opening music rumble through various speakers. Fucking hell.

Skating around the edge of the open room, I find a door and slip inside. A chrome-covered kitchen is on the other side, a white shutter separating me from the madness, but at least I'm alone. I've got roughly five minutes to slap some confidence into myself and stop being the guy that hides at the back of class.

It's not the performance or outfit bothering me; I'd re-enact this a thousand times if Harper asked me to. It's the thought of being sized up like a piece of meat and judged on my body, like always. One look and people presume I'm some dumb jock, their eyes traveling over my body as if they own it, their hands squeezing my biceps or pecs. Appearance is artificial, but if I were to walk around shirtless, suddenly my brain means nothing.

"What's going on in here?" Addy bursts in behind me. Seeing I'm not dressed, her brown eyes bug out of her head. "Clayton! I need you ready in the next three seconds and in line so get out there!"

"I don't feel...comfortable," I mumble weakly. Walking away from her, I place the outfit on a counter and lean against it with my arms crossed.

"Oh, sweetie," Addy edges closer me with a face full of concern. "Are you okay? Do you need a cup of tea and a blanket? Maybe a hot water bottle to warm your massive, sensitive vagina?" Wait, what? "Snap out of it, you dick-swab! It's a children's circus, put off by a group of disabled ten-year-olds! There's a girl with Down's syndrome out there right now in a glittery leotard doing the hula! Do you think she feels 'comfortable'?"

"Well, no....but-"

"No buts! Get your ass in that costume and go make some kids smile!" Okay, angry Addy is seriously scary. When I don't immediately move, she lunges at me to yank my top off. I step out of her reach, turning away to strip off myself. Jesus, if we were caught now, I'd be single within seconds. The costume is thrust at me as I get down to my boxers, the sound of the door clicking closed signaling I'm alone once more. Remind me never to get on Addy's bad side properly, I reckon that girl could flay me alive without blinking.

Emerging from the room, I'm instantly met with all eyes on me, like I predicted. Gritting my teeth, internally cursing fickle people, I'm ushered to the front of the line of acts waiting to go on. Wendy's husband steps through the door with their two Doberman's in mini tuxedos. Great, how am I supposed to follow a dog act? I don't have time to consider it as small yet firm hands shove me onward, a ringmaster announcing 'The Strong Man' as I step into the spotlight.

I square my shoulders and walk into the center of the room, hunting for Harper amongst the crowd. The seats are set in a circle but my eyes land on hers immediately. The pure joy I find there is worth every second of my humiliation and every inch of this spandex leopard print outfit, traveling from my left shoulder to my right hip. With my chest exposed, I consciously tug on the wide, leather belt in an effort to cover my bulge. So much for a kids show.

The ringmaster is reeling off facts about the history of the strong man and his role in the circus while I roll my neck and consider my options. I could half-ass this and let Addy kill me, or give in and have Harper love me ten times harder. I'm sold. Letting all of my inhibitions go, I flex and dab, lapping up the laughter and applause.

There's a range of fake, heavy objects displayed in front of me on a long table. A papier-mâché weight bar, an inflatable caveman's club. Yeah, no thanks. As he tries to leave, I grab a hold of the ringmaster and lift him into my arms. He's a stick skinny guy in a red jacket with gold buttons, his freckled face draining of color before I hoist him high in the air. Spinning slowly, I do a few squats and throw in a lunge before letting my captive go free on shaky legs.

Adrenaline rushes through my body, my smile wide as I play to the crowd. They go wild when I do a 'Usain Bolt' pose, but really I'm stalling as I think of what to do next. Catching sight of Harper once more, I rush forward to grab her hand and pull her into the ring with me. She fights against me but my grip is too strong, laughter bubbling from my lips.

Presuming the noise level and cheering will be too much for her to hear through, if her receivers are even still on, I quickly sign what I need her to do and drop down into a plank. Harper complies straight away, sitting cross-legged on my back while I do a round of push-ups as the crowd count along. On the sixth, an added weight joins hers, a hand gripping my hair like a horse. Fucking Rhys. My arms shake viciously but I refuse to be beaten. Not when I'm on a roll, proving to myself I can be the outgoing guy I thought had been lost. Reaching number ten, the weights hop off and Rhys helps me up with a smirk.

Punching him heavily in the chest, I notice Harper clearing off the table and grabbing two chairs for either side. She gestures for me and Rhys to sit opposite each other, taking over the act. She's practically glowing, her eyes twinkling as she addresses the crowd for an arm-wrestling competition. Holding her hand over Rhys' head first, a round of cheers sound for him, whereas when she does the same to me, the place erupts. I jerk my eyebrows at Rhys, for once feeling the level of confidence he usually portrays.

"Obviously, I'm going to let you win," Rhys leans across the table to mutter. "It's a kid's show and you're the star, for now." On the surface, he's acting carefree but I can see the monster lurking beneath the surface saying he's hating this. Not just the show, the camp, the people, all of it. Yet he's still here, smiling when he can so that has to mean something. Harper cuts me off from responding, clearly sensing the hostility growing between us.

"Winner gets to go down on me first," she bends across the table to hiss at us. Her cleavage is inches from my face, her ass tilted upwards in high-waisted jeans. A moment later, she's gone but the competition is set. This time, Rhys' smile is full, his eyes feral. Game on.

Setting my elbow on the table, I wait for Rhys to clasp my hand. The tattoo on his hand gleams in the overhead light, a crowned skull balanced at the top of an hourglass on the verge of falling. I don't have time to contemplate the image as Harper starts a countdown, the crowd joining in. Before they reach one, Rhys' tongue darts out, licking across my fingers to throw me off. And it almost works, his hand overpowering mine until I push back at the last second. I should have expected him to play dirty, especially when it's Harper's sweet pussy on the line.

We struggle for control, our clasped hands jerking side to side. I may have the visible muscle due to my larger frame, but Rhys is stronger than he looks. More than that, he has a determined mind-set that won't be denied what he thinks he's owed. His face is the picture of concentration, as if he could move my hand with willpower alone, but I'm not going down without a fight.

The audience grows louder, chanting my name. I almost feel guilty for the lack of support on Rhys' side, but Harper's hands smooth over his shoulders and his eyes flick to mine with a smirk that says he has all the backing he needs. Tensing my shoulders, I push all of my strength down my bicep and gradually force his hand downwards. A spike of discomfort shoots through my forearm, but I push onwards, shaking as his hand gets closer to the table's surface.

And that's when I see it. The flare of defeat slice through Rhys' face. The true weight of what losing will do to him evident, even though it's a stupid bet. He's lost so much of what he thought he had and who he believed he was in such a short space of time, losing yet again would make him recoil more into his tattooed shell. He's pulling away from Harper as it is, I don't want to be the reason he does it even more. So as his hand is a centimeter from the table, I roll my elbow, causing my strength to falter and he slams my hand down in a swooping arc.

There's a moment of quiet shock, quickly followed by an eruption of cheers. Harper hugs Rhys from behind, raising his arm as the victor. All the while, his narrowed eyes remain locked on mine. I rise from my seat with a shrug, bowing goodbye to the crowd before striding towards the rear door. I can feel Rhys' presence following me without needing to look back, my eyes rolling as I return to the kitchen in search for my clothes. I've barely stepped through the door when Rhys spins and throws me against the wall, his forearm across my throat.

"If I suspect for a second you threw that fight, I'll flay you alive and wear your skin to tell everyone you're a pussy-whipped bitch." I struggle to keep the smile from creeping across my face and the words of how he already is that locked in my throat. Displaying a scowl instead, I shove him away from me and barge past.

"You won, alright? Get out my face." Peeling the spandex off, I drag on my cargo pants and t-shirt before facing him again.

He's leaning against the door, watching me closely for a hint of my lie. Not spotting one, a small smile graces his lips.

"It was a good fight," he breathes as his stance relaxes. I suppose it meant more than I realized for Rhys to earn something, not to be handed it and I don't know if I feel good about the fact anymore or not. Shrugging with one shoulder, I move across the room to pat Rhys on the arm patronizingly.

"Yeah, but who's the real winner here? You get to start Harper off, but I'll be the one with her pulsing around my dick." I chuckle as Rhys' smile lessens, his elbow flying into my gut. We tussle, play fighting for the upper hand until I catch him in a headlock. After finding his struggles are pointless, Rhys' rambling about tiring Harper out too much for me to get a look in is interrupted by the ringing of my phone.

I release him in favor of yanking my phone out of my side pocket, shoving him away playfully. His retaliation is cut short upon noticing my frown at the unknown number, wondering who would call me at this time of night. Rhys also scowls at my phone, sliding his index finger across the screen to answer and taps on the loudspeaker before snarling into the microphone.

"Who the fuck is this and why are you ruining a crucial bromance moment?"

Harper

I wake with a smile already cemented on my face, stretching on my single mattress like a cat. I must make a noise, as Addy's pink hair flops over the side a moment later.

"You look refreshed," she signs. I feel it too. I don't think I've laughed so much as I did last night. The circus was a huge success and by the end of the show, even Maisy was smiling and joining with a Greatest Showman sing-along. Evelyn planted herself on my lap too, signing to the words on the karaoke monitor. Everyone here is so friendly, the atmosphere easy to lose yourself in. Jumping from her top bunk, Addy nudges me over in her fleece onesie with the rabbit ears.

"You owe me $20, by the way. I told you I'd get Clay into that leotard." I have to hand it to her, I thought that outfit was where Clay would draw the line when Addy had filled me in on the classic Strong Man act. Usually it's Jack's gig, which is why the costume was two sizes too small and provided a clear outline of Clay's dick. I'm sure most of his applause was from the girls staying in this cabin, but I can't fault that Clay looked delectable enough to make my mouth water.

Handing over the money, I nudge Addy out of the bed and make my way to the shower room. Three of the five showers are occupied, each separated by thin white curtains. A stack of freshly laundered towels sit on a shelf beside the long line of basins. A few girls are posted there too, hogging the mirror with their make-up bags and piles of hair products. It's as if, even after being here a week, these girls don't know we are in the wilderness.

After a quick shower, I towel-dry my hair and toss it into a messy bun. Addy is ready in a loose vest, cropped leggings and sneakers which are currently tucked up on my damn bed. At some point, our two separate bags became one merged pile of folded clothes. I pull out some camo shorts which are Addy's and a black t-shirt with 'Limited Edition' printed across the front. Perfect. After dressing, I snap my receivers on in time to hear my name being called for a visitor.

"Where's Clay?" I ask as I step outside and straight into Rhys' arms. He smells like cologne although I don't think he's put any on this morning, but more like his clothes are now enriched with it. He holds me a little tighter than usual, something in his posture making me step back to eye him closely.

"Clayton needs some time alone so I'm taking you to breakfast today. I don't wake up this early for anyone, so I hope you appreciate it," Rhys tries to make a joke but his fake smile doesn't fool me.

"You haven't been fighting again, have you? He'd better not be nursing a black eye as well," I scold him after the state I saw Chris and Jack in. I didn't see the two of them after the arm wrestle last night, and when I went in search, they'd already returned to their cabin for the night. I guess a part of me had supposed they might be working out some differences, and that's why I didn't bother looking any further. I didn't want my great night to be dampened by their arguments.

"No Babygirl, there won't be any more fighting." Rhys reaches out to stroke the back of his knuckles over my cheek softly.

"Well, now I'm really worried. What's happened?" I step out of his touch again, crossing my arms until he relents on a sigh.

"Can't we just enjoy a breakfast together?" I shake my head firmly with pursed lips, refusing to be assuaged. "Fine. Dekken overdosed yesterday. He's been skipping his meds and hiding them away. He left a note, the police have sent Clayton a copy so let's give him some time to-"

"No." I interrupt him. Tears swim in my eyes, my heart breaking with each heavy thud. The grief ripping through me takes my breath away, but it's soon replaced by anger. How could Dekken do this? After I believed in him, fought for him. He was on the path to getting better, he had his whole life ahead of him. I need to understand what went wrong, which means I need to see that note.

Barreling past with the first tears beginning to fall, Rhys grabs my wrist to yank me back. I'm about to protest when I'm met with his firm chest beneath my cheek, Rhys' arms wrapping around me like steel bars. And that's when the weight of my emotions crash into me, one sob leading into a full-on cry. Not the cute, reddened eyes and wobbly lip kind either. The ugly kind where my eyes are puffy, my throat feels raw and I couldn't stand the noises coming out of me so I turned my receivers off. When my knees give out, Rhys lowers me to the ground and cradles me on the dirt path, right outside my cabin.

We remain there long after everyone has walked by, eyeing me curiously and the morning sessions must have started. My entire body feels numb, yet heavy as lead. I want to curl up and go to sleep in Rhys' lap, hoping this feeling will be gone when I wake. But grief doesn't work that way. It consumes you, destroying you from the inside out and when you think you can't take it anymore, you slowly begin to rebuild. The person you were has gone, and in its place is a hardened shell that takes time to learn to love again. Time heals all apparently, but sadly not in Dekken's case.

Rhys tenderly switches my receivers back on one by one, placing a soft kiss on my forehead. "I'm sorry." Whether he means for my loss or not trying to keep it from me, I'm not sure. "Clayton wanted time to process everything so he could be strong enough to console you."

"You're strong enough to console me," I reply, my voice bland and empty. My head has lolled into the crook of his shoulder, my eyes fixed on a pinecone on the forest floor.

"I'm not good at these things. I don't…know what to say."

"I don't want you to say anything, just be there. We're a team, remember? We laugh together, we cry together." I think of Clay sitting alone, dealing with this when he'd just straightened things out with Dekken. What if he's feeling responsible? That's the overriding thought that gives me the strength to stand and start walking, flopping one boot in front of the other.

The men's cabin is empty and dark, no sign of life until Rhys' hand on the small of my back ushers me to the end bunk. Clayton is tucked beneath the covers, his face hidden from view but his laptop on the side table is open. Tapping on the mousepad, the screen flashes to life and I find a scanned image of the note waiting there. Rhys tries to deter me, but I need to know what it says. I need to understand.

Clayton,
I know when you made me promise to write,
this isn't what you intended. But your words played
on my mind long after you left, and you're right. I am
free now. I'm free of the guilt, I'm free of the revenge
that drove me through each day, and I'm free of hurting
those I care about. I've grown to care for Harper, and
even you, yet I hurt you both the most. I can't continue
to live in a world where all I have to offer is pain.
I don't expect you to understand, but I do
hope you can forgive me for this one day. Please
know it's what I wanted, to be with my parents,
Antonio and my uncle. I'm at peace now.

I slowly close the laptop, pressing my eyes closed to hold back the water gathering there. There's so much to take from Dekken's words, the most obvious how even now, he's still asking for forgiveness from a world who failed him, but I can't think anymore. Instead, I stretch onto my tiptoes, dragging the mattress off the top bunk and placing it onto the hard wood floor. Attacking the bed Clay is laying on, Rhys steps in to help me haul his mattress onto the floor as well. Clay thumps onto the ground but doesn't move or look around, which is how I know he's awake. Just numb, like I was and still am.

Stripping to my underwear, I crawl beneath the cover and press my back into Clay's front. When he doesn't hug me, I nestle in deeper until my legs mirror the curve of his, my head buried beneath his chin. Rhys rolls into the make-shift double bed on the floor a moment later in just his boxers, scooting his butt back to join our triple-stacked spoon. I pull him closer, pressing my lips into the center of his back and winding my arms around to trace patterns over his chest. And even though I've recently slept for nine hours, I drift back to sleep.

The sun is setting over Lake Everwood on a day wasted. We slept together all day, except from the brief moment when Addy came to check on me or to all roll over in unison. I was like the hot dog in a testosterone packed bun, warm and secure between the men who own my heart. If this morning's shock has taught me anything, it's to cherish what I have, right here and right now. No holding back, I'm going to give my all and then some to make sure neither of these guys ever question if their lives have a purpose.

Addy has cleared everyone out from this section of the lake's shoreline, giving the three of us privacy. The graveled outcrop is supported by wooden beams and hidden by an arch in the trees. In my hands is a tribute the children made this afternoon upon hearing I'd received some sad news, and it couldn't be more perfect. A leaf shaped cardboard base supports a range of petals and tiny flowers they picked, with a tealight candle in the center.

"Should we say something?" I ask no one in particular. It's not standard practice to mourn someone who initially had ill-intent towards you, but Clay and I know it's more than that. Whether he was at the beginning of his rehabilitation or not, Dekken mattered. His mental health mattered. And we're the only ones left to honor that.

"Don't ask me to. I'm not going to mourn someone who tried to hurt the one I love." I nod along with Rhys' words, having expected them, which is why I have already thought out my answer to that.

"Fair enough. But you can mourn someone who became another victim of your father's manipulation." This silences him, other than a grunt and I turn to Clay. He hasn't spoken much, unless necessary and only to me. "What about you?"

"I can't stop thinking if my mother had been able to bring Dekken home that day," his black eyes move slowly from the horizon to mine. "He would have been like my brother and we'd have grieved our losses together. It could have all been so... different." I link my fingers with his, pulling him to crouch with me. Rhys kneels too, producing a lighter to light the candle. Together, with our hands overlapping, we ease the mini boat into the water and push it out onto the lake.

It's a touching moment, no words needing to be said. Even when the boat begins to warp and take on water, inevitably sinking and the light sizzling out. Yeah, in hindsight, it wasn't the best idea, but the thought was there. Falling back onto our butts, we huddle together. The boy's arms are overlapping across my shoulders, their hands on each of my thighs. This is how it should be. Us united against the world.

Time seems to freeze, allowing us as long as we need. But after a while, my ass is numb and shivers have taken control of my limbs. The arms comforting me are starting to grow heavy and for once, the silence is stretching on for too long.

"What's going through your minds?" I ask eventually.

Rhys answers immediately.

"How many fish do you think we've just poisoned?" I can't contain the giggle that escapes me, feeling bad for the glimpse of light burrowing its way into my heart. Clay chuckles too, despite his efforts not to, smacking Rhys on the back of the head.

"Dick," he comments. I laugh fully this time, bending forward to hold my sides. I do hope Dekken is watching now, laughing along with us as he would have been one day if he'd stuck around. But I'm determined to live by the words he left us with, seeking for the good in the world. Like the men laughing either side of me. In the depths of darkness, they've have shone the light to guide me back and that's how I know, no matter what we face from here on out, it's all going to be okay.

Rhys

I get it. Dekken saw the error of his ways and was ready to change, and topped himself instead of actually doing it. The shame. The tragedy. What-fucking-ever. I might have been able to feel remotely upset if I wasn't so pissed off at the squirmy little shit. It takes a real pussy to duck out of life early instead of face the path to retribution. Regardless of what his note said, Dekken has hurt Harper once again and I can't even punch him in the face for it.

What's worse is I've been staring at the most miserable motherfucker for the past two days. Between lying around in bed and ignoring the fact he needs a shower, I've had to share a bunk with Clayton's mopey face and his overriding stench. But if I say that, I'm the bad guy. So instead I'm here, on the basketball court filling in for Clayton Cockface. This session is for the "troubled youth" aka, asshole teens with attitude problems.

"What you looking at?" I snap at a boy giving me evil eyes across the court. Hey, I said I'd help. I didn't say I'd be nice about it. Besides, from Evil-eyed Eddie to Hand-me-down Harry, these kids need someone who won't pander to their 'feelings' with a fucking mindful coloring sheet, but to tell them how it is. Life's shit, get over it. Try not to kill yourself.

Bouncing the basketball between my legs, I challenge someone to tackle me with a hard stare. No one out of the six boys skulking around steps forward. Pussies. Dribbling to the arc, I shoot and catch the ball as it swoops through the net.

"Sorry about that," the member of staff returns after the longest toilet break to have ever been taken. Honestly, I could have pulled Harper into a cubicle, had her on her knees and blown my load over her face quicker than this fucker takes to shit. He's older than most employees, around forty I'd guess with ginger-ish hair that glints in the sunlight and his pants belted tightly over his midriff. I didn't catch his name on account of ignoring him, but I've labeled him Suckass Steve in my mind.

"Where were we? Ahh yes, passing and dribbling. Boys, form a line along this side of the court. If you have the ball, you dribble to the other end and back to the center, where you'll pass to the next person waiting and so on. Rhys, would you like to demonstrate?"

"No." I don't think that was the answer he was expecting judging by the way his eyebrows touched his hairline, and when I refuse to give up my ball, he retrieves his own from the gym bag. I fall into line with the others, watching skeptical Suckass Steve crouch low to dribble the ball with some weird-ass lunge steps. When he stops in the center and throws the ball at me, I sidestep for it to bounce off into the tennis court behind us. This is hopeless.

"Right, listen up sad saps," I walk forward. "I don't want to be here as much as any of you do. So I'll make this real simple. The first one who manages to get this ball out of my hand can leave. The rest stay with Pedo Pete here until sundown." That's all it takes for all six to rush at me in a flash of sports shorts and scuffed sneakers. I twist away before a range of snotty hands land on me, bouncing the ball with each step. I have to appreciate their efforts, but they are obviously slow as shit. For most of them, I think this is the first time they'll have committed to anything in their crappy, little lives.

Not bothering with shooting, I round the edge of the court with a cluster of lanky teens chasing me. Skidding to the side, a smile has graced my lips as I continue to evade them over and over. Putting a distance between us and getting cocky, I slam dunk the ball into the net and immediately grab it again. A boy with a face full of braces comes at me at the front, but I already clocked the fucker trying to sneak behind me. I lift the ball high in the air as his arms flail around me wildly.

"If you wanted a hug, you'll have to ask Ranger Rodney over there." I catch the employee's eye as he tries to shout his real name at me, but I'm not listening. I don't do names, I do instincts and my instincts say this suckass ranger pedo has a stupid name anyway. Instead of darting away, I continue to hold the ball high out of reach and walk through the crowd with a mocking smile.

A body collides with mine, thumping into my side and shoving me back a few steps. He's as skinny as the rest from lack of a stable diet, with dirt patches on his cheeks and forehead beneath shaggy brown hair. There's an untamed wildness to his eyes, one that reminds me too much of myself. When I don't react, the shoulder-height teen throws a punch into my gut. Hah. I like this kid, even though it hurts my soul to act weak, I fake a wince and not-so-accidently tip the ball in his direction. He grabs it with a victorious grin until the boy beside him grabs a fistful of his hair and tosses him aside like nothing, snatching the ball as he falls. Nah, I've changed my mind – I like this kid better.

"Wow, how did you get them to do that?" I raise an eyebrow at Suckass Steve as I step off the court, following his eyeline behind me. Now the proud winner of the ball, the one I'll call Mohawk Mike is pivoting and ducking as the others race after him. He misses a shot, landing the ball in the hands of another and like magic, the little fuckers are actually playing basketball together. Sure, there's no teams and they're little savages, but I like that better. Look at me, I did a thing. Harper's going to be begging me to get inside her when she hears what a great fucking job I did today.

Movement by the cricket field catches my eye, Evil-eye

Eddie stomping away from the pack. I take off after him, refusing to let him out of the deal so easy. He lost, he stays. Stepping onto the grass, he diverts towards the woodlands which lead towards this side of Lake Everwood. My lengthened steps catch up to his in no time as we enter the tree line, my hand on his shoulder spinning him roughly into a nearby trunk.

"Where'd you think you're going?" Aside from the narrowed blue eyes staring back at me, this kids couldn't be more different from me. Olive skinned with a birthmark claiming his left cheek and jaw. A frizzy blond mess sits upon his hair, probably tempting the birds overhead looking for a new nest by the state of it. Is there no one here who could have given his asshole a hairbrush?

"Get the fuck off me," he snarls and shoves out of my grip on his shoulder. Turning, he throws a punch into the tree with a yell before storming away again, but I'm rooted to this spot. Something about his outburst threw me into a memory of a younger me punching my wooden bedpost. My father had refused to let any of the staff treat my fractured knuckles as punishment. That was also the first day I stole one of the gardener's cigarettes and lighter to give me a distraction from the pain, inside and out.

"What you here for?" I call after him as I jerk back into action, drawn towards the boy for some reason. He doesn't answer, nor does he stop until I cut in front of him and ask again, more sternly this time.

"Whatever game you're playing to try and get me to talk, forget it. I have nothing to say to any of you people. Leave me alone." He tries to side-step me again but I refuse to let him. His eyes drag across my tattoos briefly, interest flickering in his gaze but he quickly hides it in favor of irritation. Thrusting my arm out towards him, I grit my teeth and look away.

"Touch my arm." He scoffs at my order, which makes me snarl this time. "I'm not some fucking weirdo who wants boys to touch him in the woods. Just do it for fuck's sake, you'll see."

Growing frustrated, I brace myself for his hand to quickly skate up my arm. I resist to pull away as his eyes widen and he repeats the action, feeling them properly this time.

"What are they?" he breathes, almost fearful to hear the answer.

"Burns, mostly. A few breaks, a chain my dad used to whip me with. And you wanna know the worst bit?" Eddie swallows thickly, not confirming or denying the truth I see in his eyes. Recognition. "I let him." Yanking my arm away, I stride towards the closest tree to lean against and shove my hands into my gym shorts pockets.

"Why?" Eddie edges closer. I shrug, wishing I had one of the gardener's damn cigarettes now.

"Thought I deserved it, I suppose. I only found out recently I didn't, and I'm twenty. Between me and you, I could have taken revenge on my dad so many times before now, but I'm still scared of that fucker. He makes me feel so...small." I look to watch a squirrel clambering through the branches over head to get a grip of myself. Jesus fuck, what am I doing talking to some brat about stuff I've never even said before. It probably has something to do with the fact I could wring his scrawny neck if he ratted me out to anyone. Clearing my throat, I find him standing in front of me with understanding in his gaze.

"Point is, I'm not some counselor or do-goody volunteer. I'm a damaged piece of shit dragged here by my girlfriend. But feel free to take a good look as to how you'll turn out if you don't fight back early enough. There's no chance for me, but you might still have one."

His gaze trails over me slowly, from the tattoos poking out around my jersey, to my lip and eyebrow piecing and back again. He nods slowly and a rush of breath I didn't realize I was holding escapes me. Is this how people feel when they do something selfless and utterly for the good of someone else? I share a lopsided smile with him, fighting the urge to ruffle his hair or some shit. Then he opens his mouth and shatters it.

"Shit. You have the tatts, the money and the girl. I wanna be like you when I'm older." My eyebrows crease.

"Didn't you hear what I said? You have to fight back before it's too late." Eddie leans against the tree next to me, kicking a rock with the toe of his sneaker. From this angle, I can see the shadow of his wide smile.

"I do fight back. Every day when my momma tries to tell me what to do, I put that bitch back in her place. I do whatever I want because she's terrified of me." He looks back at the demons on my bicep again, pure awe in his expression. Fuck, I've done this all wrong.

"You hit your mom?" I ask quietly, my nails digging into my palms.

"Fuck yeah. I held a knife to her throat last night she disrespected me in front of my friends. That's why I got sent here," he chuckles. *Chuckles.* Was I that much of a little prick? If I'd had a parent who gave a shit about my future, maybe I'd have been sent to a camp like this. Can my past justify the way I've hurt others or am I as bad as this arrogant little prick?

Changing tactic, I spin in a flash and grab Eddie's t-shirt in my fists. Hoisting him up, I slam his back into the tree, growling at him to fight back now. To show me what a real man he is. When he doesn't respond, I throw him to the floor and press my shoe across his throat. Kneeling low, I push on the point that has his blue eyes popping out of his skull and he begins to struggle.

"How do you think your mom would feel seeing this? Would she help you or watch? Maybe next time you think about hurting her, you'll remember what being a victim feels like." I replace my foot with my hand, holding him in place but not squeezing. He's not even fighting me that hard, because he knows he can't. With my free hand, I grab a handful of dirt and sprinkle it over his face, making sure it goes up his nose and into his mouth as he tries to breathe.

"What the fuck are you doing?!" Clayton roars a moment before he hauls me to my feet by the back of my jersey. I laugh, watching the kid flinch as Clayton tries to help him. Eddie scrambles away, running back towards the basketball court while I shout how I'll be seeing him later. Clayton smacks me on the back of the head to shut me up but I don't even care at this point. I tried to do a good deed, it blew up in my face so I went another way. Sue me.

"Are you out of your damn mind? You scared that boy!" Clayton's pacing and running his fingers through his hair like he does when he's really stressed.

"He should be scared; the world's a fucked-up place where no one wins and the losers drown in their own misery." I shrug and fold my arms, watching him with a smirk.

"What's gotten into you? You know what, no, I actually don't give a shit. You don't get to unload your baggage onto everyone else. Not me, not Harper and especially not some poor kid who needed someone to look up to. You're a grown ass man, deal with your shit and go apologize."

"For your information, I was only being honest and this is the best version I can be. If you don't like it, fuck off back to the cabin. I'm already sick of your depressing face again." Clayton swivels on me, getting close enough for our chests to brush. If he still thinks I can be intimidated after all this time, then more fool him.

"For once in your life, couldn't you pretend to be a decent human being? These kids need help, not a fucking bully with daddy issues."

"I didn't even want to come here!" I shout and shove him back a step. I'm so sick of people telling me how I should behave and who I should be. Clayton's gaze shifts from mine to the forest behind me, and that's when I turn to see her. Fuck. Harper's hair is whipping around her as the wind starts to pick up, her stance too still. What are the chances she didn't wear her receivers today and missed what I said? But the hurt swirling in her green eyes shows I have no such luck. Fuck it.

"Harper, I didn't mean-" She lifts a hand to silence me,

moving closer slowly. Stepping in between Clayton and me, she regards me for so long I begin to fidget. I hate when she looks at me like that, like she can see straight through me. When she eventually reaches up to stroke my arms, I have to fight the urge to curl in her arms and ask for forgiveness, although she seems to sense that anyway.

"It's okay Rhys. I made you a promise and I've done what I came here to do. It's time to go find your mom."

Harper

I'm usually the first to fall asleep on a car journey, particularly one in the middle of the night, but my thoughts won't let me rest tonight. Rhys is up front with Clay, neither speaking to the other so I remove my receivers and pull up my hood. Slouching against the Ford's window, I watch the crescent moon follow us.

I still can't believe Wendy personally thanked Rhys for his breakthrough with Spence, the boy he shouted at. Apparently, the kid was on a downward spiral and the camp was a last-ditch attempt to straighten himself out before he ends up in Juvie. I'd like to think Rhys sensed another lost soul when he decided to scare the boy shitless, that there was some poetic nature to his actions, but I'm not so sure. Either way, we've all been welcomed back anytime.

I meant what I said, I was ready to leave, but that doesn't stop it from hurting my pride. To think of the kids waking in the morning and asking for me sucks, especially Evelyn. Even though I hate goodbyes, I'm a grown-ass adults and she's just a child. I should have stuck around like Addy protested I should. But with the weight of Dekken's early departure still heavy on Clay's shoulders and the decreasing moods I've witnessed with Rhys, it was time to go for all of us.

The road seems to go on forever. We rarely meet another vehicle, only the passing streetlamps showing we're still on the freeway. I don't know where we're heading, my mind hasn't caught up to that point yet. As per usual, I'm along to enjoy the ride wherever it may take me.

My eyes have started to grow heavy when Clay pulls off the main road, winding through a darkened town. Pulling to a stop outside a large house, I sit upright at the sheer size of it. Must be one of those converted boutique hotels the quieter towns are doing these days. Realizing Clay and Rhys are already retrieving the bags from the trunk as I take in the Victorian structure, I slide out of the cab. Rhys takes my hand first, his gaze searching mine like he has been since I found him in the woodlands back at camp. I give him another reassuring smile, letting him guide me towards the porch.

Anyone else might demand to know where we're going or how he found this place, but not me. I find it refreshing to fully let go and know I'll be taken care of. The building is beautiful up close. The perfect mix of red brick and white stone, a turret-like cylinder on either side of the detached home. A woman bustles to the door, pushing open a mesh shutter in her nightdress and fluffy slippers.

"*Come on in,*" I lip-read her say as she ushers us all in with a warm smile. Clay places down the bags to shake her hand while I take in the lavish interior. I wonder how many guests must come through here for the owner to seem so happy about receiving us at stupid o'clock in the morning, or why they'd need two living rooms which mirror each other. There are bookcases implemented into the curved walls on both sides, separated by a cushioned bench behind a large window. I'm already drifting towards one when Rhys pulls me back with a knowing smile.

"*Tomorrow,*" he promises. Drawing me up the staircase, I see Clay up ahead with a numbered key in his hand. Pushing it into the lock and opening the door, he waits for me to near and enter first before following. I walk straight for the king-size bed, flopping onto my front on a groan. I haven't done anything but sit for hours yet my energy tank is running on empty. My biker boots are eased off my feet and I roll over to see I'm alone with

Clay. Halting his actions, I pull him down to lie beside me.

"How are you doing?" I ask, brushing his waves behind his ear. I love he has the confidence to wear his hair free now, although the beanies might play a role in the bedroom from time to time.

"*I'll always be good as long as I'm with you.*" I feel like his words were a bit of a cop-out but my thoughts vanish when the most delicious scent reaches me. Bolting upright, I see Rhys has joined us again with a large plate of cinnamon buns in his hands. He sits at the foot of the bed, my legs draped over his shoulders and holds up the drool-worthy treats. They're warm to the touch, which I hope is from being reheated and not because that sweet lady baked them in preparation for our arrival. Taking the plate, I ask Clay to fetch my receivers from my backpack. He returns a moment later, gently easing them onto my ears and switching them on while I stuff my face with sugary goodness.

"How did you find this place?" I finally ask, my curiosity getting the better of me. Rhys pulls my socks off to massage my feet, his answer rumbling against my calves.

"I had a PA looking into my mom before we went to camp. This town is the last place she was in according to records, and that's where the trail stops." Rhys shrugs but my chest tugs uncomfortably, not liking what that might mean. "We're only a state over from my dad's estate, so it's a good place to start."

Having demolished another cinnamon bun, I pass the plate to Clay to set down for me. When he returns, I lean into his torso as a thickened silence descends. We're all thinking it, but no one wants to be the one to say it – people don't just disappear if they are happy and loving life. I'm starting to worry what this path might uncover and if Rhys will be able to handle it.

"Have you had any thoughts on what you think we'll find?" I have to break the silence. Rhys shrugs, staring into the distance. Sharing a nod with Clay, we shift onto the floor to join him. Curling up in his lap, I nestle my nose into Rhys' neck and try a different tactic. "Okay, how about this. What are you hoping for?"

"I don't know," he breathes heavily by my ear, causing my receiver to crackle slightly. "On one hand it might be nice if she's some suburban housewife who bakes and has been waiting for me to knock on her front door. But realistically, if she could be paid to have a baby and walk away, she's most likely a hooker or drug addict." I scrunch my nose, tracing patterns over his arms with my fingers.

"Your dad is too meticulous for that. He wanted you to be his perfect puppet. He wouldn't have chosen someone with a history with addiction or who lives in poverty. Ew, what if it's some upper-class snob? What if we've met her at the investor's meeting?"

"Not making me feel any better here." Rhys drawls but it drew a chuckle from Clay's chest.

"Plot twist. Your mom had a sex change and she is your dad." Clay adds, dissolving the heavy atmosphere instantly as we all burst into laughter. This is the first time I think Rhys has laughed wholeheartedly and without abandon. It's raspy and deep, like a rumble rolling straight from his gut. I think it may be my new favorite sound. Settling down, I rub my cheek against Rhys' chest as my eyebrows knit together. I don't want to ruin the lightened mood, but I know Rhys doesn't open up like this often. Swallowing thickly, I sit upright to lock his gaze in mine.

"I'm hoping I am wrong about this, but it needs to be said. All of Della-Mae's belongings were packed up in an abandoned house in the middle of nowhere. I saw the dusty boxes and piles of clothes. I'm not trying to upset you, but I think you should prepare yourself." Instead of the denial or sadness I expected, Rhys smiles. He draws my face into his hands, brushing his thumbs over my cheeks.

"I'll be fine. Can't miss what I never had, right? Besides, I've got everything I need right here." Rhys nudges Clay's shoulder, before his gaze drifts to my mouth. Running his thumb across my bottom lip, I feel the icing sugar collected there before he pushes his thumb into my mouth. Sucking hard, I maintain Rhys' gaze to watch it turn heated instantly. His pupil dilate, his tongue darting out to wet his lips.

Knocking his hand aside, I attack his mouth with mine. There's nothing sweet left about this moment, Rhys' hands gripping my hips roughly to make me straddle him. A third hand slides beneath my thigh, pulling me half across Clay too until I'm central between them. Suddenly, my appetite is back and it won't be sated with food. Curling my tongue around Rhys', his hand grabs my jaw and swivels me to make out with Clay so he can ravage my neck.

Hands run over my body, all of my clothes being removed between the fierceness of Clay's kisses. My lips tingle from their roughness, a gasp escaping me when Rhys latches onto my pierced nipple. He doesn't grant me any mercy, starved by our forced separation in the camp's quarters. The pair of them suck and bite my skin, one yanking on my hair and the other clasping my hands behind my back, baring me to their joint assault. I fight against their hold, kept immobilized as a hand dips in between my legs.

Raw heat and seeping wetness allows the fingers to slide through my pussy and back to my clit, making me groan. With the advantage of my legs pinned open by their thighs, the digits push straight inside of me. Curling them around, my g-spot is being stroked and a thumb circles my clit while another hand moves around the back. I tense as I finger strokes firmly over my puckered hole, earning me a joint pair of chuckles.

"Not tonight, Babygirl. But we will be working you up to taking both of us in these tight little holes." This finger I'm supposing is Rhys' dips inside my ass ever so slightly and I gasp, finding I didn't hate it like I'd expected. Relaxing, I remain still except for the unstoppable roll to my hips to their movements, my teeth sunk into my bottom lip.

"Yeah, you like that, don't you Angel? You like us pleasuring you together, picturing us fucking you together." I moan at Clay's words, a flush working its way across my chest. I'm used to Rhys' filthy mouth, but hearing Clay's dirty talk does weird and wonderful things to me. Bucking, I try again to be freed, much to their amusement. My nipples are licked, my tits kneaded tightly. Hands and mouths roam my heated skin while I'm forced to stare at the ceiling, my climax building into an inferno in my core.

"We're not going to let you go until you cum," Rhys mutters, the smile on his face as evident as the solid cocks pushing against my thighs. Fuck that. If these guys wanted a submissive, they could have had their pick.

"You'd better start trying then," I mock. The responding growls do something wild to me, the vibrations felt deep inside. I'm released so suddenly, I drop forward into the pair of chests in front of me and Rhys delivers a smack to my ass.

"Stand," he barks. He looks genuinely pissed, which only makes me smile more. As I rise to my feet, the boys move simultaneously to strip and surround me. Clay is at the front, staring at me with a cocky raised eyebrow that screams 'challenge accepted'. Lifting my leg over his shoulder, he buries his face into my pussy, eating me like a man starved. My hand grips his hair for stability, holding him in place by the roots.

Rhys' tongue rolls between my ass cheeks, directly over the hole back there. I gasp, unable to hide my pleasure as I push back against him. I vaguely hear a comment about being a greedy bitch just before he dives into me without shame. His nails dig into my ass as he separates the cheeks, opening me for him. I've never felt so dirty, yet I've never felt so alive.

Fingers plunge into me, the wetness dripping between my legs slickening the movement. It's only when I feel a strange push and pull motion inside me do I realize I have both of my men fingering me, their hands bumping against the other. The speed picks up as I'm feasted on, my climax crashing through me on a scream. I judder and shake as they refuse to stop, Clay's teeth scraping against my hooded bud.

"Okay, okay! You guys win!" I shout, my legs threatening to give out beneath me. The fingers are removed so quickly, I jerk forward and crash into the mattress, panting as they loom over me.

"That wasn't so hard, was it?" Rhys mocks with a panty-melting smirk. Luckily, I'm not wearing any. Grabbing Rhys by the shoulders, I throw him down beside me and straddle him in one fluid motion.

Clay kneels in behind, one hand circling my throat and the other on my hip, impaling me onto the pierced cock primed beneath me. I can't describe how much I love it when Clay breaks out of his shell to take control like this, his hand directing me to grind onto Rhys. I lay my head back on his shoulder, relishing the unashamed connection we all have. But this is just the beginning. I won't be satisfied tonight until I've exacted my revenge. They'll both be begging *me* for permission to cum and scream my name in turn before sunrise, I swear it.

Clayton

The dining table is starting to fill up, the delicious smell rolling through the house calling everyone downstairs. I place another bowl into the centre, having set the table and helped Miss Travis cook the dinner. We slept most the day, curled up with Harper between us, so helping out is the least we could do. Every time I walk back through the open archway from the kitchen, another woman is seated and eyeing me suspiciously. It's a good thing Rhys is elbow deep in oven right now if they find me intimidating.

Harper is at home on the window seat, a book in her hand and small smile on her face. I take a moment to appreciate her like this before scuttling away. She's breath-taking all the time, but something about her softened expression when she's lost in a book makes my heart expand. Of all the fake and materialistic women in the world, she's like the freshest breath of air breezing through.

Rhys emerges with the crowning glory plated in his hands, a large chicken on a bed of colorful vegetables. I hear the collective intake of breath as the women see him, no doubt associating his inked skin and piercings with something in their past. I agree he looks like a thug, but now I know the man beneath the mask, I'm firmly in protective mode. Ignoring the stares, Rhys places the platter in the center and makes his way to Harper, kissing her gently to rouse her from her reading.

"No need to be alarmed ladies," Miss Travis says as she

too joins us, clearly feeling the hospitality in the air. "These men are here as my guests, and I have no doubt they'll protect each of you as fiercely as they protect their girlfriend whilst staying with us." I smile at the older woman, pulling out a chair for her. She's barely five feet tall with silver strands claiming most of her mid-length hair, her cloudy eyes a mix of blue and green. What's more is her blind acceptance of us all, separately and together, restoring my faith in the world.

Rhys copies my actions with Harper, remaining glued to her side. I can sense he's uncomfortable, although from the gawking or the apprehension of finding his mom, I'm not sure. Sitting beside her, Miss Travis leads us in prayer before we dive into the feast before us. I take the opportunity to offer the food to the timid brunette beside me, barely out of her teens and shaking like a leaf. On her nod, I spoon mashed potato onto her plate and continue to present her with dishes until her plate is full. Only when the women have finished do I start on my own, splitting the leftovers with Rhys. Harper smiles at me the way she always does when I eat properly, as if she's proud of me or something.

"So, I have to ask, what kind of hotel is this?" Harper looks around skeptically at the woman-heavy table. Some giggles, some balk but its Miss Travis that answers with on a laugh.

"This isn't a hotel. It's a women's refuge shelter." All of the color drains from Harper's face, her cutlery dropping onto her plate so she can sign at me in a flurry of gestures.

"Why would you bring us here?! Oh god, I was screaming all night and have fingerprints bruised into my neck!" It's my turn to chuckle at this, my eyes drifting to the handprint in question. Rhys slinks an arm around her shoulder, pulling her in while he continues to eat. Miss Travis watches them closely, her head titling wistfully.

"I remember Della-Mae clearly; you remind me of her." Rhys' eyes settle on Miss Travis, placing his fork down slowly. His shoulders tighten, his hand gripping onto Harper whether he realizes it or not.

"I doubt she looked like this," he motions to his tattoos and pushes his lip ring forward with his tongue. Miss Travis isn't fazed, probably having dealt with all types of defensive behavior in her role here.

"Not in appearance, although you have her dainty nose." I snigger under my breath at Rhys' offended look of being called 'dainty' anything. "And your spirit. She was tenacious and wild too. In fact, she was pregnant with you while she was here so I'm glad I get the chance to meet you finally." Many of the table's guests have finished their tiny plates of food and quickly squirrel away, still nervous in our presence. Through the mic clip on our t-shirts, Harper smiles sadly and links her fingers with Rhys' on the table.

"If she was here, does that mean..." Rhys' voice trails off.

"Oh goodness, no! Nothing like that! Della-Mae used to volunteer here, and she was fantastic. The women staying here at the time loved her, myself included. She always had a smile at the ready, her warm heart shining through. Everyone felt nurtured by her kindness, until one morning, she didn't show for work. No one knew what happened, all that she left was a cheque in my name for a sizable donation. I always wondered where the money came from." I share a look with Rhys, the bigger picture coming into view but the question still remains. Where is she now?

"Have you heard from Della-Mae since, or have an idea where she has gone?" I ask, starting to scrape food back onto the platter and stacking the empty plates. Miss Travis shakes her head, standing to join me.

"Afraid not. It's been a burning question for me too. I tried to look for her, but she was ...gone." I don't need to look to sense Rhys' slumped shoulders or hear his loaded exhale. I carry the plates into the kitchen, switching on the tap to fill the sink with hot water. Harper slides in beside me, tipping in some washing up liquid and nudging me aside.

"He's outside. Can you make sure he's not doing something stupid?" I question why me but all I receive is a knowing smile. Kissing the top of her head, I nod to Miss Travis as I pass and head for the front door. I can't see Rhys at first, the porch dark once again. It's a quiet street, nothing like the one I grew up on. I notice a cherry bud flare to life by the truck, jogging down the steps to join Rhys.

"Thought you quit," I jest, leaning against the trunk.

"Stressful times," he replies darkly. Offering me the cigarette, I decline on a scoff. We both know Harper won't kiss him again tonight if he tastes like nicotine, and I'm not going down with him. I'll take all the kisses on his behalf, make him watch too. We fall into silence, the balmy night air enjoyable without the need of jackets. I hear Harper's laugh bleed out through the mesh shutter, finding myself smiling too.

An elderly woman with a tiny dog edges towards us on the footpath, the little cloud of white on legs taking an interest in Rhys' shoes once they've approached. He grumbles irritably, but the woman pulls to a stop too, eyeing him closely.

"You're that Waversea kid," she states, squinting in the dark. The light streaming from inside the windows puts her at an advantage to see us, but her face is hidden in shadow. Dropping his cigarette and grinding it beneath his shoe, Rhys stands straight and folds his arms. I step in behind him, although I doubt he'd need assistance from a frail woman with a ball of fluff for a dog. "I wondered how long it would take before you came around here." This grabs both of our attention. The woman holds out her arm to Rhys, and after a beat he takes it. Rounding her other side, we walk with the old woman further down the street.

"You know who I am?" Rhys asks for a while, clearly at a loss for what else to say.

"Oh yes, dear. All over the news, aren't you? In the papers sometimes and I say to my daughter, look Kenna, its Della's boy again." Rhys' gaze turns to mine over the woman's head, the overhead streetlamp revealing not only his surprise, but the sudden burst of hope that shines from him.

"I don't suppose you know where my mom went, do you?" he asks, almost dejectedly. I'm worried about what we might find on this ghost hunt, but I'm starting to think finding no clues at all is going to be harder on Rhys than any end result. Continuing on with 'what ifs' is a terrible way to live.

"Of course, dear. Della grew up in this town, went to school with my Kenna. They keep in touch now and again. Lovely girl, your mom is." Leading us to the end of the street and crossing the road, the woman uses Rhys' assistance to reach a detached bungalow with the lights on inside. She doesn't release him when she is at the front door, her bony fingers pulling down the handle. Catching the door, Rhys holds it open and I crouch to unleash the fluffball when I see her struggling to do it. Stepping inside, the smell of candles fill an open plan living area dressed in aged décor.

"Momma, what did I say about trusting strangers?" A younger version of the woman stomps over from the sofa to kick us out I imagine until her gaze lands on Rhys. "Oh my, it's you." Her dark eyes are transfixed, her hands clasped in front of her tightly. She has the ebony skin of her mother, but smoother and a beautifully wild afro.

"I told you he'd come back," the older woman muses, hobbling towards the armchair. The air thickens with a building tension as the three of us are left standing on the doorstep awkwardly. The white fluff ball is fascinated with Rhys' sneakers, probably smelling the expensive leather and refuses to leave him alone.

Blowing out a frustrated breath, Rhys bends to scoop up the tiny dog with a pink studded collar, cradling her in his arms to scratch behind her ears. His tattoos are a stark comparison against her white fur and I wish the situation wasn't so tense so I could whip my phone out to take a photo. Maybe I could sneak one when he's not looking? Ignoring us, Rhys walks through the house like he owns the place and sits on a sofa beside the woman who found us. The dog curls in his lap, lapping up his strokes.

"With all due respect," he turns back to look at Kenna, "you're the only lead I've had in regards to finding my mom. I'm not leaving here without some answers so you might as well show Clayton where the kitchen is. We're all gonna need some coffee."

Harper

"So what did she say?" I ask eagerly. When I couldn't find the boys last night, I took the book I was reading to bed and fell asleep waiting for them to return. Once they finally did, they'd been happy to crawl into bed, distracting me with their hot kisses and muscled bodies pressing against mine.

"Do you mind?" Rhys asks Clay, rubbing the back of his head. "I'm still computing. Gonna have a bath and do a mud mask." Rhys leans down to kiss me before heading into the en-suite with his toiletry bag.

"Woah, a mud mask. Must be serious," I try to smirk but not sure I pull it off. Clay grins though, dropping onto the bed after pacing the way he does when he's thinking.

"Kenna is a childhood friend of Rhys' mom. She grew up around here, went to the school down the road, worked in town and volunteered in this shelter. Everyone knew her, but apparently no one except Kenna knew who she was pregnant by. She wouldn't tell anyone, and like Miss Travis said, one morning she vanished. She did, however, stop to say goodbye to her best friend." I twist to cross my legs, waiting for him to continue.

"Kenna doesn't know where Della-Mae, or should I say Catherine, is. But she does have a contact number so she's going to reach out, let her know Rhys is looking for her."

"Changed her name?" Clay hums his answer, tucking my hair behind my receiver. Clever, but I can't help to worry what forced her to make such a decision. If Rhys' conception was as simple as a payment transaction, why would she run? Why was her stuff left in the house Phillip told Dekken to stash me in? Leaning into Clay, I sigh and try to find some positives in all this. "At least we know she's alive, and contactable. It's a start."

"Sure is, Angel." My hands fidget, the need to do something riding me hard. And as sexy as my men are, I don't think this restlessness will be sated with another orgasm. God, did I just think that? Looking around the room, I spot Rhys' phone on the dresser and perk up, formulating a scheme as I dash to grab it. That's what I need, to have fun. To be carefree and mischievous.

Clay eyes me as I run back to him with a giggle, settling myself on his lap. His arm locks around my waist, holding me in place to unlock Rhys' phone with the passcode he forced me to learn, something about needing to know I can trust him. Opening the camera, I flip it to face us and proceed to fill Rhys' camera roll with images of Clay and I. Some smiling, other's stupid with tongues out and bunny ears. When Clay bites my neck, I fake my best cum face.

"Give it here," Clay chuckles. Taking the phone, he quickly applies the last one as Rhys' lock screen image and changes his passcode. I have to cover my mouth to contain my laughter, slipping the phone back on the dresser before Rhys walks back, dry in with a towel wrapped around his middle.

"Couldn't be bothered," he mumbles, grabbing some clothes to pull on. I bite the insides of my cheek, waiting for the moment he checks his phone but it doesn't come. Soon he's dressed and looking at us with a scowl. I hate seeing him like this when we've come so far. Pushing to my feet, I link my fingers through his and place a kiss over his heart.

"Let's go for a walk."

The town is beautiful in the daylight. Wondering through the avenues, each street is as tranquil as the last. Flowers line every sidewalk, bird houses hanging from the spaced-out trees in the concrete. I can't believe I've been here almost two days and am only just discovering what a hidden gem this place is, and I don't know why Rhys' mom would have wanted to leave. The buildings are clean, the roads are quiet, the people are friendly and I've said good afternoon more times today than I have in my whole life.

Rhys walks out of the ice cream parlor with a double scoop cone in each hand, offering me both with a sheepish look.

"I got a different combo I like on each so you can choose your favorite and I'd still enjoy whatever is left." I burst out laughing, linking my fingers with his as Clay emerges from the shop with his own ice cream.

"I feel like that's cheating when I said to surprise me, but I love it when you're thoughtful." I press a kiss to his jaw before we start to walk, licking my mint choc chip topped Oreo ice cream. Rhys is too cute sometimes, like a charred marshmallow. All dark and crusty on the outside, but inside he's melted gloop.

Clay's shadow is cast over me as he walks a step behind, my human sun shield as per usual. Considering he was the one who opposed this relationship in fear of being upstaged, Clay rarely gets jealous. I hope that's because he knows how I feel about him without needing the constant reminders like Rhys does, and not because he's hanging back on purpose and suffering in silence.

Turning off the main street with a church spire visible at the far end, we find ourselves breaking free of the buildings. A sprawling green lays before us, a pond glistening before a white band stand. Clay whoops like a child, grabbing my arm to yank me towards an empty play park opposite.

"Really?" I laugh, shoving the last of the ice cream cone into my mouth. Pushing the gate open, Clay drags me towards the swings. Once seated, he pushes me and I can't contain my smile, my heart fit to burst. Rhys sits on the next swing along, his voice seeping into the microphone clip and sounding inside my head.

"When I said we should get her a swing, I meant of the sex variety. And she'd be permanently naked." I giggle, not objecting while Clay's firm hands push my ass gently with each swing.

"I think the townsfolk would have something to say about that," Clay responds. The sun beats down on us from a purely blue sky and Rhys swings beside me, making this the perfect day. I wish every day could be like this. Carefree and relaxed. And when Clay delivers me a sharp spank, it gets even better.

"You wanna play dirty, big man?" I mock, jumping high off the swing and landing on a crouch. I didn't know where I was going with that, but the matching stares of hunger I receive are going in the right direction. Rhys hops off his swing too, slowly advancing on me like a tiger stalking his next meal.

"I'll do you one better. Rhys, give me your t-shirt." Rhys complies without batting an eyelid and chucks it to Clay, who also removes his own. "Jeremy and I used to play a game like this, capture the flag. First person to get all of the flags wins." Clay walks over to me, slipping off my leather jacket. His fingers brush my arms, leaving a trail of goosebumps in their wake.

"And what do I get when I win?" I breathe. His smile is dazzling, the playful mirth dancing in his dark eyes.

"Whatever you want," he mutters before planting a toe-curling kiss on me. His lips are firm and demanding, drawing the breath from my lungs as he steps away. Winking, Clay jogs off to hook our 'flags' in different areas of the playground. Planting himself in front of his, Rhys and I follow suit with challenging smirks. My jacket is hung on a step on a climbing frame. Way too easy. Grabbing it, I dive into the structure, climbing upward and squeezing through tunnels I know the guys can't manage. Reaching the top, I hang off the side of the climbing frame to hook my jacket on the tallest spire, then take the winding slide all the way to the bottom.

My satisfied smile drops when I realize the guys have also disappeared to hide their t-shirts in areas I won't be able to reach. Clay has claimed a wooden castle for his territory, while Rhys is sitting on top of the swing set with his shirt tucked into his jean's waistband. His cocky smile is in full force and for a moment I want to enjoy him like this. But the moment ends when Clay jumps to the ground heavily in his boots and cargo pants, my mouth filling his drool at his ripped torso. Holy hell, I'm going to lose so hard if I can't focus.

"Ready?" he asks. Holding up my index finger, I flip my hair forward to tie it into a high ponytail, hike up my denim shorts and tie a knot in my tank top to reveal my mid-section. Now I'm ready. Crouching, Clay chuckles and starts running for me, only to dodge me at the last second. I shriek regardless, turning to see Clay jump high in the air and grab onto Rhys' foot. He yanks him to the ground and jumps on him, but I don't wait around to watch any longer.

Running across the wooden drawbridge, I fly over an open slate bridge which wobbles beneath me. Latching onto a wall on the other side, I scale it using the hand and foot holes provided. I search every wooden turret but I can't see the white material of Clay's t-shirt anywhere. Ducking low, I peer over a short wall to look for the boys scuffling around on the floor, but they're nowhere to be seen. I realize now I will only be able to hear through the microphone clips, and not if someone is to creep up on me.

Arms grab me from behind, dragging me to the floor. Clay is over me, his body strained against mine and his hands pinning mine above my head. My fingers brush a bundled ball of cotton which Clay is clutching onto, the cologne scent drifting to me telling me that's Rhys' shirt. Tightening my hand around it, I push my chest upwards and push my tongue into Clay's mouth. He tries to resist, but we both know he can't. Grinding into me on a groan, his tongue tangles with mine just as Rhys tackles Clay off me.

I lay still, catching my breath and smile to find the t-shirt clasped in my hands. Rolling and jumping to my feet, I race to the other side of the castle. The sounds of grunts and laughter fill my head while I continue to search, clearing the top level and dropping through a hatch to the middle floor. This floor is enclosed by walls on all sides, with thin slits for windows to let streams of light pierce the darkness. I'm forced to duck so I don't hit my head on the wooden beams, creeping further through the maze.

Another opening in the floor shows me a ladder which I ignore, dropping onto the bark covered ground below. There, I find a tire swing hanging on a thick rope and tucked inside the wheel is Clay's t-shirt. I let out a victory noise before clamping my hand over my mouth. Snatching the second t-shirt, I shove them both into the back of my shorts like a kinky little fox and make a run for it. There's no point trying to suss out where the guys are now either my mic clips are out of range or they've gone full stealth mode, so I take my chances.

Strangely, I make it back to the climbing frame without any trouble, which only makes me more suspicious. Sliding into a yellow tunnel, I peek through a window in the center to look around. Even with my loss of hearing, I can sense it's too quiet. Either one of them has been knocked out or they've teamed up. Inching out of the tunnel, I climb towards the top of the frame, wondering why I didn't wear my own flag the entire time. Idiot.

Breaching the top level of the tower, I find Rhys perched on the open ledge with one leg either side. My jacket is swinging from his index finger.

"If you let me win, I'll go full 69 with you as my prize." I bat my eyelashes innocently. Edging around the circular space, I stand in front of the slide for a quick getaway.

"As incredible as that sounds Babygirl, I don't lose. Ever." Laying my jacket over the ledge, Rhys hops down and stands between me and it, crossing him arms. I lick my lips, unable to keep my eyes from his body. I know every defined muscle and the deep V dipping into his waistband from memory, my fingers itching to reach out and touch him. Swallowing, I try to find some of the spirit I had before I knew how good his pierced cock felt stroking over my g-spot.

"Even if it meant no sex for a month?"

"You couldn't hold off for a month," Rhys steps closer, a knowing smirk on his face. "We've awakened a sexual minx in you. You'll be begging for my cock in your throat while Clayton fills you from behind."

"Just like this," Clay's voice sounds as he grips me from behind, seemingly climbing out of the slide's opening. Shoving me forward into Rhys' chest, Clay arms band around mine and he rolls his hips into me.

"I thought you didn't lose." I stare in Rhys' crystal blue eyes as he peels the two t-shirts out of my shorts. Throwing them onto the ledge with my jacket, his hands grip my body, his thumbs brushing beneath my vest to stroke the outline of breasts.

"I don't consider this losing. I have to share you with him either way, might as well be on my terms." His mouth lowers towards mine as his phone begins to vibrate in his pocket. Neither of them releases me, leaving me sandwiched between their growing erections. The phone call is brief, a series of grunts mostly until Rhys ends with 'I'll be there.' Hanging up, he catches a glance at his screen's new and improved wallpaper, his eyes darkening.

"Oh Babygirl, now you're in for it."

Rhys

Clayton pulls into a parking bay next to the sidewalk, the sky-scraper of a glass building outside reaching for the full moon. When Kenna had asked me to stop by her house, I thought she'd have a message for me, not an address. I've backed out at least ten times since then, but Harper knows deep down I need to do this. It's what I wanted but I hadn't expected my mom to want to meet me. Why would she, except for curiosity? She sold me like a calf sent to a slaughterhouse. The darker my thoughts become, the more I push against the leather seat and refuse to get out the truck.

"It's going to be okay," Harper slides her hand over my slack-covered thigh and squeezes firmly. I don't know why I felt the need to make an effort, donning a shirt and loafers, but I'd wanted to make a good impression I suppose. Fuck, why should I care about any impressions at this stage? Harper notices my internal struggle, swivelling my face back to hers.

"And if not, like you said, you haven't lost anything. But if you don't go in there, you'll have to live with the not knowing which will be worse." Looking into her emerald green eyes, I can't help the smile she brings out of me.

"Will you come in with me?"

"I think you need to do this without me leading it for you. There's a restaurant right across the street. If you need me, text and I'll come running. But we both know if I'm in there, you'll hide behind me and the great Rhys Waversea hides from

210

no one." Harper beams at me this time, pressing the sweetest kiss on my lips. Even the light touch of her mouth and the nerves swirling in my gut can't stop my cock from stirring.

"You got this buddy," Clayton chimes in like the condescending prick he is and I toss my middle finger up at the rearview mirror. He chuckles, hopping out the cab to open Harper's door and extend his hand for her. With one last reassuring smile, she slides out and makes her way to the restaurant with Clayton as promised. I stare at the open door, tempted to slam it closed and shove my headphones in, but now's not the time to become a pussy. Tomorrow, perhaps.

Jumping out, I shut the door and see the headlights flash as Clayton locks it from their booth in the window. Walking with long yet slow strides, I approach the security guard posted at the revolving door. I open my mouth but he holds a hand up, listening intently into his earpiece. Stepping aside on a nod, I eye the camera above the door before walking inside.

Glass pillars face a long line of elevators tucked into a granite wall, a water feature behind the empty main desk on one end. In fact, there isn't another person around as I step into the waiting elevator. The doors close once I'm inside and I travel upwards, narrowing my eyes on yet another camera fixed on me from the corner.

I did my research before coming so I know as much as the basic online bio would tell me. Catherine Lawson is a chartered account, one of the best around apparently. Basically, she makes money sorting other people's money and is a regular participant in the stock market. So what the hell was she doing selling babies? If I'm to believe I was the only one, that is. I could have a whole family of misfit siblings out there.

The elevator halts and my heart is set to implode, hammering in my rib cage when the doors slide open. Finding myself at the back of a corridor with glass offices on either side, I walk towards the one at the far end with the only source of light inside. She sees me coming, given the transparency of the walls, rounding a desk to stand in front of it. Pushing open the door, I keep my eyes trained on the wall until her Louboutin's come into view.

The silence drags on until my pulse is pounding through my ears. I don't know if I wanted her to squeal and run at me with open arms, but when I don't get it, my heart sinks slightly. Licking my lips, I bite the bullet and look up, staring straight into the blue eyes opposite. Fuck, she's beautiful. Like supermodel beautiful, despite barely wearing make-up. Her brunette hair floats down to her mid-back, a designer navy and white pant suit tailored to her slender body. My eyes snag on the tie hanging open either side of her shirt collar, covered in a repeated pattern of fried eggs.

"Oh," she laughs, noticing my eye line. "It's casual tie Friday. I like to get involved." Pulling the tie free and tossing it onto the desk, I can't help but stare at her smile. The backs of my eyes sting but I can't look away, picturing a life where that smile was a constant factor. Where I'd have grown up shooting Nerf bullets around these glass offices, been snuck extra cookies by the employees and waited all week for casual fucking tie Friday.

Turning away, I pinch the bridge of my nose. I'm not crying here. I'll hold it at bay, waiting for the moment I'm in a hotel room with Harper's arms around my neck and Clayton hunting for the nearest bottle of whiskey. But fuck if those scenarios won't stop playing in my head. Hearing Catherine move closer, I bite the inside of my cheek hard enough to distract me before turning back.

"I'm..." Whatever she was going to say doesn't come out, her eyes looking everywhere except at me for an alternative. "I didn't expect you would want to find me, in all honesty."

"And why is that?" I ask, my voice sounding too gravelly. Like a slap, hearing the desperation for answers in my tone snaps me out of the state I'm working myself into. Straightening my spine, I cross the room to lean my forearm against the external glass, looking down forty-three flights.

"Well," Catherine begins. Moving over to a white sofa, she sits and straightens her skirt before gesturing for me to join her opposite. Chewing on my lip ring, I sit with my legs wide and rest my elbows on my knees, waiting for her to continue.

"I've watched you grow up through a screen and read many articles written about you in the media. I even joined Instagram to follow you. You seemed happy, albeit guarded and toughened but that was to be expected. I suppose I thought there was nothing else I could provide for the boy who had everything."

"Except a mother," I mutter. I study her face, watching the regret course through her. I'm thankful she's strong enough to hold herself together, but the misery is clear. Hanging my head, I know there's no point arguing. What's done is done, but she's here now. I'm here, and I want to make it count for something. "No, you're right. If you'd approached me even a few months ago, I'd have told you where to go because I don't need anyone."

"What changed?"

"I fell in love." And there's that stupid smile again, the one I get every time I picture Harper's face. Catherine's expression softens too, her lips turning upwards and the overbearing tension is broken.

"She must be a special girl."

"She's incredible. But she's shown me the world through her eyes, mainly how to perceive myself and I didn't like what I saw. I've spent my life rebelling against everything my father considered moral, but turns out this is who he wanted me to be all along. A fuck-up. I was manipulated, and without Harper, I have no place in this world."

Catherine nods as if she knows that feeling all too well. Her eyes trail the inked demons on my forearms and I want to know what she's thinking. Is she repulsed? Does she care for the story behind the tattoos? Given she's seen me portrayed through the media, my appearance won't be a surprise but I want her to see me, the real me.

"Can I show you something?" Catherine nods, sitting forward as I unbutton my shirt. Pulling the left side down, I point to the angel inked below my sternum. She's dressed all in white, her wings fending off the blackened demons clawing at her as she cradles a wrapped bundle in her arms. "I...that's kinda you, I suppose. I always hoped you might come save me."

Catherine's hand flies to her mouth, trying to hold back a sob but the tears have already escaped her eyes. Moving to sit beside me, she hovers with her arms wide for me to lean into, which I do. I have to. This is all I've dreamt of for so long, and why my own tears begin to fall. And fall. And fall until I'm fully crying into the crook of my mother's neck while she does the same into mine. Years of heartache and despair pour from me, leaving a raw ache in my chest. I've built myself on the pain I can't hold onto anymore, hidden behind it. But from here on out, it's all on me.

"Rhys," Catherine chokes out. "I know it's fruitless, and nothing I can say will fix what you've clearly had to endure. But I want you to know, I am so sorry. I tried harder than you'll ever know to be a part of your life, and I've loved you since the moment I found out I was pregnant."

"You loved me?" I have to ask again, my head refusing to believe what my heart knows is the truth. "You didn't sell me?"

"Sell you?! What- I would never do such a thing!" Catherine urges me to sit upright but her hands clasp mine tightly. Her mascara has run but I know it's nothing compared to the state I must look. Swallowing loudly, I compose myself on a long exhale.

"I need you to take me back to the start. Tell me everything."

A short while later, Catherine and I are sitting cross-legged on the carpet, looking at the moon-lit view beyond the glass. The Chinese food she ordered is laid out between us, although we have yet to eat any. Now initial appearances are over,

Catherine popped into the ladies bathroom to change into a set of yoga pants and t-shirt she had stashed away. Her hair is tied back in a slick ponytail and I can't stop looking at her. Just a boy and his mom, camping out on a Friday and reminiscing. I just wish the topic was a happier one.

"I met Phillip on a visit to the city. As you must know, I grew up in a small town where everyone knows everyone and the general aspirations start at the local farms and end with the pharmacy. I was always too motivated for the life I was born into," Catherine spares me a sympathetic look. "So, I took night classes and did online courses. I watched the stock market like my favorite sitcom, learning it inside and out. After months of applying, I finally received an interview for an entry level position so I traveled here. Needless to say, I got the job and twenty years later, I bought out the company." Catherine pauses to uncork a bottle of wine, pouring us a glass each.

"Anyway. Phillip was here on business too, meeting some friends in a fancy bar. I was ready to celebrate, but I didn't want to risk the seedy clubs alone so I found myself in the same bar and that's where it all started. I'd call it a summer romance, but it was more than that. I don't know your father anymore, but back then he was a perfect gentleman. He showed me a life I would strive for later on. Whisked me away for holidays and dinners, bought me huge bouquets every time he came to visit. I believe he genuinely loved me the way I fell in love with him."

I listen quietly, but I can't picture the man Catherine is describing. I've never even seen my father smile. Could it all be through some sense of heartbreak? Sipping the wine, I notice Catherine is staring out of the window, seemingly lost in her memories.

"So what went wrong?"

"That's what went wrong. He loved me," Catherine breathes a laugh but it's filled with bitterness. "Phillip wanted out of the expectations of the legacy. He wanted to be free of the debts, to build a life for us even if it meant walking away from what we had so hard worked for. And I've have done it too. But then we discovered I was pregnant, our romance suddenly turned into a business transaction. He found what he'd always wanted, a way out. And there was no room for weakness in his plan."

Sighing heavily, Catherine downs her wine and turns to rest her back against the glass panel, facing the room instead. I nibble on some food to fill the quiet, although I'm not hungry. I'm pissed. Oblivious to my mood, Catherine continues as if she's been waiting years to get this all off her chest.

"He found his way out from everything, even me. Where I saw hope, Phillip saw dollar signs. He could keep borrowing against the college; have a life so lavish, he'd be untouchable. Instead of trying to solve his debts, he decided to expand on them and I couldn't have any part of it."

Rising to her bare feet, Catherine walks over to a tall filing cabinet. Hunting through the top drawer, she returns with a folder so thick, I have to use both hands to take it from her. I open my mouth to ask what I'm looking at, but the first sheet of paper inside gives me the answer.

Court orders and legal documents. Hundreds of them. Flicking through, I see paperwork dated back to the months before I was born. Catherine tried to expose my father's plan by filing police forms and talking to the media so he had her done for defamation. The bastard.

"Phillip sued me for everything I had. Even the deeds to an old house I inherited in the sticks. Not because he needed it, because I wouldn't have any other choice but to back off. Once the charge stuck, it was easy for him to get full custody of my unborn child. The state deemed me to have insufficient means to raise you. I fought him in every court case, but the jury was always on his side. He had the college, the investors, the charisma. I was an apprentice who could barely afford her rent at the time. I got one night with you in the hospital before the officers came to take you away." Another tear falls down her cheek which I wipe away with the back of my hand.

"I left my hometown for good and changed my name, started again. You were almost five when I was well off enough to file for full custody, so I did. Annually until you were twelve, and it was the same every year. He was believed to be the better parent. I even came to the house a few times, tried to climb the gate before the security team caught me," Catherine laughs. "Phillip is too powerful and I guess I hoped you were happy so… I gave up."

"You didn't give up, mom." Pushing the file away, I offer out my hand to her. Standing, we walk to the back of the office where Harper will be far below, worrying about me. Catherine's arms wind around me and I lean my head on her shoulder, watching the flashing lights of an airplane trail across the midnight blue sky. I'm murder-level furious with my dad after hearing everything that's been said here tonight, but I force it to take a backseat for now.

What's important is I was always loved. I always had someone in my corner and I wasn't the only one to suffer. I hope sooner or later, even without Harper's help, I'd have sought out my mom because I needed this. I feel rejuvenated and ready to fight, to beat the bastard who created me no matter the cost.

Harper

Stepping into the penthouse suite, my eyes widen and my jaw drops. Holy shit, this place is amazing! Rhys' mom said we can stay here as long as we like and I'd like to move in. Clay and I finished dinner hours ago, turning to shots to stay awake. After the restaurant cleared out, the manager gave me free rein over the speaker system and we danced until they were ready to lock up. Not romantic, slow dancing either. The nasty grinding kind until I'm sure the fiction on my jean-clad ass rubbing against Clay's cargo-covered dick would start a fire. And what a tragedy that would have been.

Clay moves further into the suite to investigate, a bag in each hand. Rhys is still downstairs, saying goodbye to his mom. I met her briefly on the way in, but it was the look on Rhys' face that captured all of my attention. I can't describe it; he looked brighter yet darker at the same time. Full of hope yet even more haunted.

Running a hand over the glittery black surface of the kitchen's island, I slowly walk into the main living area. Every outer wall is made of glass, but not in an intrusive way since we are over forty floors up. White sofas fill the main room between a stone fireplace and projector screen that fills the opposite wall.

Traveling to the windowed wall, I stare at the horizon. We're closer to sunrise than I realized, the deep blue of the sky beginning to pale. The city stretching before me is littered with polka-dot lights, as if the stars have fallen directly from above.

Electronic shutters start to come down, making me jump. Spinning back, I see Rhys standing beside a panel on the wall by the elevator.

"Hey," I start back towards him, studying his face. Clay also reappears, meeting us by the kitchen. For a moment, no one says anything even though there's so much to discuss. Running a hand through his hair, Clay decides against asking any questions and heads towards the fireplace instead. I smile as I watch him go, also figuring why not? This lifestyle is different for both of us, we should embrace it while we can.

"Come here," Rhys breaks the silence with a soft demand, holding out his inked hand. Accepting it, Rhys guides me over to the sofa and slumps down, dragging me onto his lap. His cheek rests on my head, his arms tightly caging me in, not that I would try to escape anyway.

"Do you want to talk about it?" I ask after a while. The alcohol leaving my system is giving way to a weariness I refuse to feel. Rhys needs me, possibly more than ever. When I don't receive an answer and the rhythmic movements of his chest deepens, I figure Rhys has fallen asleep. Attempting to slither out of his arms, he holds me firmly in place.

"There's a big gala happening at my father's place tomorrow night, we have a plan and the arrangements are being taken care of. It's all going to be okay now, Babygirl." I twist my head to stare into his blue eyes with a questioning look. Sighing heavily, Rhys swivels his eyes towards the fireplace Clay has now lit. "Look, I love that you care, you've always cared. But right now, I need to get out of my head if we can drop this until morning?" I nod, having heard him loud and clear through my receivers. Wriggling out of his hold, I slide down until my knees hit the plush rug on the floor.

"Consider it dropped," I smile seductively, reaching for his waistband. With only a moment's hesitation, Rhys lets me unbutton his slacks and slide them down his thighs with his boxers. His dick bobs free, instantly hardening. Kicking his loafers off, Rhys frees his legs off the restrictive material and spreads his thighs wide, reclining back in the sofa. I take a moment to look at him like this, completely at ease and carefree.

Starting with his shins, I slowly scrape my nails up his legs, across his thighs and dodge his dick at the last moment. His hiss gives me a sense of satisfaction, so I do it again and again. Not once does Rhys stop me, remaining as still as he can beneath my touch. Reaching upwards, my chest brushes against his solid cock as I unbutton and remove Rhys' shirt, leaving him bare to me. The power I have over him makes me heady at times, visions of tying him down and tease him for all eternity flashing to life in my mind.

A hand grips my hair roughly, yanking me back on a growl. Apparently Clay's bro-code has kicked in with full force. Releasing my hair, Clay drags my t-shirt over my head and unclasps my bra while Rhys' heated gaze watches. Gentler this time, Clay gathers my hair and holds it in one hand, easing me forward to Rhys' throbbing cock. The piercing glistens in the flames from the fireplace, my tongue darting out to wet my lips.

Starting from his balls, I lick a steady path from the base to the tip. Thank god for male grooming. Rhys' shaft is smooth beneath my tongue, his bulbous purple head silky as it glides into my mouth. I've practiced enough now not to gag as his piercing grazes the back of my throat, taking him deep and slow. Rhys' guttural moans would be enough to spur me on enough on their own, but Clay rubbing his knuckles against my nipples makes me suck harder. I can feel the wetness seeping into my thong, my hips grinding in time with Rhys' every time I take him into my throat again.

Clay's hand on my hair forces me off Rhys with a pop, causing us both to shout at him. Pulling me upright, Clay undresses the rest of me until I'm fully naked in front of Rhys, like he's unwrapping a present in front of the birthday boy. Nudging my legs open with his thick thigh, Clay bends me over to continue sucking Rhys' cock. Behind me, I hear the muffled sounds of him stripping, and the shriek of the coffee table being pulled closer for Clay to seemingly sit on. When his tongue runs the length of me from clit to ass, I release Rhys on a gasp.

"You stop, I stop," Clay growls, his breath fanning across my opening. Locking eyes with Rhys, I lower myself onto him and feel Clay's tongue spear inside of me. Moaning with a cock down my throat isn't easy, but fuck, it's hot as hell. Whether he wants to admit it or not, Clay was made for this. Rhys and I act like we have our shit together, but in reality we are the ones floundering and Clay is the glue keeping us all together.

Clasping my knees to lock me in place, Clay uses my exposed position to his advantage. His stubble rubs my clit, his tongue feasting on me. He sucks and bites at my inner thighs, no doubt leaving a trail of hickeys across my inner thighs. But I don't care what he's doing back there, as long as he doesn't stop. The salty taste of Rhys' precum spreads across my tongue, his face strained as he fights to stay in place.

"Rhys, touch me," I plead, done with this game.

"Fuck yes," he responds, his hands plunging into my hair. I can't fight my smile, my teeth accidently grazing his shaft but he moans loudly. Not seeming to know what to do with himself, his hands travel from gripping the sides of my head to my cheeks, across my neck and down to knead my tits. His thumbs flicking over my nipples, driving me to finish this. An insatiable hunger has built within me, and in this moment I'd do anything either of them asked. I want them everywhere, their hands on me, their dicks in me.

"I need one of you in me, or both of you in me, right now." I say a little too loudly, bolting upright. I feel hot, knowing a flush has claimed my chest and neck, my skin tingling all over. I can feel how wet I am, my teeth pushing into my bottom lip at how horny these guys make me. It's Clay who stands first, turning me slowly to face him. His thumb pulls my lip free before he coils his hand around my nape.

"You're not ready for that, Angel. One day." My hooded

eyes lower to his thick cock nudging into my stomach, and I wonder if I'm able to beg. Reaching for him, I hear Rhys grumble something inaudible behind me but it makes Clay smile. Resting his hands on my hips, Clay eases me backwards until my legs bump into Rhys' and I'm lowered onto him. "Finish Rhys off before he ruins the upholstery," Clay whispers into my receiver with a wink before walking away.

I open my mouth to ask where he's going but Rhys has other ideas. Flipping me unexpectantly, I'm thrown over the arm of the sofa and Rhys plunges into me in one, hard thrust. My wetness welcomes him, his cock reaching my core instantly before he tears out and does it again. And again. I can't contain my cries as Rhys takes me hard and without abandon. The climax Clay started crashes into me with the force of a tidal wave, blinding me with its intensity. I scream through the unrelenting pounding Rhys delivers me, my walls squeezing him too tightly. On his own roar, I feel him explode inside me and the sensation was almost as good as my own orgasm. Without slowing, Rhys pumps his hot cum into me until he's empty, steadily bringing slowing pace. I shake beneath him, fraught with the tremors of what just happened.

"Holy...shit," I breathe, flopping against the arm of the chair. Rhys leans over me, sweeping my hair aside to place kisses along my spine. When his arms are around me, we simply remain there, covered in sweat and softly panting together.

"I can never lose you," Rhys murmurs against my back. My eyebrows crease at the sudden change in atmosphere, Rhys' arms tightening around me desperately. "I don't know who I am without you."

"Well, that's bullshit. You're Rhys fucking Waversea. You can do anything."

"I'm serious, Harper," he growls. Elbowing out of his hold, I turn as much as our connected bodies will allow, the evidence of our union leaking down my thighs.

"So am I. You've been a survivor long before you met me.

The only thing that's changed is you've allowed yourself to realize it." Rhys' eyes hold mine for a long moment, his mind working over my words. Cupping my cheek, he bends to kiss me thoroughly and passionately, his lips portraying the words he can't seem to say. I drown in everything he is; his touch, his smell, his taste. The man no one else could see even though he was begging to be noticed.

Breaking away, Rhys ducks his head as if I didn't see the glisten of a tear on his cheek or feel the slight tremble to his hand as he held me so preciously. Grabbing Clay's t-shirt, Rhys holds it between us as he pulls out of me. Ever the romantic. Scooping me up in his arms with Clay's shirt still nestled between my legs, Rhys carries me through the suite until I hear the sound of a shower growing louder.

Nudging the door open, I spot Clay under the spray with his eyes closed, leaning against the tiles. The whole room is like one big shower, divided in half by a glass separator. There is a drain in the middle of the floor and the shower head is built into the ceiling. Setting me down, Rhys unhooks my receivers from my ears and places them on the counter beside the basin. After removing and tossing Clay's shirt, he nudges me towards the shower. Without looking back, I link my hand in Rhys' and drag him with me, refusing to be separated from one of my men for a second time this evening.

Clay opens his eyes when my hand touches his chest, greeting me with a wide smile. Pulling me beneath the spray, he begins to wet my hair and wash me without a word. But I can't help to notice his now soft dick and the coolness of the water, putting two and two together.

"Why did you...we could have..." I suddenly find myself anxious as well as curious. Did I do something wrong? Did I push Clay away subconsciously, or not make him feel included enough? Gripping my chin gently, Clay lifts my face to look at him and the relaxed grin he has waiting for me there.

"*Rhys needed you tonight,*" he mouths. I turn to look at

Rhys who is playing ignorant while he washes himself, despite being right next to us.

"But you didn't have to be left out," I respond, my eyebrows knitted. My hand still on Clay's chest feels the chuckle rumbling through him, his expression turning serious when he answers.

"*It doesn't always have to be all or nothing with the three of us. I love you as much as Rhys does. As long as you're pleasured, happy and taken care of, that's all I care about. I know I was...hesitant at first, but that was before I realized you were compassionate for the both of us. I don't need to be with you all the time to feel you in here,*" Clay shifts my hand to cover his heart. Leaning into him, I blink through the spray of water to see Rhys staring at me with the same sentiment in his eyes.

"*Once my father has been dealt with, I'll second that. But I have to make sure the world is safe enough for you first.*" I frown at him, not liking the way he said 'I' as if we aren't doing this thing together. Smirking slightly, Rhys reaches over to pull mine and Clay's clasped hands out from between us. Linking his fingers on the other side so my hand is sandwiched inside theirs, Rhys presses a kiss on my forehead before leaning back. "*Don't worry your beautiful brain about it Babygirl. This ends tomorrow night.*"

Clayton

"Okay, run me through the plan," I say, fastening my tie. The penthouse suite is huge, giving us enough rooms to change separately but we're all together in the master bedroom. Harper steps out of the en-suite, halting our conversion for everyone to take a leisurely admiring look. Even PC Haynes and detective Steiner lose their professionalism at the sight of her, and I can't blame them.

A form fitted navy dress covers her hourglass frame from her bust to the floor. Over the top is a layer of floral lace, stretching to her neckline. Giving us a spin, the spaghetti straps open to expose her back in a low V. Her hair shines in the light and bounces around her in loose curls, her face glowing with a light dusting of make-up and mascara. Absolutely breath-taking. I must admit, despite his downfalls, Rhys has exceptional taste.

He's currently striding towards Harper in his unbuttoned slacks, pulling her into his arms. The officers suddenly remember themselves, turning towards the desk with a united grunt. They've set out a range of gadgets, one of them being the wire Rhys is going to wear beneath his suit. It's kind of genius really; hiding a wire behind a microphone clip in case there is security on the doors. I slide my own clip onto my black tie, smoothing it carefully.

"It's simple," PC Haynes finally answers my question, distracting me from the pair as he flashes a glossy invitation into the air. "We all attend today's high society gala at the Waversea house. Steiner and I will be undercover, posing as potential investors."

"And all I need to do is be my arrogant self until my father pulls me into a room to tell me how pathetic I am, and then I'll get him to talk about the loophole he's pursuing again for the surveillance team to enjoy." Rhys joins us by the vast windows, looking down on the city below. We're around fifty miles from Rhys' home, waiting for the police van to get into position long before guests begin to arrive. Apparently, we need to be 'fashionably late' to make our appearance believable.

"Is that enough of a case to stick, legally I mean?" I ask dubiously. Shrugging on the black suit jacket, I drop down on the edge of the bed beside Harper and take her hand in mine.

"If Phillip Waversea has been making purchases and taking out loans against the college for the past two decades, knowing he wouldn't be paying them back, it's fraud and embezzlement. Not to mention if he does get physical with Rhys, we could prove he's been abusive. Maybe get the staff to testify." PC Haynes shares a confident smirk with Steiner.

"Yeah, we'll make it stick." The bald man replies. The pair arrived after breakfast this morning, already dressed and ready to go. Steiner is the older one of the pair, pale and round in the middle. Haynes is taller, in his late twenties with tanned skin that speaks of many holidays in exotic places. I'm hoping that works in our favor, allowing him to look well-traveled and loaded even at his young age. I'm presuming Phillip Waversea isn't easily fooled, and that's only one reason there's a ball of nervous churning in my gut about today.

Harper and I watch in silence, leaning on each other as Rhys is fitted with the wire and the officers try to reassure him. I can't tell if it's an act or not, but Rhys has slid straight back into his cocky, own-the-world character with a constant smirk and straightened spine. Even so, I'll take comfort in the surveillance team listening in and the squad of cops waiting in a concealed van further down the road. It was agreed reinforcements should be on standby should the plan go to shit, given that the mansion is so large, it would take too long to find Rhys if his dad turns on him.

Fastening on his Rolex and smoothing a hand over the longer section of his hair, Rhys turns to us with a cruel smile. Not even looking at Harper softens it like usual and I wonder if the Rhys that comes out of today will be the same man who went in. Packing away, the officers lead us to the penthouse elevator while I take one last look around.

This is my first, and probably last, time in a suite like this. I didn't think they existed in such splendor, only shown this way in movies. The kitchen is larger than my entire childhood apartment, chrome appliances and black surfaces cover every inch to match the central island. What's more, it costs months' worth of rent to stay here one night, and it's insane to me to see how the other half live.

Traveling down in the elevator, Harper's hands stay gripping in Rhys' and mine all the way to the Ford. I'm so on edge, the thought of driving seems impossible but I reckon it'll be a decent distraction. Besides, this beauty is mine now and I've refused to let Rhys drive it again in fear he might total it without a second thought. Not everything is easily replaceable for me, and I'd never afford another truck of this magnitude. Sliding behind the wheel, I adjust the wheel to lock eyes with Harper in the back seat, giving her a small nod.

The journey is quiet, the atmosphere thick with unspoken words. We are literally driving Rhys towards the man he hates in the hopes he'll get beaten up, and as much as he's pretending not to care in the backseat with his arm around Harper, I'm worried for him. Even if today goes well, we manage to trap Phillip Waversea, get him arrested and Rhys escapes with a busted lip, then what? What's going to happen to the college and all the students who go there? What will happen to me if I lose my scholarship? Waversea isn't just providing me with weekly funds and an education, it's my current home.

Nearing the tree lined pathway bordering the Waversea estate, my anxiety kicks up a notch and I feel physically sick. Stopping briefly in front of the mansion, I'm fully aware this time I'm walking into the lion's den. Fuck, I wish Harper was as far away as possible from here but she refused to even consider staying behind. Rounding the house, I follow the concrete round to the ramp and glide into the underground parking. It's heaving, not a parking space free due to the expensive sport cars filling every spot. Figuring we're not welcomed anyway, I pull up right in front of the doorway and park, blocking several people in.

Rhys nudges me with a whoop before we get out, bobbing on his feet as I round the truck. Sliding my arm around Harper's waist, Rhys links their fingers and leads us into the house. Classical music fills the air and draws us along the empty hallway. Turning a corner, waiting staff rush between the kitchen and an open set of doors, trays of champagne flutes and tiny canapés in their hands. We hang back, allowing a young woman in a black pencil skirt and white shirt pass first, her long brown ponytail swishing with each step.

Following her, we walk into a grand ballroom. My mouth drops open at the pure size of it, masses of tables and chairs sitting either side of a polished dance floor in the center. Chandeliers glimmer along with the gold flourishes covering the ceiling. White tablecloths match the organza bows on each chair, making this event look more like a wedding than a function. A small podium with a microphone stand has been erected across the far side with a live orchestra playing beside it. Even though the dance floor is full of couples swaying, the seats are mostly full too.

Edging around the room, we find a spot to stand and grab a glass each from a passing tray. I spot Steiner and Haynes walk through the doorway, having stayed at the hotel a while longer to put some distance between us. They blend into the crowd, meandering through the tables looking for a place to sit.

Harper's fingers on my chin draw me back to her waiting smile.

"Stop looking, focus on me." I grin, despite the trepidation I feel. If only she wasn't here, Rhys and I could face this Bad Boys style. I vaguely notice over her shoulder a reporter strolling around, followed by a cameraman. They take interest in Rhys until he snarls at them like a wild animal, forcing them to move along. A few flashes catch my attention as another reporter spots the exchange, taking some snaps before slinking away.

"I didn't realize there would be paparazzi here," I whisper-shout to Rhys who is focused on tipping back the content of his champagne flute. Stopping a waitress, he pushes the glass into her hand and demands something stronger before turning back to me.

"More media, the better when daddy dearest is carted out in handcuffs." Rhys half shrugs and leads Harper towards the dance floor while I hang back. The main man in question is yet to be seen, if he's even in the ballroom at all. Maybe fashionably late runs in the family. Sipping the champagne, I spot a recently vacated seat and make my way over to it. Spinning it around, I sit with my back to the rest of the table's occupants to watch Harper.

She's a vision, taking the spotlight between everyone else on the dance floor. I don't know why I'm surprised Rhys can dance, but my focus is fixed on her as she twirls and sways in his arms. Her hair bounces around her, her fingers stroking Rhys' biceps as she talks into his ear. And when she laughs, I hear it all the way down to the pit of my stomach. It doesn't bother me in the slightest when she's with Rhys anymore, because I know she's being loved. A girl as precious as Harper obviously needs two people to adore in the way she deserves, both of us bringing different aspects she needs.

"Ugh, what a slut," I vaguely hear from behind me. Spinning in my chair, I lock eyes with the busty blonde across the table for the first time. She's sausaged herself into a red satin dress way too small for her ample chest, showcasing more skin than a naked mole rat. Her hair is tightly bound to the back of her head, and the disgust written across her features makes me sneer.

"Keep your thoughts to yourself, Klara, if you don't want Harper to put you on your ass again in front of your fancy friends." I should have known she'd be here, her mother is one of Waversea's biggest investors. The rest of the table is surrounded by females our age, all pretentious and caked in make-up. They look me at with unhidden interest, probably presuming I'm of their high-class status thanks to Rhys' expensive suit. If this is what being high class consists of, count me out. Fake attention and prearranged balls have no place in my day-to-day life.

The music behind me comes to a gentle close, the couples dispersing to find seats or stand around the edge of the room. I raise a hand to catch Rhys' attention, the pair approaching with Harper's head on his shoulder. Spotting my company, Rhys straightens and his easy smile slips.

"Move." At first, I thought his bark was at me, but the girls jump up and scatter at his demand. All except Klara.

"I'm not moving. I got here early for this table." Rhys doesn't argue as expected, instead he shrugs and gestures for Harper to take the seat beside me and tucks her in. Twisting his chair to look solely at Harper, he tucks her hair behind her ear and I see a blood vessel burst in Klara's temple. Opening her mouth to comment, the room is suddenly hushed and I turn to see the man we've been waiting for approaching the podium. Phillip Waversea.

Harper

Seeing Rhys' dad fills me with rage so quickly, I feel physically sick. The more I learn about him, the more I hate him. I hate this kingdom he's built around himself. From the mansion to the Caribbean holiday homes, the jet and the college, Phillip has sat himself on a throne made of other people's money and doesn't intend to pay any of it back. What a cock.

Even the way the ballroom has been decorated in such ridiculous splendor makes me nauseous. Only an arrogant bastard would waste so much money on stupid spends such as the ice sculpture I see across the far side of the room in the shape of the Waversea logo. I am in love with this dress though, savoring the feel of the satin gliding against my skin like butter. After tonight, Rhys will possibly be as poor as the rest of us, so I'll enjoy it while I can. Besides, I'm just as happy with a cheesecake and Netflix binge in bed between my men. 'Easily pleased', Aunt Marg always used to say.

Shifting in my seat, my knees press into Clay's thigh and Rhys' hand is glued to my ass from behind. I can feel the heat of Klara's death stare hitting the back of my head like a pair of lasers. Hah, bring it bitch. I lean back into Rhys, lapping up his attention as his dad's voice bleeds from the speakers and into the boy's microphone clips. Wait, who was meant to be the bitch here?

"Thank you all for coming this evening. We have a full night of music and fine wine to enjoy, so I won't keep you too long." The room chuckles low, everyone falling for his fake charm. What Phillip means is, let me get this over with so I can take your money and run.

"Many of you here tonight are interested in claiming a stake in the Waversea legacy for yourselves and investing in our beloved College. Along with tying your name to our ever-growing list of successful sportsmen and prized scientists, you would also receive a sizable return and shares for your invest-ment. Now, I'm not naïve enough to think you all won't have seen the recent events in the media, the actions of the few sullying those of the many."

Phillip's eyes search the crowd either side of the room, settling on Rhys and me with pursed lips. At this, everyone else turns to stare too, clearly deciding we are to blame for every-thing to have happened, despite most of it happening to me. I grit my teeth and narrow my eyes at Phillip, ignoring the rest of the room as he continues.

"But I assure you the college is and will continue to thrive. Once you're finished enjoying the dance floor and can-apés, please make your way to the drawing room down the hall where you'll find The Waversea prospectus, year books, awards and trophies, and more information if you should wish to join us. The current board members and I are around if you should have any questions, and I wish you all a lovely evening." Rais-ing the glass in his hand, the room copies to cheers him and the music begins to play again. I roll my eyes on a scoff, turning back to the table but Rhys remains transfixed on his father.

A breadbasket is placed in the center of the table with a tray of butters and vinegars in small dishes. Diving in, I tear my teeth into a small, plaited roll while Klara continues to glower at me. What? I can't even enjoy carbs now without doing some-thing wrong? Refusing to be intimated, I stare right back at her as I eat my entire roll with sound effects.

"Honestly, what is your problem?" she finally exclaims, slamming her hands on the table.

"Me?!" I nearly choke on my last mouthful of bread. Clay hands me a glass of champagne to wash it down, Rhys absentmindedly patting my back without looking. The display makes Klara growl something inaudible to anyone who isn't part canine and stands. Leaning her hands on the table, I can't help but look down her exposed cleavage as she snarls at me.

"You know what, you deserve everything Kenneth, or whatever his fucking name was, did to you. You've been harassing me since you stepped foot on campus and stole my boyfriend from me! I don't deserve the way you treat me, and I won't stand for it." Stomping away in her six-inch heels, I gape after her. Rhys tries to stand, no doubt wanting to go after her to defend me, but my hand on his wrist stops him.

"Oh, god," I breathe. What if she's right? Ignoring her possessiveness over Rhys, have I been wrongly blaming her this entire time? That makes me the bully, and my conscience can't allow that. I was happy to out-bitch her when I thought it was deserved, but this changes everything. Rising, Rhys tries to stop me this time with a stern look. "I won't be long. I need to clear this up." Slowly releasing me, he looks to Clay for back up but finds none.

"Hurry back. The show's about to begin." I follow the jerk of his chin to see his dad shaking hands and smiling falsely, working the room in our direction. Promising Rhys I will, I share a quick sign with Clay to watch out for him and slip away.

Stepping out of the ballroom, I see Klara at the far end of the corridor staring out of a bay window. Sensing me approach, she storms off once more and I'm soon following her through the mansion's internal maze.

"Klara, wait! I just want to talk." A door slams in my face as I reach it, but I won't be dissuaded so easily. This is being sorted, tonight. Pushing down the handle, I let myself in to a massive bathroom. Klara is perched on the side of the bathtub, a scowl sour enough to churn milk plastered on her face. Holding my hands up in defeat, I slowly pull my phone from where it was sandwiched between my side boob and the tight dress, and turn on the microphone app.

"I do just want to talk. What you said back there...well, it confused me to be honest. I thought you had it out for me this whole time." My voice trails off, the words I want to say not forming proper sentences. Klara stands and crosses her arms beneath her chest, her hip popped to one side.

"I admit I was pissed when you showed up. I saw the way Rhys looked at you. He'd been with me for close to a year, and he never looked at me like that. So yeah, I started a fight with you in the bathroom that first day I met you so you might back off. But that was it. Everything after that was you." I rack my brain, trying to clear out the champagne's influence. Leaning against the basin, I list the incidents I'd accused Klara of.

"You didn't steal my receivers before the after party?" Klara shakes her head. "Fill my locker with dog shit, scribble on my notepads, rip the pages from my library books? Any of it?" She continues to shake her head, the sorrow creeping into her gaze making me frown. "You just wanted Rhys back."

"I couldn't understand why he liked it so much when you fought against him. I've seen you physically hit him, and he loved every second of it. But I couldn't do that, so I thought fighting with you might spark whatever flame he has burning for you in my direction. Nothing worked." Klara shrugs, focussing on a spot on the floor and I suddenly feel like the biggest bitch ever. If I'd spared one moment to speak to her before this, we could have settled our differences a long time ago.

"Klara, I'm so sorry-"

"Save it," she interrupts me, leaning her head back on the marbled wall. A bathmat thicker than most carpets separates us, seafoam blue like the rest of the bathroom's décor. The claw-foot bathtub is so deep, I would probably float to the surface and never be able to touch the bottom. Spotlights shine above a huge mirror in front of the basin I'm leaning on to give my feet a brief reprieve from these heels.

"Despite the blonde hair and the big boobs, I'm not stupid. I know he never wanted me, but I tried so hard to be good enough. Our families expected us to be together, but I wasn't able to keep his attention. Something my mother is still furious about. And then I saw how he looked at you, how much he enjoyed the way you insulted him. It doesn't make sense to me, but it seems to work for the two, or three, of you. You're so fucking lucky, how could I not be jealous?"

I can't help the small smile creeping across my face. I never thought someone might be jealous of me; the orphaned deaf girl who would prefer to read than socialize. But meeting Clay and Rhys has changed everything, changed me. Now I have a future brighter than I could ever have hoped for, the least I can do is try to help Klara achieve the same.

"Klara, listen to me. Rhys isn't like other guys, and it's not that he didn't notice you. I don't think he noticed anyone, he was too busy fighting his own demons. Doesn't mean you're not worthy or good enough, it just means he wasn't the right one. And if your mother doesn't like that, that's her problem. But everyone deserves to be loved, you just have to find that special person who accepts you for the jealous bitch you are." We share a laugh, Klara's eyes swimming with the tears she won't let fall in front of me. "Everyone is good enough, but not everyone is the right fit. It's important to know the difference."

"Thank you, Harper. I'm sorry I was a cow." She smiles sadly, walking towards me as if to clutch my hand or give me a hug but decides against it. Settling on an awkward arm pat, I decide to screw convention and pull her in for a hug.

"No, I'm sorry I blamed you for everything. And...especially for the prawny cheese mix I dumped on your head." Klara gags against my shoulder, pulling away with her nose crinkled and I laugh again.

"Let's never talk about that, ever again." She smiles, holding out her pinkie finger. There's a twinkle in her eye that says this might not just be a reconciliation, but possibly the chance for a friendship in the future. Linking my pinkie in hers, I start to laugh again.

"Deal."

Rhys

I keep my eyes glued on the graying man taking his sweet fucking time to gravitate towards me. He knows I'm here. I can see it in the way his posture is a fraction too tight and his face is purposely turned away from me at all times. Every time I down the whiskey in my glass, Clayton prises it out of my fingers and replaces it with a full one from the tray of drinks I stole. I won't admit it out loud, but I'm thankful for his company. Especially with the way my teeth are grinding due to how long Harper has been gone. I know she could take Klara if needed, I just miss her when she's not by my side where she belongs.

As Daddy Dearest nears, I shrug off my suit jacket and roll up my sleeves to expose some ink. Fuck it, I loosen my tie and pop open my top buttons too, careful not to go below the microphone clip, but uncovering enough skin to piss him off. He hates everything I am, which only encourages me to go further with each tattoo. Make them more grotesque, cover myself in hideous images. I want to offend people, stop them from looking at me in fear of tainting their nightmares. All that matters is I didn't discourage the beauty who's come into my life, the one Clayton aptly nicknamed Angel. The rest of the world can go fuck itself, especially the man who has finally come to a stop in front of me.

"No handshake for me, father?" I ask with a mocking smirk. He looks at me with unreserved disgust. Perfect.

"Those are reserved for welcome guests, son." He grits

out the last word as if it physically pained him but I can't help to laugh at the irony. I've never been a welcome guest in my house. He tries to sidestep me but I refuse to let him, noticing Clayton close in on his other side. I've been picturing ways to irritate my father for years despite this being a recent plot, but never in my wildest dreams did I think I'd have back-up.

"I want to talk," I mutter into his ear. Not because I think he'll accept, but so I can blame my following actions on his refusal. My father barges past me as expected, looking for the missing guests at the table when I knock the tray in an approaching waitress' hands to the floor. The orchestra and long-time investors don't react, used to my 'childish outbursts' at these bullshit conventions.

"Rhys," my father warns in a low tone that used to scare the shit out of me. "Don't start." Turning, he begins to walk away and I rush for a way to get our plan back on track. Make my dad furious, get him to beat me up and spill his secrets. My eyes dart around as the whiskey suddenly hits, making me feel dizzy enough to hold onto my chair for support. My gaze snags on the butter knife Harper used, maybe I could stab myself with it? Get that butter all in the wound, infect the shit out of it. Wait, no. That's stupid, my dad wouldn't care about that either way. Clayton steps closer, trying to ground me but instead I have a better idea.

"Quick, put your tongue in my mouth."

"What?!" Clayton jerks back, his eyebrows knitted close enough to form a unibrow. "Fuck no, you're drunk." His hands on my shoulders don't deter me. I slip underneath his grip and grab a hold of his suit jacket, yanking him into me. Puckering my lips, Clayton twists and shifts his head wildly, trying to get as far away from me as possible.

"I need to anger him enough to drag me out of here," I hiss through my teeth. Grabbing Clayton around the back of the neck, I lean over his puffed-out chest and my lips scrape his stubbled jaw. Oh god, I might throw up myself doing this, but

I'm out of time and options. "For fuck's sake Clayton, you've tasted my cum in Harper's mouth. Just tongue fuck me already."

The next thing I know, I'm being slammed face-down onto the table. Fear consumes me as a heavy body leans over mine, pinning my hands behind my back. Fucking Christ, how far is Clayton going to take this ruse to infuriate my dad? Being hoisted up, I see Clayton's worried gaze opposite a moment before a baton connects with my thigh. Oh, thank fuck. I was sure my chocolate starfish was about to lose its purity. Well, if you ignore the anaconda size-shit I took this morning. Laughing manically at myself, a security guard drags me from the room while I shout over the classical music.

"They can't keep us apart, Claybake! Hold onto my erection for me, I'll grab the diamond-studded douche kit! I need to dive into your brownie hole-" a fist connects with my jaw the second my foot is yanked over the ballroom threshold. My vision swims, the copper tang of blood filling my mouth. I hoped to see my father on the delivering end, but another guard is here instead. Grabbing a fistful of hair to drag me along by, I laugh like a psycho as blood dribbles from my mouth.

I'm thrown into the study and the door is slammed shut behind me, my father already seated behind his desk. The room is cast into shadow by a table lamp, used to intimidate me as if I were still five. I sneer at the range of stuffed animal heads covering the wall above the unlit fireplace, knowing that if he could have gotten away with it, my head would have been up there too.

"What do you want, Rhys?" my father drawls, sounding bored as he lights a cigar. "Clearly you want my attention, but I'm busy so spit it out." Turning to face him, I see two versions of my dad through blurry vision. What a nightmare. Stumbling into the armchair, I cover my eyes with my arm briefly as a wave of nausea rolls through me.

"I just wanted some Waversea-style bonding time," I smirk beneath my arm. "You know the type. You whip me, I refuse to cry, you burn me, I crash your golf caddy into the swimming pool. Like the good old days." Not only do I hear his sigh, I feel it. Like a balm washing through my system, the plan knitting together perfectly. Now I just have to wait for the first blow to the gut.

"I'm growing too old for this shit," he mutters instead. I bolt upright, regretting it instantly as I wince but it was needed.

"You cursed," I breathe. My jaw has dropped into my lap, my heart skipping a few beats. "You cursed!" I clap my hands like one of those crazed symbol-holding monkeys, bobbing in my seat with a shocked smile taking over my features. After all these years of beating me shitless for my foul mouth, my father has cursed in front of me. I feel like I've won something, although I'm not sure what. Just a sense of satisfaction I suppose.

"We're finished here. Either enjoy the party or leave Rhys, but don't get in my way." My father stamps out his cigar and pushes to his feet, striding across the room. I suddenly remember why I'm in here, rushing to intercept him from reaching the door.

"Wait. I thought you'd be happy. I'm doing what you wanted; forcing the investors to see me as a flight risk to their precious college. Helping you get it stuck down so you can skip naked into the sunset. No more loans, no more debts. That's the dream, right?"

"Do I look stupid to you?" he scoffs with narrowed eyes. I bite on my lip ring, my head screaming at me from the inside. Don't answer that. *Don't* answer that. I open my mouth on a nod when he continues. "I've had guards on the grounds since sunrise and they spotted your precious surveillance truck a mile off. Let me guess, you're wearing a wire. Otherwise, you'd already be naked by now. It's typically pathetic you thought you could outsmart me."

My father reaches for the door handle but I refuse to move, needing a plan B right fucking now. I shove him back a few steps, challenging him to retaliate. I'm a grown-ass man now, albeit slightly drunk, but I could still take him. Instead, he shakes his head in the 'what did I do to be burdened with his dickstick for a son,' kind of way.

"Get out of my way, Rhys. I'm not giving you what you came here for and I have other business to attend to. Wash up before you show yourself out." This time, I let him push past, knowing defeat when I hear it. The plan was fucked before it even started, and I almost made out with Clayton for nothing. Scratching the back on my head, I hurry towards the desk and start pulling out drawers. There has to be something here we can use, anything. I don't give a shit what my father has done to me, he targeted Harper and that will ultimately be his death wish. But not today it seems.

"Fuck!" I yell, kicking the last of the drawers closed. Stalking into the joined bathroom, I splash water onto my face and scrub the blood from my chin. I can't stand to look at my reflection for more than a few seconds at a time, words tumbling through my mind each time I do. Pathetic. Worthless. Failure. I can't blame my father's words or the whiskey for them, this is what happens each time I'm away from Harper too long. The self-doubt creeps in along with the fear she might realize the truth for herself one day too.

Switching off the basin, I smear the remaining blood across the white hand towel and chuck it into the basin. Rushing back towards the ballroom, my heart kicks up a notch until I'm almost panting. I need Harper in my arms. I need her to look at me as if I'm her world long enough for me to believe I can be too.

Spotting Clayton slumped in the same chair as before and nursing a whiskey of his own, I scan the room quickly for my father. There's no sign of him so I make a beeline for Clayton, needing his help to fix the mess I've made. Surely we can salvage something of tonight? Ignoring the stares, I shove through the couples swaying on the dance floor as a shortcut to the table. Only once I'm by Clayton's side do I realize he is still alone.

"Is Harper not back yet?"

Harper

"No way, you're lying!" Klara exclaims, slapping her hands on her thighs. I'm not sure how we managed to get down onto the tiled bathroom floor in these dresses, but we sure as hell aren't getting up.

"I swear it's true! Fuchsia pink on every toenail, and he kept it on for weeks." Our laughs ring around the spacious room and echo through the mic app on my phone between us.

Now it's just the two of us like this, sharing stories and laughing easily, I feel terrible for the way I've acted. I was so ready to fight off girls with a nail-embedded stick, I went on the defence without giving her a chance. More than that, I actively sought to blame her when, for the most part, she was innocent. Aside from yanking my hair out in the girl's bathrooms but I've done worse than that to her now.

"Damn. You know what, you're right. I was never the one for Rhys. You are." Klara nods thoughtfully and I take her hand in mine.

"Your one is out there. Hey, maybe you'll have two or a whole harem."

"Ha! I think I need one to handle all of this," she jiggles her tits at me. Her laughter is cut short by something she must have heard, but whatever it was is too far away from my phone. I can't tell what emotion floods Klara's face, but it's not a good one. Fear? Horror, maybe. Her hands grip onto mine and she mouths she's sorry just before my world goes black.

I jerk back against the thin, smooth material covering my eyes, trying to twist away as it's tightened but Klara keeps my hands locked in place. A hand clamps over my mouth so tightly, fingernails dig into my cheeks. I'm confused as to what's happening until a rough voice has the blood freezing in my veins.

"Sounds like you were having a little too much fun in here. When I ask you to do something, don't fuck about. Just get it done." Phillip Waversea heaves me up by hair on a squeal, his rough hand not leaving my mouth. There's a scuffle sound inside my head from my phone, which I presume has been snatched up and placed in Phillip's jacket pocket due to the volume and clarity of his voice.

"Why are you still here?" he snaps.

"It's just...I really don't think she-" A sharp slap cuts through the air and silences Klara. Tears sting my eyes behind what I'm guessing is a tie, shivers rolling through my body. "One more word and I'll ruin your family so fast, you'll be on a street corner by the end of the month."

When I don't hear Klara again, I presume she's left. Gone. I'm torn between hating her for leaving and understanding why she did. No one denies Phillip, and I wonder how many times Klara's spunky attitude has found that out the hard way. It occurs to me if he is here, not in handcuffs, then Rhys mustn't have got what he needed. The plans a failure and this monster is still free. My heart plummets as my arms are suddenly wrenched behind my back and I'm shoved forward.

"It's just me and you now, Miss Addams." I fight back as Phillip moves me onwards, but the more I struggle, the harder he yanks on my arms and tightens his grip on my face. My shoulders scream with pain, my heels unable to stay balanced. His voice filters through my skull self-commentary style, and it's at that point I realize he doesn't know I can hear him.

"It was all going to plan until you turned up. I thought you'd be Rhys' downfall when I approved your application. Who knew you'd find the soul I've spent years beating out of him?" I fight the urge to react, not wanting to let on I can hear every word. I'm used to being underestimated, but I still refuse to give up. Digging my heels, I attempt to shove myself backwards to catch him off guard. The hand dislodges from my mouth long enough for me to scream, until my head is slammed into a wall.

Pain so visceral assaults me, colors bursting to life behind my eyelids. My legs give out, allowing Phillip to drag me along by my arms while my head lolls. Spike after spike of agony pounds into my temple until I think my skull will explode. Phillip's voice fades in and out, only the odd word filtering through.

"Little bitch...ruined everything...spent too long...defective slut...You're no one." I try to focus, try to hold onto the pain as a way to keep me conscious, but it's exhausting.

An image of a little boy fills my mind, his brown hair falling into his swollen eyes. He stretches out to me, the raised scars visible on his small arms. My Rhys. The one who never stood a chance. A large hand lands on his shoulder, my mind drifting to the understanding eyes and shaggy blond hair standing behind him. I nod stupidly, tears collecting beneath my eyelids. Whatever happens, Clayton will protect Rhys now, even from himself.

"The board are already having meetings about closing the damn college. I'm so close to my cash-fueled retirement away from all of this bullshit. And I'll leave Rhys with absolutely nothing. Not even you." And there it is. The confession we needed, and it's already slipping away from my memory as my forehead throbs again. I drift further towards the floor as I'm heaved upright, my stomach churning. I retch behind Phillip's strong hand as he drags me further. Finally, he throws me down and I collapse in a heap on a mattress.

I want to curl up and cry, but the fight or flight in me has other ideas. Scrambling forwards, my fingers hook over the far side of the bed until my ankle is caught in his unyielding grip. I scream now, shoving the blindfold off but the brightness makes my head spin. My dress has peeled up, giving me room to kick wildly with my heels. A weight drops on top of me, forcing the air out of my lungs before his hand circles my neck and squeezes. Holy shit, I'm going to die here. Phillip's an abusive tyrant, but a killer?

"Just like Rhys, I think you're my undoing. But if I'm going down, I'm taking the memory of your tight cunt with me. It's time to finish what Dekken didn't have the balls to." Bile clogs in my airway, my body immobilised as he shifts and leans on me to rip the side of my dress open. How is he so deceivingly strong? His hands are on the back of my thighs, his whiskey-infused scent making me heave as it consumes me.

Static sounds as I guess Phillip removes his suit jacket and tosses it away with my phone inside, but I don't want to look back. If I see him behind me with my own eyes, that will make this too real. Too unforgettable. So I scrunch my eyes shut and fight with everything I am. I wriggle upwards, causing my dress to slip further down, kicking violently. My heel connects with something firm, the grip on my thighs lessening enough for me to shoot forwards.

Leaving my dress behind, I squint to see a wooden doorway directly in front of me. Running in my heels, I reach out for my fingers to brush the brass handle before a weight collides with mine. My entire body slams into the wall beside the door, agony claiming every inch of me as I crumble onto the floor. This time, I don't fight. I lie in a heap, accepting I can't outrun a man who clearly keeps in shape behind his sharp suits whilst sporting a head injury. My chest is on fire, my shoulders pulsing and legs limp. I'm done, I think as my eyes drift closed.

But nothing happens. I try to open my eyes, but they're too heavy to open. I try to call out, my throat raw from screaming and being choked. Then, hands touch me and I flinch so hard, I let out a groan. Sounds attack me as I rouse back to full consciousness. Arms scoop me up like I weigh nothing. I try to lash out but all I manage is a pathetic wiggle. It's only when a kiss is pressed to my forehead do I still, focusing on my senses.

A uniquely masculine scent fills my nostrils, a smooth cotton shirt cushioning my cheek against a firm chest. Not trusting myself in my deluded state, I push all of my concentration into cracking an eyelid. And there he is. My savior, my faithful protector. The light shines around his blond waves like an angel, his face concealed in shadow but I can feel his frown. I smile like a crazy person, snuggling into the half of my soul I worried I wouldn't see again. But where's the other half?

Clay sits with me nestled in his arms, allowing me to take in the scene around the room. A swarm of uniformed police officers surround an incapacitated Phillip Waversea on the floor of a lavish bedroom. Skirting around them is the tall butler I remember from being here last time, Reid, in his penguin-like suit. He waddles towards me, unless that's my mind playing tricks on me, with a red first aid bag in hand. I try to bat him away but Clay holds my arms in place. Not in a restrictive way, but in an 'I love you so hold the fuck still' kinda way. An icepack is placed on the bump on my forehead and my limbs are checked over until I've had enough.

"Where's Rhys?" Clay takes over holding the ice pack as he bats Reid away, reaching across the bed for my dress. I frown, having forgotten about being mostly naked except for my heels, thong and boob tape. Hugging the material to my body, I look to Clay with an impatient stare.

"They had to handcuff him to the bannister when he couldn't find you. He was flipping tables and smashing windows," Clay says into his microphone clip, snapping me out of my daze. My thoughts race around my head too quickly, my eyes darting around the room. The investors are here. With Phillip arrested and Rhys losing his shit, their decision will be easy. Would Phillip still be able to access the funds to make bail? I'm on my feet before Clay can stop me, although I do use his shoulder for balance when a wave of dizziness makes me sway.

"Help me," I plead, gesturing to the dress but I meant for

more than that. After a moment of concern, Clay nods and holds out the dress for me to step into. His movements are unhurried, shimmying the satin up my body and delicately placing the straps over my tender shoulders. His arm wraps around me for stability, helping me to escape the room with as much dignity as I can muster. But once I'm outside, my steps are frantic.

Half running down the hallway, I come to a fork in the corridors. I know left will take me to the main lobby and Rhys, but the ballroom is right. This may be our last chance, if anyone is even still here and it's not about saving Rhys. It's about saving the college, the students, the scholarships, the staff. Bouncing on my heels, I order Clay to fetch Rhys and dart right. Now unsupported, I stumble slightly, looking like something out of a horror film hunting for fresh human brains to snack on.

The waitress by the ballroom entrance gapes at me as I pull to a halt, needing a moment to compose myself. Breathing deeply a few times, I smooth my hair and dress down before stepping into the hall. I can't hear the quiet fall over the room since I'm stuck in silence anyway, but I feel it. Every eye turns to me, the expressions of those closest speaking for the general population of investors still present.

Straightening my back, I walk through the centre of the parting crowd. Lifting the ripped edge of my skirt which I'm going to pretend is an intentional high-slit, I step onto the podium to face everyone. I can see whispers being passed around, although they need not bother, and several reporters rush forward with cameramen on their heels. Swallowing thickly, I tap a finger on the microphone before me and take everyone's responding wince as a signal it's on.

"When you leave this mansion, you're all going to discover what took place here today. But before the truth becomes misconstrued, I want to give you my account. For longer than anyone you realize, Phillip Waversea has been tricking you. Everything you see around you, every glass you've sipped from and the canapés you've enjoyed, are paid for with your investments. He doesn't own any of this, you do." At the back of the room, I see Rhys skid to a halt. His cheeks are glistening with tears, his features drawn but he doesn't move any further into the room. Gently rubbing the bruising lump on my temple, I try to remember my train of thought.

"Phillip's wealth comes from a string of sizable loans he's acquired, using the college you all fund as collateral. He doesn't care about the success of the students, he doesn't care about the scholarships. He doesn't even care for his own son. He only cares for the lavish lifestyle he wants to continue to lead, so he used Rhys to make you close the college and have his debts expunged. You may think many things about Rhys, but he is a product of his father's plan. A pawn on his chess board.

We came here today to expose Phillip's plot. Rhys came here, hunting for another way out. He doesn't want to be the next in line, he wants all of you to continue allowing the college to thrive. To continue giving futures to those who have run out of options. If you decide to close it down, Phillip wins and us, the students, lose. I'm imploring you, regardless of where your loyalties lie, to do what's right for the thousands of young people relying on their degrees. Those desperate to make their way in this world. But mostly, from a personal standpoint, I'm begging at least this of you. Don't make Rhys Waversea into the monster who created him, give him the chance to be free of corruption and abuse. Let him be a normal guy."

I take a wobbly step back, not knowing what else to say. There isn't anything else, and I can see in the eyes of those staring at me, it's fruitless to try. My head is throbbing, a tear falling as movement catches my eye. At first it's from a few to my left, but soon enough the entire crowd is mimicking. They're clapping. I scan the audience, my gaze snagging on the red flashing from a camera.

A body slams into mine, sweeping me off my feet into a fierce hug. Rhys's body is racked with shudders as he sobs into my shoulder, Clay stepping in behind. Now the boys are back in range, the symphony of applause echoes through my head, but I don't care anymore. I've done what I can. Ultimately, it's the three of us against the world. Three lost souls drifting through life until we found one another. Even the boy's bromance has blossomed past the point of walking away, we need each other. Although Rhys seems to still need convincing, muttering a string of apologies into the mic clip about bringing me here but I refuse to give it any thought.

"I go where you go, remember? I love you Rhys, and one of these days you're going to learn to love yourself."

"What could I possibly love about this?" He pulls away from me and gestures to himself with disgust etched into his features. Roughly grabbing his shirt in my fists, I give him a hard shake.

"Rhys, listen to me. When I look at you, I don't see the external. I see your heart and your light. As battered and dimmed as they are, they're mine. I've seen you at your best and worst, and I'm still right here promising you tomorrow." Rhys presses his forehead against mine, Clay's hand clasping his shoulder in solidarity.

"I don't wanna butt in and turn the tables here," Clay rests his cheek on my sore head to say, "but in about an hour, the entire country will be watching a video of you professing your love to Rhys. Is there still room in that big heart of yours for me?" I glance towards the cameraman who has crept forward for a front row seat to my love life, snorting softly. Was that a hint of jealously I heard in Clay's statement? Turning in Rhys' arms, I brush Clay's waves aside to have a clear view of his endless black eyes.

"You don't need pretty words to know how I feel about you. Let the world see for themselves." Without hesitation, I tiptoe upwards and Clay meets me halfway as I capture his mouth with mine. A soft touch turns heated, my hands gripping Clay's collar to pull him closer. My tongue pushes into his mouth insistently, needing to reinforce our connection. The weight of what I've just been through and what could have happened crashes down on me. In my hopelessness, it was my men who came to me in my mind and now they're here. I'm safe again. Rhys stays glued to my back the entire time, holding me tightly.

Releasing Clay, I link our fingers with a beaming smile and twist to place a kiss in Rhys' hair. I'm ready to leave, to be alone with my men to show them exactly how much I love them and let them do the same to me, over and over.

"I know that look," Clay raises his eyebrow at me despite his smirk. "You have a concussion and you will be resting until you're over it." I punch him in the arm weakly, making my way off the podium. Why'd I have to pick a man with such a high set of morals? Although I didn't have a choice in the matter, his heart undeniably was made for me.

Most of the crowd has dispersed and filtered out by now, leaving open gaps between the remaining guests to stride through. Now the adrenaline is deserting me, my limbs begin to feel heavy again and my head is pounding. The door is in sight, my escape within reach when a small group step into my way and block me from it. A tall woman with straight blonde hair and red claws for nails commands my attention with her shrewd gaze. Her mouth is pursed tightly, the abundance of wrinkled lines around her lips suggesting it's a permanent fixture.

"You must be Harper Addams," she raises an eyebrow as if she doesn't know what to make of me. At that moment, a timid-looking Klara steps out from behind her, keeping her hands clasped in front of her.

"Yes mother, this is Harper." Klara's face emits a range of emotions from sorrow to guilt, so I leave the comfort of my men's arms and close the distance between us. Pulling her into me for a hug, I whisper in her ear it's not her fault. I've done so many undeserving things to Klara over the past few months, and I truly believe she's as much as a victim tonight as I was.

Turning back to her mom, I nod and return her impatient expression.

"It's rather…impressive what you did here this evening. You should consider a future in diplomacy. As for your request, I have spoken with the other board members," Klara's mom looks at the sheepish men standing around her. I can tell in that one move, she is the one calling the shots within the group.

"A few of us have suspected something has been at play for a long time, but we will need evidence to confirm the accusations you have made. We have agreed not to act until the dust settles, leaving the college functioning as normal until we come to a decision. However, Phillip Waversea has been voted out and will no longer benefit from our goodwill. Our loyalties also lie with the students." Spinning on her skinny, six-inch heel, the woman walks away, beckoning Klara to follow.

Once she's disappeared from view, my shoulders sag as if my body was forcing itself to keep it together in the board's presence. Yawning loudly, I lean into Rhys as we finally emerge from the room. My movements slow to a sluggish crawl until Clay scoops me up and carries me the rest of the way. My eyes drift closed on a smile, despite only an hour ago I thought I'd never smile or feel safe again. I expect to be placed into the backseat of the truck, but when my body is lowered onto a spongy mattress, I look around me.

Black satin sheets slip against my dress as I crawl up Rhys' circular super king-size bed, taking a shameful moment to inhale the scent of his cologne imbedded into the pillows. The sweet abyss of sleep is calling to me, but the fingertips trailing the length of my spine have me holding it off.

"Sleep, Babygirl. Clayton's going to run you a bath for when you wake, and we'll take turns washing every inch of your precious body." Hands delicately peel off my shoulder straps and ease the dress down as the other removes my heels. Turning me onto my side, I find Clay there, softly removing my boob tape with unadulterated love in his gaze, Rhys taking care of my thong until I'm completely naked. Their eyes worship me but neither makes a move to get closer.

I'm about to beg for them to touch me when a thick, fluffy blanket is placed over me and I groan at the feel of it on my skin. Nestling into a ball, I realize the pair have vacated the bed and are striding towards the door.

"Wait, you're not going to stay with me?" I question, a frown pulling at my eyebrows. Both throw me roguishly hand- some smirks over their shoulders, the two of them suddenly looking like the carefree college guys they should be.

"The police are still here Babygirl so we need to go keep them at bay. Don't worry, we'll be back before you wake."

"You promise?" My voice comes out small as I pull the cover tighter to my chest.

"We promise, Angel. We'll both be there every time you wake, every time you fly and every time you fall. You're our sal- vation, and we'll spend forever proving we're worthy of being yours." Clay throws his arm around Rhys' shoulder, pulling him through the doorway and closing it behind them with one last heart-stopping smile. I'll never tire of seeing my men happy. Their pasts have been as tragic and tortured as mine, only in different ways, but together we fix one another. Together we're stronger. Together we're beautifully boundless.

Epilogue

Four Years Later

"Hold still for one more second, annnndddd done!" Klara jumps up and down, clapping at her handy work. I swivel on the stool, looking in the handheld mirror she passes me to see a reflection of the masterpiece she's created with my hair in her dresser mirror. Rose-shaped buns cascade from the top of my ear to my nape in a swooping motion with the rest tucked into a chiffon bun underneath. At the front, one long curl falls either side of my face. She picks up my receivers and gently snaps them into place on either side, careful not to mess her design.

"I don't want to sound vain, but I'm fucking amazing," she giggles once they're switched on. I laugh with her with a roll of my eyes.

"You always sound vain," I joke. Well, mostly.

"Next time I do your hair like this, it had better be for your wedding and not some poxy graduation." This time, I laugh wholeheartedly, standing in my black robes.

"Excuse me, my boyfriend is the valedictorian for this 'proxy graduation'," I finger quote, "and you're as excited for today as I am."

"Only because the handsomely new trustee will be giving out our diplomas and he is a H. O. T sugar daddy. 'Hunkier Over Time'." Walking over to her bed with a roll of my eyes, picking up our yellow sashes and handing Klara hers. After a public trial, the boards of investors were forced to have a change of hands to avoid conspiracy charges, due to many of them having a close connection with Phillip. A whole new Board of Trustees has taken over, and the students couldn't be happier. There's thirty-three in total, all of which being wealthy past alumni's from Waversea. It was their decision to make the college public to all once more, awarding more scholarships than ever recorded and revamping the archaic rules.

"What did I miss?" A flustered Addy bursts through the door still dressed in the leggings and tank top she left in this morning with her robes flung over her arm.

"Have you been setting up this whole time? Why didn't you message me for help?"

"I did, slut bag," she retorts, and I check my phone to see the 13 messages and six missed calls. Oops. "It's fine. A bunch of meatheads with muscles for days saw me bent over in my Tik-Tok leggings and came to assist me." There's something about the way she said that last part has my suspicions rising. Now I look closer, I don't think the crazed ruffle to her pink hair has anything to do with prep work after all.

"You've been doing the nasty with some stranger while the rest set up the ceremony, haven't you?! And you called me a slut bag." I drop onto the edge of the bed with a fake scoff in her direction.

"What?!" Addy shrugs with widened eyes. "He was ripped to death, wearing just a pair of cargo shorts. You know what they say; thick calves, thick cock."

"Literally no one says that," I drawl.

"Agreed," Klara chimes in. "But, was it? Thick, I mean?" The three of us burst out laughing as Addy snatches my coke can to re-enact her mouth stretching skills. *Yeah, thanks, I was drinking that. Biatch.* Striding into Klara's bathroom, the shower is switched on before Addy closes the door.

Since Addy rooms in a quad dorm with Clay, Rhys and I, we'd decided to get ready together here while the boys did whatever they do when I'm not around. Play Xbox until five minutes before they need to rush to get ready and leave, I suppose. It's not too bad sharing with Addy considering she spends more and more nights lately sleeping with and at other people's places. She drifts between men and women, going wherever her inhibitions take her, but I'm starting to grow concerned her inhibitions will take her too far one of these days.

A considerable while later, we are all ready in matching robes with hairstyles fit for royalty. Addy opted for a plait-formed crown, rounding her now bubble-gum pink head as an excuse not to wear her mortarboard. She's become a rebellious minx these past few years, whereas Klara has gone the opposite way. After quitting the cheerleading team and dressing more modestly, she became a different person overnight. Heading up the student council, Klara is the board's inside eyes and ears to ensure the college is running smoothly on both sides, giving the student body a voice and is an inch closer to following in her mother's footsteps.

The campus is buzzing with excitement. Fellow classmates wave as the three of us pass by arm in arm, the sun shining brightly overhead. Paparazzi are loitering on the outskirts of the buildings, not allowed on campus to get their prized shot of the disgraced former owner's son on this special day.

Phillip is currently rotting in a state prison where he belongs. Being such a high-profile case that was reported on internationally, the judge wanted to make an example of Phillip by giving him three consecutive ten-year sentences back-to-back for fraud, attempted rape and child abuse. Rhys and I both had to take the stand which wasn't easy on either side, but luckily the surveillance team had tapped into my phone when they realized I was missing and recorded Phillip's whole confession.

The central courtyard is beautiful. Floral displays in all shades of orange and yellow hang over each doorway of the four surrounding buildings, including the Dean's offices behind a raised stage. The fountain is dressed similarly, blooming lilies floating within the watered tiers and omitting a glorious smell through the breezy summer's day. The Waversea flag flies proudly overhead, filling me with a sense of gratification as it has every day I see wide smiles pass in the corridors. I'm not one to brag and I feel awkward receiving compliments, but that doesn't stop me from having a mini-victory dance inside. I did this. We did this. And my knight once shrouded in shadow is ahead in the robes and cap I never thought I'd see him in.

"Rhys!" I shout, racing towards him, all composure forgotten. He spins with the biggest smile and I fly into his open arms, being swept off my feet. Anyone would think it had been weeks since we'd seen each other, not hours, but it's like this every time. I can't help the butterflies that still churn in my stomach whenever I see him, the excitement of having found my soul mates so early on in life sometimes too much to bear.

"Get a room," Addy remarks and continues walking. Her relationship with Rhys hasn't changed much, but they tolerate one another for my sake. I grab onto Rhys' thick biceps as he plants me back on my feet, marveling at the firmness against the satin. He's been on creatine shakes and hitting the gym daily with Clay, and not because he felt threatened by Clay's size. One outrageously-camp café owner in Paris called him 'Baguette Legs' a few summers ago and that was it. A gym-obsessed monster was created, but I love he has a hobby.

"*You'd better be naked beneath these robes*," he signs fluently as I still grope at him.

"*Why don't you find out?*" I reply with a raised eyebrow. Rhys grabs my hand the moment I'd finished signing, dragging me through the crowds of proud parents and families hoarding around their graduates.

"There'd better not be a single hair out of place when you get back!" I hear Klara's voice fade out in the distance and fail to supress a laugh. Pulling me around the side of the cafeteria and into an alcove in the brick, Rhys hoists me up for my legs to circle his hips. His hands glide beneath the robe to find my ass bare underneath, a groan rumbling through his chest as his tongue invades my mouth. I grind against him shamelessly, our kiss turning brutal on my lips.

"Wait," I breathe, pushing at his chest as I come to my senses "Where's Clay?"

"He's practicing his speech and gave me full permission to sate you beforehand. Something about getting too wet for him in the aisles."

"He did not say that," I smack his shoulder. Rhys' fingers dip inside me, forcing a gasp to cut my words short.

"Okay, fine, I paraphrased. But it is my turn. He got all your attention last night." My eyebrows crease but my back is arched, his fingers leisurely working their way in and out of me and circling my clit.

"He was nervous about his speech," I groan. Rhys' lips drag across my neck, nibbling at my jaw. His fingers are soaking with my wetness while they toy with me and my head lolls back against the wall. Sorry Klara.

"Well, I'm nervous too," Rhys murmurs into my receiver. I manage to flop my head forward and crack my eyelids, checking for sincerity in his gaze. It's there, waiting for me. The thought of him having come so far as to feel anxious on Clay's behalf pulls me out of the moment, making me want to treasure him. "Nervous I might explode if I don't get my dick inside you in the next five seconds." And there it is, illusion shattered. Punching him in the chest, I grind against his hand now a third digit has slipped inside me.

"Do it then, asshole," I bite out. Sandwiching me against the wall with his torso, Rhys shifts his robes aside and fills me instantly. Looks like I wasn't the only one going commando today. His piercing drags inside me deliciously, his fingers teasing my puckered hole at the back. I didn't used to be the kind of girl who wanted to try anal, but having two boyfriends means it comes with the territory. Now I have a thick cock knocking at my back door most nights and I gladly let them in.

Unlike with his fingers, Rhys doesn't hold back. He slams into me over and over, my back thumping against the brick with each delicious impact. My g-spot is singing but the building climax hangs back, balancing frustratingly on the edge. Our breathing is labored, our skin slapping together, so it's no wonder I don't hear Clay approach.

"I thought the after party was supposed to be...well, after the ceremony." And it's all he says. Without hesitating, his hands are on me. His fingers dip between Rhys and me, circling my clit while the other hand slips beneath my robe to pinch and twist my pierced nipple. Instantly, the orgasm rips through me on a scream I don't hold back, Rhys' cock swelling within me a moment later. Subconsciously, I know there was something missing. My body is fine tuned to their touch, accustomed to the pleasure they jointly provide. Basically, I'm a demanding bitch now, and I'm cool with it.

"Ahh, might not have thought this one through," Rhys comments as he remains nestled inside me. The three of us share a look before bursting into laughter, the force of it causing cum to seep down my legs.

"I'll get some tissues," Clays smiles with a roll of his eyes. I shout after him as he walks away.

"My hero!"

When we emerge into the courtyard, everyone is seated and looking bored. Klara spins in her chair, tapping a pen on the clipboard in her hand to signal Clay should have been on stage already. And that's before she sees my hair. Kissing Clay good luck, Rhys and I slip into a spare pair of seats on the aisle and duck our heads like naughty school children.

"Ahh, here he is. Ladies and gentleman, your valedictorian!" The audience claps as Clay takes the stage, my heart expanding to the point of bursting. I couldn't be more proud of my men for how far they've come, succeeding against all odds.

"Board of Trustees, Principles of Colleges, Deans, Directors, our beloved teachers, parents and my fellow graduates, I'm honored to be addressing you all today. Before I begin, I'd like to spare a moment to remember those who could not be with us today, as they were taken from this world too early. But in their memory, we honor them with our success. We cherish them with our perseverance to rise above our grief, and with our ability to love and live."

Clay stands tall, his wholehearted smile making a lump form in my throat. Following the direction of his eye line, I see his mom already crying in the front row with Rhys' mom on one side and Huxley on the other. Even after Hux finished Waversea, the two of them have remained as close as brothers. So much in fact, it was mutually decided Hux would visit Rachel with him, posing as Jeremy. It may seem deceitful or unethical, but as her condition worsens, seeing her 'sons' together again is the only thing that makes her smile anymore. As soon as they enter the room together, she practically glows with the magnitude of her love.

I can't hold back my sobs as Clay continues the speech I've heard a hundred times in practice, but it doesn't compare to today. Using Rhys' sleeve, I wipe my tears away while he places kisses on top of my head. Bullshit aside, Rhys is as affected by Clay's words as I am. His chest shakes on juddered exhales, his fingers knotted tightly in mine. These two aren't just bound as my partners, they are united as best friends, thicker than thieves and each other's lifelong confidant.

As the speech comes to a close, the entire courtyard are on their feet in applause. I lose sight of Clay as a sea of mortarboards fly into the air, mine and Rhys' joining them. Cheers fill my head and joy beats through my chest. This is it, the start of a new chapter and I can't wait. As the crowd form a line starting with Klara at the edge of the stage, Rhys kisses my cheek and says he'll be right back. Addy replaces him within a second, linking her arm in mine.

"Nice girls finish last, right?" she muses as she draws me towards to back of the line. Shrugging, I hunt through the people to see my men taking turns to hug their moms.

"Are you sure you can't come to New York with me?" Addy pouts as we take mini steps forward when the line moves. I tilt my head at her, trying to force a stern look.

"We've been through this. Rhys starts his entry level position for Chicago's top forensic science labs next month. He's got to pay off his student loans somehow." I can't fight my grin as those words leave my mouth. Filling out those forms with Rhys was the day I saw the biggest change in him, and he's never once regretted it. In fact, he's excited to earn his own money, make his own way. When Catherine offered to pay the deposit on the cozy apartment we're going to rent in Chicago, Rhys did a few modeling shoots to make the money instead. Who knew women liked stock photos of sexy, tattooed men so much?

"And what about you?" Addy scolds me. I knew it was coming, I've heard it all before. "You can't put everything on hold while Rhys pursues his dreams. You have dreams too."

"I'm not putting anything on hold, but even if I were, I wouldn't care. Rhys has come so far and I'll support my men in every way. I've got a little gig lined up as a teaching assistant in a school for the deaf until I find a suitable apprenticeship. Clay has a few interviews lined up in some pharmacies when we get there, hoping to work his way up. It might all work out, it might not and I don't care Adds. I'm living my best life over here and I've never been happier."

"That's all I wanted to hear," she comments with a weird smirk, turning her back on my frown. I shake my head at her, edging forward while I ponder her words. Sure, the three of us have had our ups and downs over the years, mostly when the guys are horny enough to eradicate all rational thought, but I try not to let them get to that state often. Only as punishment once in a while for making decisions on my behalf or leaving the toilet seat up. It's all about the training. But I meant what I said, I'm thankful every day these men barreled into my life.

Reaching the steps at last, I glance up to see Clay and

Rhys on stage waiting for me, my diploma in their joint hands. I narrow my eyes, slowly walking onto the stage to join them. I spare a glance around, noticing everyone who has received their certificates has sat back down and are watching me in an eerie silence. Okay, now I'm freaked out. Stopping in front of the pair, I glance down to take my certificate when I notice the glimmering diamond ring attached with the red ribbon. My hand flies to my mouth as they drop to their knees in unison.

"Harper Addams," Clay starts. *Holy shit. Holy shit! This is actually happening.* "We've been trying to think of the perfect thing to say for months, but it all comes down to this."

"You're our everything, Babygirl. From the first moment we saw you, we knew you were perfect. Even when we've been giant assholes, your faith and love in us has never wavered. All the time in the world wouldn't be enough to express how much we love you, but we can start by making you smile every day of the rest of our lives." Rhys' voice quivering affects me more than his words, a sob locked in my throat at the pure love shining through his crystal blue eyes. Clay pats him on the back tenderly, causing the first tear to spill from my eye. My men, my world.

"Will you marry us?" Clay finishes, removing the ring from the ribbon while Rhys reaches for the hand still covering my mouth. My knees shake a moment before they give out from beneath me, my hands covering my face as I cry. There have been so many points in my life where I've been close to giving up. Close to hiding away so I can never be hurt or feel grief again. But to grieve means I've had love pure enough to mourn for, and I'd give myself to these men a thousand times over before I let myself run away in fear of losing them. Rhys peels my hands from my face, his expression filled with worry.

"Please?" I suddenly realize I haven't answered and throw myself into the pair of them.

"Yes! Yes, of course, yes!" I cry. I feel them both sag in relief and their laughter fills my head. Clay draws me onto his lap, holding my hand out for Rhys to push the ring onto my finger. It's beautiful, even through my tears I can see the two intertwining bands crossing with a row of diamonds.

Pulling me to my feet, the guys face me towards the crowd I forgot was there. Random graduates stand in different rows, each one pulling out a brass instrument from beneath their black robes. I can't contain my laughter when they begin to play 'Thinking Out Loud' by Ed Sheeran, this moment impossibly more perfect. Other than Clay pulling me in for a deep kiss, of course. His tongue explores my mouth in unhurried movements, uncaring of our audience. As soon as he pulls back, Rhys spins and pushes me against Clay's chest, his actions more feral. He attacks me with all the passion of an animal, desperate to leave his mark and claim me as his.

I join in with the applause as Rhys releases me, beaming at each of the brass band in turn. Leading me down the steps, I'm lunged at by Klara first and then Addy. Sneaky bitches, they set me up. Hugging them tightly, I find Huxley next in line to congratulate the three of us.

"I can see why he calls you Angel," Hux bumps Clay's shoulder. "You've been a god-send for him. I'll never be able to thank you enough." I blush at his words, even though it's not the first time he's said similar to me. Avoiding his direct gaze, I suddenly notice Addy eye-fucking him so hard, it could be considered rape. I thought she'd dealt with the Shadowed Souls before, when they attended here, but her investigation of Hux's t-shirt contained muscles would suggest otherwise.

"Um, Huxley, this is Addy by the way." I say, watching the pair closely. His eyes travel from her shoulder-length pink hair to the gem-studded converse poking out of her robes, the interest reciprocated.

"Pleasure to meet you, Addy."

Thanks!

That's a wrap on Waversea College! I'm not crying - you are!
I am so sad to have come to the end of the Waversea Series, I
hold these characters close to my heart. But I'm thrilled with
their HEA and ready to move onto more exciting projects
in the future! Thank you all so much for your continued
support and time, I couldn't do any of this without you!

A special thank you to my editor Teresa, proofreaders Gemma
and Oriance, and the ARC team and bookstagrammers
who always post and share on my behalf.

Books by Maddison Cole

The Moon Bound Series

Exiled Heir
Privileged Heir

The Shadowed Souls Series

Devilishly Damaged
Decietfully Damaged
Dangerously Damaged

The War at Waversea Series

Perfectly Powerless
Handsomely Heartless
Beautifully Boundless

Printed in Great Britain
by Amazon